Ohan Gaidzakian

Illustrated Armenia

and the Armenians

Ohan Gaidzakian

Illustrated Armenia
and the Armenians

ISBN/EAN: 9783337287474

Printed in Europe, USA, Canada, Australia, Japan

Cover: Foto ©Andreas Hilbeck / pixelio.de

More available books at **www.hansebooks.com**

Illustrated Armenia

and the

Armenians

BY THE
REV. OHAN GAIDZAKIAN, M. D.

BOSTON
1898

ILLUSTRATED
ARMENIA AND THE ARMENIANS

SPIRIT OF ARMENIA

REV. OHAN GAIDZAKIAN, M. D.

THE WRITER.

A SKETCH OF HIS LIFE AND OCCUPATION.

I was born January 7, 1837, in Albastan in the state of Aleppa. When I was a young man, 17 years old, that was in year 1854 some strangers came to my own town Albastan. After staying at an inn for a few days, they left the city, but they left four copies of the New Testament and several religious pamphlets in their room. The inn was kept by my cousin; so he got those blessed books and pamphlets, and a few days after that he presented a copy of the New Testament to me. I learned also that the strangers, who visited our city, were missionaries of the American Board. I read this book or New Testament always secretly in some private place. I always kept it in my pocket, for fear that I would be persecuted for reading it; and besides if I had read it in public it might have been taken from me and thrown in the fire, because in that time Armenian patriarchs in Constantinople had given special command and orders to all Armenian churches all over Asia Minor against missionaries and all their publications also. For that reason nearly two years I kept reading my New Testament, which worked its wonderful result upon my heart. I was convicted of my sinfulness, repented of my sins and found forgiveness for my sins, and peace to my disturbed soul. That Bible was the only means of my conversion and subsequent happiness and blessing of my life.

After a few years, Rev. Beebee and Rev. Perkins, American missionaries of Marash, had visited my native town, Albastan, and had organized the evangelical Armenian church with only eight members, one of whom was myself. During the first two years I had a good many troubles and persecutions

from my mother, relations and also from Armenian friends.
A few years after that I came to Marash and studied in the
College and the Theological Seminary under the supervision
of the American Board of Foreign Missions. During my theological season I married a Christian young lady, who is living
with me yet. I was graduated from the Theological Seminary
in 1869 and have been laboring in the Lord's fields in Antioch,
Kasab, Balin and Adana. For the first two years I preached
in those places, and in 1872 I had a call from the Evangelical
church of Marash. I was ordained in that church the same
year, in October. For about four years I had successful pastoral work in that church, and in 1876 I had a call from the
Evangelical church at Adana. I preached at that place until
1881, and then realizing a great demand for a medical mission
at home for that purpose, I came to America about 18 years
ago, and through the help of the Rev. Cyrus Hamlin, D. D.,
and Rev. Dr. Clark, the secretary of American Board of Foreign Missions,—these noble men opened my way to the medical department of the Vermont University where I was graduated in 1883. Soon after I returned home with better advantages in healing the sick and preaching the Gospel to the poor
and rich. For this privilege I consider myself indebted to the
American Congregational churches in this country.

So how much I was glad to get that New Testament;
and through it I have had a good many blessings in my native
land, both I and my family also.

I am, as you will see, a refugee. I have with the greatest
difficulty escaped from Turkish barbarism, after suffering the
greatest outrages, abandoning home, property and friends in
Armenia. But I have brought with me a large family, more
than 18 months ago; and have had much trouble and very hard
time always. I am now 61 years old, not able to work out of
doors. Unable to practice my profession in this country, I re-
sort, therefore, to the only method of earning for my family an
honest living that I have at hand, namely, the sale of my books,
and my Lord's prayer chart in 12 different languages, both of

8

which were prepared by myself. I wish to call your attention to the testimonials of prominent clergymen, professors and missionaries of American Board, and the Foreign Missionaries. The following few are selected:

Lexington, Mass.,

Nov. 23d, 1896.

To any Christian Minister or Private Individual:

I wish to introduce to your kind regards Rev. Ohan Gaidza-kyan, M. D., an Armenian refugee from Adana, Asia Minor—or rather, Northern Syria—where he has been a successful physician, and also a preacher of the Gospel, among his people in Cilicia, for more than twenty years.

He can tell his own story of the escape of himself and his family of seven, and lately also of relations, ten in number, who arrived from Marseilles, aided by Lady Henry Somerset.

The question now is how to keep the wolf from the door?

He has certain articles and books to sell. At the same time, he is anxious to be acquainted with the spiritual welfare of his native people in the United States, and to preach the Gospel as he may come in contact with them. He will answer any questions you may ask about Turkey and the Massacres.

If you will kindly, in any way you choose, give access to your people he is hopeful of gaining sufficient to support himself and family, also to succeed in his purpose of Christian work. I have known him for about sixteen years as an earnest worker. I commend him to your wise advice.

(Signed) Cyrus Hamlin,

Ex-President of Robert College of Constantinople.

———

To whom it may Concern:

The bearer, Rev. Ohan Gaidzakyan, M. D., I have known for a good many years in Asia Minor, as a preacher and prac-tising physician, although he has occupied a pulpit about three years under my care, namely, in Neegda, and he has been an able and always faithful man. But in consequence of the late troubles in Turkey, he has with the greatest difficulty escaped from Turkish oppressions, after suffering the greatest outrages. Abandoning home, property and friends, he has with a large and dependent family come to America. Even now he has had many months of illness in his family, and the struggle to keep the wolf from the door is no mean struggle. In his efforts to earn an honorable living by the sale of his beautiful chart of "Our Lord's Prayer" in twelve different languages, and books, I would gladly, if I could, enlist the interest of every Christian minister and private individual. I wish for him a kindly and sympathetic reception and consideration with Christian fellowship.

(Signed) W. A. Farnsworth,

Missionary of the A. B. C. F. M.
in Cæsarea, Asia Minor, Turkey.

Woburn, Mass., July 7, 1897.

---

128 Wall Street,
New Haven, Conn.,
28 Oct., 1896.

This will certify that I have known Rev. Dr. Ohan Gaidzakyan for the past sixteen years. He is a graduate of the Medical Department of Vermont University, and has been practising medicine in Adana, Turkish Empire, during the last fifteen years. He has been reduced to utter poverty by the plundering officials of the Turkish Empire, and has been obliged to flee to this country with his family. He is endeavoring to find some way in which he can support his needy family, and is anxious to gain such support in an honorable and self-respecting way. I would bespeak for him a friendly reception from all those to whom he appeals, and can cordially testify to the entire integrity of his Christian character.

(Signed) Lewis O. Brastow,
Professor in Yale Divinity School.

To whom it may Concern:

This will introduce the Rev. Ohan Gaidzakyan, M. D., who, together with his family, was among the refugees who escaped with their lives, but with the loss of all their property, from their late home in Armenia, which the inhuman Turk has rendered desolate with fire and sword. Dr. Gaidzakyan is endeavoring to support his family by the sale of a beautiful chart of "Our Lord's Prayer," in twelve different languages, prepared by himself, and also by the sale of a small but very interesting book by Frederick Davis Green, on the "Armenian Crisis in Turkey."

I am well acquainted with Dr. Gaidzakyan, and know him to be an earnest Christian man and one worthy of assistance in his struggle to make the best of his present circumstances.

I bespeak for him a cordial reception wherever he may present this.

(Signed)   Judson V. Clancy,

Pastor Congregational Church.

West Medford, Sept. 14th.

CONTENTS:

INTRODUCTION.

Armenia has generally been termed "The cradle of the human race," in view of the scriptural indication of it as the land of man's origin. In fact, the mention of the four rivers (Gen. II., 10-11) seems to point conclusively to the situation of the Garden of Eden near the source of the river Euphrates, which takes its rise in the mountains of Armenia.

Then there is the great and everlasting monument, Mount Ararat, with which will be inseparably associated the exceedingly ancient name of Armenia, destined, though the race itself be now threatened with extermination, to immortality.

In their native tongue they speak of their people as "Haik," and of Armenia as "Hayastan," derived from that great ancestor and patriarch who formed their kingdom.

By foreigners they came to be known as Armenians, from the name of King Aram, whose bravery is fittingly recorded in these pages.

Armenia can trace its origin to a period three centuries anterior to that of the Jewish nation, inasmuch as Haik, its founder, who was fifth in descent from Noah, was born 2277, B. C., whereas Abraham's birth did not occur till 1996 B. C. Its people, as a whole, were the first to embrace Christianity and, as narrated in the body of this work, King Abgar held communication with Jesus Christ. Throughout the ages they have cherished their Christian belief, in spite of innumerable trials and they still preserve it unswervingly.

So we find, after nineteen centuries, the people still living in firm adherence to Christian doctrine and discipline, submissive to their ecclesiastical head, the respected and beloved Father Mgertich I., the catholicos of all the Armenians, who now sits on the very seat of the Apostles Thaddeus and Bartholomew and of St. Gregory the Illuminator.

We may quote here a passage from Mr. F. D. Greene's work on "The Armenian Crisis and the Rule of the Turk," with reference to the adoption of national religious belief. He writes: "They (the Armenians) have the distinction of being the first race who accepted Christianity, King Dertad receiving baptism in 276 A. D., thirty-seven years before Constantine ventured to issue even the Edict of Toleration. Their martyr roll has grown with every century. The fact that the Armenian stock exists at all today is proof of its wonderful vitality and excellent quality. More then for 3,000 years Armenia, on account of her location, has been trampled into dust both by devastating armies and by migrating hordes. She has been the prey of Nebuchadnezzar, Xerxes, Alexander, and the Romans, the Parthians, and Persians, and Byzantine, Saracen, and Crusader, of Seljuk and Ottoman, and Russian and Kurd, etc. Through this awful record the Christian church, founded by St. Gregory the Illuminator, has been the one rallying point and source of strength.

Illustrated

Armenia and the Armenians.

CHAPTER I.

THE STORY OF ARMENIA. WHERE IS ARMENIA ?

Having found out, during my last visit to America, that a large majority of people in America are without any knowledge of Armenia and its historic events, and that they are anxious to know something about the country, I have intended to give, hereby, a brief account about its history.

First of all, Armenia is a very important country in regard to its connection with the Bible. Armenia is the cradle of mankind, and the venerable mother of all other countries. Our first parents were created in that land. The beautiful garden of Eden, which was planted for their enjoyment, was in that land. It was in this garden that our first parents had their first direct communication with Jehovah. It was there, that after their disobedience, they offered a sacrifice to God, and out of the skins of the sacrificed animals God made them clothes and clothed them. The first religious service, and the first plan of forgiveness by grace were instituted in the garden of Eden near its eastern gate and in the midst of seraphim and cherubim with their flaming sword.

Adam and his wife, after their fall, were driven out of the garden of Eden into the land of Armenia, which was full of thorns and thistles, that they might till the ground and thus provide their daily bread in the sweat of their face.

Our first mother rocked the cradle of her first offspring in Armenia. Therefore this country became the residence of our first parents and the inheritance of their children.

It was there that Cain and his brother Abel were born and brought up. Cain became a tiller of the ground, and selected for himself the fertile lands of Armenia, while Abel became a keeper of sheep, and led his sheep on the green pastures at the foot of Mount Ararat and watered them out of the rivers flowing from the garden of Eden.

The altar upon which Abel offered sacrifice to God with a sincere faith, was in that country.

Cain slew his brother Abel in Armenia, hence the first murder, and the first martyrdom took place in that land. On account of this murder Cain left Armenia and went to the land of Nod in Arabia, situated on the southeastern direction of Eden, and there he was settled, built cities and founded the land of Midianites.

God, after Abel's death, gave Adam another son, named Seth, to our first parents, and after having many sons and daughters born to them, and having lived their nine hundred and thirty years, died, and were buried in Armenia.

It was in that land that Enoch walked with God for three hundred years, and it was from there that with chariots and horses of fire he was translated to heaven without tasting death.

Armenia was the land of all the people living in the world during the first fifteen hundred years from Adam to Noah.

It was in that land that Noah, the patriot, was born, and for a period of one hundred and twenty years was the preacher, pastor and father of the people of that land.

The preparations for the Deluge were made in that land, as the Deluge, took place there, mankind having not yet dispersed to other parts of the world. One of the convincing proofs that the Deluge took place in Armenia is that the waters of the Deluge have left their remnants in Armenia in the form of the present Armenian lakes and especially the Caspian Sea. This fact cannot be refuted.

According to the testimony of the Bible the mountains of Ararat are in the land of Armenia, and when the waters were abated, the ark rested upon the mountains of Ararat.

After a certain time in the ark Noak looked out of the window, looked over the land and found that the waters were wholly abated, and according to the word of God he left the ark with eight persons, who were his kith and kin, and descended to his beloved land of Armenia. As soon as he left the ark he built an altar and offered a sacrifice to God. Then he tilled the earth, planted gardens and vineyards, and of their products he made wine and drank. It was Armenia that produced Noah. He lived there before and after the Deluge. It is not reasonable to think that after he left the ark he went to a distant place, but he lived where he was before; and after having sons and daughters and grand-children, and living three hundred and fifty years, died.

Gomer was the son of Japheth, the second son of Noah. Togarmah was the son of Gomer, and Haig was the son of Togarmah. Haig was the first prince or king of that land, therefore the land was named Haisdan. He fought with Nimrod, who wanted to build the tower of Babel; he conquered him, and became the chief ruler of a large region. Haig was succeeded by his son Armenag, in whose honor the country was also named Armenia.

It is very likely that you may think as though I am saying these things as historic curiosities or as fables. It is natural for you to say, "Well, here is an Armenian lunatic, we don't care what he says." It is all right if you think so. But in the way of proving what I say I want to bring before you the following two points, and wait for their answers.

FIRST. The Garden of Eden was the first residence of our first parents. The rivers that issued from the Garden bear the same old names to-day as in the days of Adam. We have them to-day in the same position and with the same old names. I cannot exactly tell in what part of Armenia the Garden stood, as the Deluge wholly wiped out the Garden. But judging by the original source of these rivers we can infer that it stood on the east of Mount Ararat. This leads us to say that the home of our first parents was in Armenia.

SECOND. According to the Bible, God spoke to Noah that he would send the Deluge to the world within one hundred and twenty years. Noah made preparations for it. It goes without saying that the Deluge took place where mankind was, and, as I said before, the first population of the world was only in Armenia. Therefore the Deluge took place in Armenia and the ark rested on the top of Mount Ararat. The traces of the Deluge are still seen in the numerous lakes in Armenia, especially in the Caspian Sea.

If there are those among the hearers or readers who have objections to these points, let them kindly tell them and I will endeavor to answer them.

But the student of the Bible will find a great delight in perusing any Biblical and historical work, for the discourses of the Assyrian, Babylonian, Egyptian, Moabyan and Persian monuments and tablets, with the decipherment of their cuneiform inscriptions, have verified much of Biblical narrative, satisfied the honest doubting minds and silenced the idle cavilers. Armenia indeed does not equally rank with these countries in the importance of its discoveries, or in its immediate relation to the land of the Israelites. Yet Armenia played an important role in the drama of the history of Western Asia in the past, and who can tell what she may still do in the future.

THE LAND OF ARMENIA; IT IS THE MOST PICTURESQUE OF COUNTRIES.

The country of Armenia lies directly north of the Mesopotamia plain. It is a mountainous country, and contains all of the great river resources of Western Asia. The Euphrates, the Tigris, the Araxes, Cyrus (Kur), the Acampsis and Holys (called Kizil Irmak) take their rise in the highland of Armenia and flow into three different seas, fertilizing the

MOUNT ARARAT.

subjacent countries through which they run. Armenia is well likened to Switzerland in its relation to the Western part of Asia, as the latter is to Western Europe.

I. Its general character is that of a plateau. On the north, Armenia reaches almost to the Caucasian mountains; on the west, the Black sea, Asia Minor and the Taurus mountains; on the south, the bay of Mesopotamia, the upper part of which was included in the Armenian provinces, "the Noire" of the cuneiform inscriptions; on the east, the Caspian sea and Midia bounded Armenia.* In the time of Herodotus, Armenia must have been about 550 miles from east to west, and 250 miles from north to south: or about 150,000 square miles. The country was divided into two parts, namely, Armenia Major and Armenia Minor. The latter lay to the west of the Euphrates; the former was again divided into fifteen provinces. But at the time of its greatest extent and power—when its people were great and its kings were great, long before Alexander's conquest—Armenia covered about 500,000 square miles, and stretched from the Black sea and the Caucasus on the north to Persia, and Syria on the south; from the Caspian and a much smaller Persia on the east, to Cilicia and far beyond the Holys (Kizil Irmak) on the west, but also including old Midia.

Armenia is a highland from 4,000 to 7,000 feet above the level of the sea. Its surface is undulating, with beautiful dells and hills, with fertile valleys and forest-covered mountains, with fecundant and extensive plains and pasture lands, and lofty snow-capped mountains with glittering snowy peaks piercing the clear, blue sky. The highest mountain of Western Asia is situated at the centre of Armenia. It is Mount Masis of the natives, and Mount Ararat of the Europeans, which is of unsurpassing beauty, magnificence and

---

*Pliny agrees with the Armenian historians in bringing the eastern boundary to the Caspian sea, and Herodotus makes Armenia border on Cappadocia and Cilicia on the west, stating that "this stream (the Holy river) rises in the mountainous country of Armenia."

grandeur. No traveller has yet ever seen it and not spoken of it in admiration. "The impression made by Ararat upon the mind of every one who has any sensibility of the stupendous works of the Creator, is wonderful and overpowering; and many a traveller of genius and taste has employed both the power of the pen and of the pencil in attempting to portray this impression. But the consciousness that no description, no representation can reach the sublimity of the object thus attempted to be depicted, must prove to the candid mind, that, whether we address the ear or eye, it is difficult to avoid the poetic in expression and the exaggerated in form, and confine ourselves strictly within the bounds of consistency and truth."

"Nothing can be more beautiful than its shape, more awful than its height. All the surrounding mountains sink into insignificance when compared to it. It is perfect in all its parts; no hard, rugged feature, no unnatural prominence; everything is in harmony, and all combined·to render it one of the sublimest objects in nature."

Mount Masis or Ararat is situated on the wide and fertile plain, which is watered by the Araxes with its tributaries. This river traverses the plain, running on the north of the mountain, and fertilizes the plain which it dotted by numerous villages. This plain is, in fact, a plateau about 7,000 feet above the level of the sea. The mountain still rises over 10,000 feet higher than the plain, thus making its total height over 17,000 feet from the sea level. It is, therefore, perpetually covered with snow ice that dazzles in splendor the eyes of the spectators.*

Mount Ararat and other mountains have been visited at times by violent earthquakes and eruptions. Though Mount Masis itself is formed of volcanic rocks, no record of its volcanic activities is preserved for us by the ancients. How-

---

*Sir Layerd saw the mountain from a distance of about 145 miles on the south side of it; and a German traveller from the Caucasian mountains on the north, a distance of 150 miles.

ever, a German traveller makes mention of his seeing a ter-
rifying sight more than a century ago; and says, "Some distant southern volcanoes, or Ararat itself (the terrible gorge
of which, distant from Caucasus in a straight line 150 miles,
one can hardly look at without shuddering; and which, on
the 13th of January and 22d of February, 1783, began again
to throw out smoke and fire) must have burned the top of
Caucasus, and thrown upon it those mineral ashes."

In the year 1840, on the 20th of June, a terrible earthquake shook the foundation of the mighty mountain. The
monastery of St. James and the villages of Aicuri were buried
in the ruins; and the inhabitants of the villages, about one
thousands in number, were buried alive. The towns of
Nakhjevan and Erevan did not escape the calamity. In both
of these towns hundreds of houses were thrown down;
and thousands of human beings, unexpectedly, within a few
minutes were swept out of their earthly existence.

Undoubtedly such calamities must have been repeated
in the past; but we are not informed concerning them by
the ancient visitors. But sad it is still to hear such news as
the following:

"Paris, May 17th, (1891), The Dix Neuwine Sircle,
states that commercial advices have been received at Marseilles from Trebizond to the effect that a new volcano has
appeared in Armenia at the summit of Mount Nimrod, in
the District of Van, vomiting forth flames and lava. The
villages at the base of the mountain have been destroyed,
and many persons are said to have been killed or injured.
The fugitives are camping outside the range of destruction.
They are almost entirely destitute, and the greatest misery
prevails among them."

The earliest name of Armenia, by which it was known
to the ancient Hebrew and Assyrian writers, was Ararat.
We are told, in connection with the Deluge, that when the
waters of the great flood subsided, "the ark" of Noah "rested
upon the mountains of Ararat." The language of the Bible

is both accurate and precise:—not upon Mount Ararat, as it is generally and incorrectly said and written by many—but upon the mountains of Ararat.

The author of the book of Genesis is accurate in his expression and precise in his knowledge of the fact that Ararat is the name of the country upon whose mountains the tmpest-tossed vessel of the patriarch rested. Whether his knowledge was the result of Divine inspiration, or is a historical fact, preserved and handed down to the author's time, we cannot tell. The accuracy of the statement, however, which stood the criticisms of centuries, and especially this age of criticism, has a rightful claim to its acceptance by all.

The following is a specimen of such absurdities and blunders so often ignorantly, or by carelessness, committed.

A traveller, well known in this country, writes to one of the daily papers as follows: "At daylight we were in a broad flat valley, lying between the greater and the lesser Caucasus. The latter, to our south, lifted not far off, from twelve to fifteen thousand feet, and were clothed in snow. In the far distance were others. I saw a sharp, conical burnished peak, which I took to be Ararat. I could not help thinking what a hard time the mighty line of living things had when marching by twos, male and female,, from those cold, bleak heights down into the plains below, after the great flood had subsided; and what a time good old Noah must have had to keep some of his warm-blooded pets from freezing on that lofty sixteen-thousand-feet-high pinnacle. What a pity our theologians do not boldly preach that the Bible is a mighty system of truth, but that its truths came to us clothed in Oriental legend and fable:—that the truth is there, pure and undefiled, as the grain is pure and uncontaminated by the chaff in which it is housed, instead of trying to make a reasoning world swallow the chaff for solid kernels."

Undoubtedly our honorable traveller will claim to belong to that "reasoning world" of which he speaks. But if all who make up that "reasoning world" will reason as he does, namely, take that erroneous expression of the common people, and call that highest mountain peak—which is over seventeen thousand feet from the sea level—Mount Ararat, and add to this error, or comparatively modern designation, another, namely, that the ark of Noah rested upon this mountain; then turn around and condemn the Bible as an "Oriental legend and fable," it must be said that this kind of "reasoning" of the so-called "reasoning world," is absurdity, and not reasoning at all.

Ararat is mentioned in three other books of the Old Testament, beside the above, in connection with the flood: 2 Kings xix: 37; Isaiah xxxvii: 38; and Jeremiah li: 27. None of these passages speak of it as a mountain, but as a country. The first two passages, identical in import, speak of the escape of Adrammelch Sharezer "into the land of Ararat," after having committed the crime of assassinating their own father, Sennacherib.

The prophet Jeremiah summons the forces of Armenia to combine with the Medes to overthrow Babylon, in these words:

"Set ye up a standard in the land, blow the trumpet among the nations, prepare the nations against her (Babylon); call together against her the kingdoms of Ararat, Minni and Ashchenaz.

"Prepare against her the nation with the things of the Medes." Li: 27, 28.

The following is from an inscription of Assur-Natsir-Pal, the King of Assyria; and the date of his reign is assigned by Professor Sayee, from B. C. 883 to B. C. 858.

"The cities of Khatu, Khartaru, Nestum, Irbiri, Mitqia, Arzonia, Tela (and) Khalua, the cities of Qurkhi, which in sight of the mountains of U'su, Arua (and) Arardhi mighty mountains are situated, I captured." Professor Sayee remarks that "Arardhi seems to be the earliest form of Arar-

dher (of later Assyrian inscription), the Biblican Ararat."
(Records of the Past, Vol. 2, page 140.)

These passages from the Bible and the Assyrian inscription, show, beyond doubt, that Ararat was the earliest name of Armenia, and it was not the name of mountain; and finally, that the ark of Noah rested upon the mountains of Ararat or Armenia. Thus the history of the human race began anew from the land of Ararat.

II.   It has been said that the great rivers of Western Asia take their origin from the highlands of Armenia: Euphrates, Tigris, Pison, Araxes and many others from the jewels of her crown. These rivers penetrate to every corner of the land, traverse many hundreds of miles to give life to the field, the vineyards and the orchards, to turn the mills. The river Acampus of the ancients identified by some with the Pison of the Bible, has its sources from the southeast of Erzurun. It receives several streams and with beautiful winding flows into the Black Sea. About the Arapes, according to some the Gihon of the Bible, there is an interesting statement in an Armenian history. "Aramais (King of Armenia) built a city of hewn stone on a small eminence in the plain of Aragay, and near the bank of ariverbefore mentioned, which had received the name of Gihon.

The new city, which afterwards became the capitol of his Kingdom he called Armatvir after his name, and the name of the river he changed to Arat, after his son Arast."

The river Arakes is fed and swollen by many streams, rivulets and brooks, which run from the sides of numerous glens, through picturesque ravines, and mingle with it. Along its tortuous course it carries a great fertility, and finally mingles with no less than the famous river Cyrus (Ker) and pours itself into the bosom of the Caspian Sea.

The two rivers of Armenia are the Euphrates, and Tigris, whose identity with those mentioned in connection with the Garden of Eden is beyond doubt. Both of these rivers take their origin from the highlands of Armenia.

The Euphrates from the springs, which are not very far from Mount Misis (Ararat so-called), takes a westward course along the Taurus mountain chain on the northern side of the mountain. Near Malatiyeh the river turns towards the southeast and approaches the source of the Tigris, but within a few miles distance. From this point onward, with a southeasterly course, these rivers flow and finally they unite and pour into the Persian Gulf.

The student of the ancient Babylonian and Assyrian history and civilization knows what fertility these rivers carried along their course through the Mesopotamian plain and hold with numerous canals and channels, they irrigated the land of the Great Empires and became the means of commercial intercourse with the neighboring nations.

The claim of Armenia to the possession within its bosom of the Garden of Eden ought not to disputed. No country, indeed, has attempted to contend with Armenia for this honor. Her natural beauty, salubrious climate, her exuberant fertility, the fragrance of her flowers, the variety of her singing birds, above all her mountainous bosom and overflowing breasts from which the mighty water run down on her sides and fill the great channels of those rivers which fertilize the subjacent counties and replenish the three adjacent seas, all these do justify her claim and render it almost a historical fact that Armenia was the cradle of infant humanity. "Ancient traditions place the province of Eden in the highest portion of Armenia, anciently called Ararat, and it appears to furnish all the conditions of the Mosaic narrative."

If variety makes beauty, Armenia furnishes such a variety, making her one of the finest countries in the world; not only has she those gigantic mountains with their snow-crowned heads looking down upon the clouds that envelop their skirts while they mock the ambient air and the wind, not only has she hundreds of murmuring streams and rippling brooks gliding along the sides of thousands of hills

which swell those kingly rivers and cause them to overflow
their banks, but, she also has some beautiful lakes, like jewels set in their respective caskets.   The lake of Sevan, which
lies between the Arapes and the Cyrus rivers, occupying the
centre of a fertile plain of the northern part of Armenia, is
called "Street lake," in contradistinction to the others, which
are salt-water lakes.   Lake Sevan, near the city of
Erevan, is now in the Russian provinces of Armenia.   The
lake of Ormi or Orumiah, lies in the southern part of the
country, now in the provinces of Armenia.

These lakes and some others are surrounded by romantic views and poetic scenery, but the lake of Van, surpassing them in size, in importance, and splendor, causes us with
her to linger a little longer.

The area of Lake Van is about fourteen hundred square
miles, its surface is over five thousand feet high above the
sea.   It is embosomed at the centre of a verdant and rich
plain, which plain also is encircled by an exceedingly beautiful, romantic, undulating mountain chain, which culminates
on the north in the sublime monarch of mountain of Western Asia, Mount Massis (Ararat).

The beauty of Lake Van and its surroundings always
did and will more intensely enchant the poets and artists
who are more fortunate and enjoy the beauty of nature more
than the rest of us.   The following is the language of a distinguished explorer: "A range of low hills now separated
us from the plain and lake of Van.   We soon reached their
crest and a landscape of surpassing beauty was before us.
At our feet, intensely blue, and sparkling in the rays of the
sun, was the inland sea, with sublime peak of the Subbon
Dagh (Mountain) mirrored in its transparent waters.   The
city (of Van) with its castle-crowned rock and its embattled
walls and towers lay embowered in orchards and gardens.
To our right a rugged snow-capped mountain opened midway into an ampitheatre in which amid lofty trees stood the
Armenian Convent of Seven Churchs.   To the west of the

lake was the Nimrod Dagh, and the highlands nourishing the sources of the great rivers of Mesopotamia, the hills forming the foreground of our picture were carpeted with brightest flowers, over which wandered the flocks, while the gaily dressed shepherds gathered around us as we halted to contemplate the enchanting scene."*

Many a scene like the above has enchanted the foreign traveler and inspired the native authors and poets, and caused the wandering, expatriated sons and daughters of Armenia to remember her former majestic beauty and splendor, but marred by the vicissitudes of the ages and especially under the iron heel of the present tyrant, her indescribable misery, and weep like Jeremiah, "Mine eye runneth down with rivers of water for the destruction of the daughter of my people." (Lamentations, 3-48.)

III. The climate of Armenia is the very healthiest in the world; I do not say one of the healthiest, but the very healthiest. The climate is excellent all the year round, and though the winters are severe and much of the country is covered with snow, yet on account of the elevation, which is from four thousand to seven thousand feet above the level of the sea, and in latitude 35° to 42°, or say from North Carolina to Massachusetts. It might easily have been understood that the climate of Armenia cannot be mild in winter, on account of the altitude of the country, which is from four thousand to seven thousand feet above the level of the sea.

In general it is very healthy, but in winter the cold is severe, and it lasts from the middle of October until the beginning of May. But the air is dry, pure and agreeable always in the whole year, a preventative of disease, and conducive to languity. The dread disease, consumption, does not exist there, while dyspeptics, if any are to be found, must have been imported. The perfect type of physical vigor is to be seen there.

In the valleys the weather is a good deal milder and very

---

* Layard's " Nineveh and Babylon," pages 333-4.

pleasant. The summer is short, but warm and dry; this especially is so in certain valleys, which are far away from the reach of the sea breeze, too much enclosed by high mountains and too deep for the mountain breeeze, for neither is it uniformly long, nor is the degree of warm weather the same all over the country. Generally the people of Armenia in all the ages are tall, powerful, ruddy cheeked, full of endurance and energy, shrewd and honest too. They are longer lived than any other people of countries. I know a good many people in Armenia lived from 80 to 125 years of age. They are full of life and they are greatly enjoyed in that country. The most of the American missionaries in Armenia would be sure to echo these words. A returned missionary gave a striking testimony to this effect. He was addressing and lecturing in this country as follows: — "Before I became a missionary, I had very poor health; most of my family died of hereditary consumption, and I was attacked by it. My house physicians strongly protested against my becoming a missionary, saying that if I went to a foreign land I would grow worse, and probably die there, but I paid no attention to this; I presumed they were right, but I was determined to go anyway, and if I must die, to die in my chosen work. When I offered myself to the American Board, I was allotted to Armenia, and thither I went. My disease disappeared and now I am as healthy as any missionary in the world. You see how stout and vigorous I look, and I do not expect to die soon. But I feel sure that if I had stayed in America to save my life, I should have lost it before this time." He is still living in Armenia, and I hope will live to be over a hundred, as many of the natives do there.

The reader will smile at all this as the patriotic boastfulness of an Armenian, and say, perhaps, that he can make as fabulous declarations for his land, wherever he may be; but such claims cannot be substantiated by records and personal observations as these for Armenia can. Take the Bible; some of the patriarchs lived to be 600, 700, 800—one even 969; if in-

deed he ever died a natural death; some were taken up to heaven
without knowing death; and all these long lives, as will be
shown, were lived in Armenia. God's judgment was good.
He did not create man in America, Europe, or India, or anywhere but in Armenia. He came down there from
Heaven, planted the Garden of Eden there, and from the dust
of that land created the first man. When the race had become
sinful and only Noah's family were preserved, the ark was not
brought to rest on the Rockies, the Alps, or the Himalayas,
but on Ararat in Armenia.

The natural resources in Armenia are very rich.
The mineral wealth of Armenia is very great; but like the
other potential riches of the Turkish Empire, it profits nobody,
not even the greedy despot, whose word is death. Gold, silver, copper, iron, and minor metals, besides marble and other
beautiful stones, are present in abundance.

The reader might well have anticipated that a mountainous country might possess some other valuable things beneath
the surface. Such an anticipation is decidedly justifiable
when we remember the fact that the mines of Armenia are
rich, numerous and varied.

Traces of old gold mines are found midway between
Trebizond and Erzerum. Some even think that the locality
of "Ophir," from whence King Solomon fetched gold to decor-
ate the temple, was in this region. It may be interesting to
some to mention that the ancient river Acampsis, identified by
some with the Pisom of the Bible, "which compasseth the
whole land of Havilah, where there is gold," does really run
through this part of the country. About three miles from
Marsahan is a mountain caller Tarshan Dagh (rabbit mountain), rich in gold; another in central Turkey is a mountain
called Baalgar Dagh, among the Taurus mountains very
rich in gold and many years since, are used by Turkish Empire.

There are very rich silver and copper mines in the vicinity
of Harput (Harpoot), the copper mines alone annually yield

two million two hundred and fifty thousand pounds. There are rare mines of sulphur, sulphuret of lead, antimony, and silver. The mines of iron and coal are found in abundance, but the coal mines are entirely neglected and the iron and other mines are very poorly operated. There is a little town situated among the Tauraus mountains called Zeitoon; about ten miles from Zeitoon is a mountain called Beraut Digh, rich in soft and abundant iron mines. The people of Zeitoon almost live through that iron mine.

The mineral springs, hot and cold, at various places with their peculiar curative powers, have become the "Bethesdes" of the invalids, and are frequented, like the places of pilgrimage, by those who suffer anyq ailment and are able to repair to such restorative resorts. Rock salt and salt springs also abound in Armenia. They are especially inexhaustible in the vicinity of Moosh. A salt stream, whose springs are from the salt rock, which would bring a good income in the hands of a wise governor, unprofitably flows into and mingles with the waters of the Euphrates.

The country has all the old fertility which made Asia Minor under the Byzantine Empire the garden of the world, till the Turks half turned it into a desert, as they do every spot accursed by their presence.

Such a variety of climate combined with a naturally fertile soil will produce a vegetation rich in quantity and splendid in quality. There are indeed, a very few large forest and timber lands left on account of their being inaccessible to the people and for want of good roads. The government is entirely indifferent, but in cultivating or protecting the people who would cultivate such forest trees for the two-fold use of them as timber and fuel. Consequently the people suffer very much for the want of these, especially is this true in certain districts.

But such vegetations as wheat, barley, cotton, tobacco and grapes, and every kind of fruits are almost unexcelled in quality. The matermilons raised on the banks of the Eu-

phrates and the Tigris are the largest and sweetest of their kind;
two melons are sometimes a camel's load. It is impossible
for a family to use the whole of such a melon, which has to be
cut up and sold in pieces. The grapes, either fresh or in the
shape of wine or raisins and dried as raisins exceed in size the
plumpest grapes of other lands. Nearly everything is raised
or grows wild in Armenia which is to be had in the Northern
or Southern States of America, though of course, each country
has some things peculiar to itself. The products of the North
are paralleled by those of the rugged picturesque highlands of
North Turkish and Russian Armenia, with their cold snowy
winters, short, hot summer, and mild intervening season; those
of the South find their counterparts from the rich upland valleys, or the lowlands plains needing irrigation, of Kurdistan and
Persian Armenia, with its semi-tropical climate, and alterna-
tions of wet and dry seasons. The Indian corn and oats and
rice are raised, and sugar is made in the Persian port. In the
fields and gardens you can find not only the wonderful melons I have just spoken of, but pumpkins and squashes, lettuce
and egg plant, and indeed most of the vegetables that come
to an American table. As to fruits, all that you know we
know also, only of finer flavors. Asia Minor is the original
home of the quince, the apricot, and the nectarine, and I believe of the peach too; while our apples, pears, and plums are
incomparable, the muscot apple of Amassea are exceptional
even there. After eating them, one hardly wonders that
Adam and Eve could not resist the temptation of doing the
same, at the cost of innocence and Eden. The pears of Malatiah keep them company; and the quince grows sometimes as
large as a man's head. Another fruit equally important is the
mulberry for silk-worms. The olive and fig are cultivated and
also grow wild, and filberts and walnuts can be gathered anywhere in the woods, as well as orchards; of course not the
American "hickory nuts," but the "English walnuts" of the
groceries.

The fertility of the country is unquestionable when we

remember the fact, that not only the country is very old and therefore more or less would naturally decline in its productivity, but the method of cultivation itself is also very old, started by Adam, Noah and Abraham, and their immediate descendants, compelled by the necessities of life.

It has been said ancient traditions place the province of Eden in Armenia. Such a statement itself might have aroused an expectation in the mind of the reader to know something about the environment and conditions which will give a paradisaical aspect to a place. The flowers of Armenia will, not a little, contribute to this aspect, which, though growing wild and uncultivated, are of rare beauty, fragrance and hue, and hardly known to the Europeans and American. Though one of them has a Latin scientific name, no plant of it has ever been in Europe, and by no manner of contrivance could we succeed in carrying one away. This most beautiful production was called in Latin bananca, or philipea coccinea, a parasite on absinthe or wormwood. This is the most beautiful flower conceivable; it is in the form of a lily, about nine to twelve inches long, including the stalk; the flower and the stalk and all the parts of it resemble crimson velvet; it has no leaves; it is found on the side of the mountains near Erzerum, often in company with Morans orentalis, a remarkable kind of thistle with flowers all up the stalk, looking and smelling like the honeysuckle. An iris of a most beautiful flaming yellow is found among the rocks, and it, as well as all the more beautiful flowers, blooms in the spring, soon after the melting of the snow.

In regard to the singing birds of Armenia we do not attempt to say much, but undoubtedly must they have performed a noble service, by their melodious music in that great assembly of all creation, gathered to witness the nuptials of our innocent parents.

Many of the children of Adam and Eve even now do not have any other musicians than the same. The birds in general are numerous, belonging to various tribes, "which," says the

author above quoted, "in thousands and millions, would reward the toil of the sportsman and the naturalist on the plains
and mountains of the highland of Armenia."

Nothing was more delightful and amusing to the writer,
when a child, than to watch the armies of birds flying towards
the north with spring, or south in the autumn in a beautiful
array, led by a general, as it were, until they were lost out of
sight in the clear and bright Oriental sky; nor even now would
it give him little delight, if it were possible, to retire into one
of those solitary watchmen's cottages in the vineyards and orchards of the East and listen to the most melodious anthems
of those songsters, who were then, it seems to him now, vying
more with each other to render their praises acceptable to
their Creator than many of our noted singers in the magnificent churches and cathedrals.

The animals that are generally found in a temperate
climate like the climate of the Northern states are also common in Armenia. In the days of old the Armenian horses
were as famous as are the Arabian horses now. The rich
pastures of Media and Armenia furnished excellent horses
for the Medo-Persian army. See also (Ezekiel xxvii, 14).

According to the rule of Sultan Hamid II. there is no
land of Armenia at all in that district.

The present Sultan forbids the use of the name altogether,
and insists on the district being termed Kurdistan, or called
by the names of its vilayets, Diarbekr, Van, Erzroom, Harpoot,
etc. Many maps do not have the name Armenia at all. But
the reader knows and we know the name of Armenia has been
used more than four thousand years to that district; at the same
time some of the ancient cities of Armenia are still in existence,
however, not in their former magnificence, and some are in
complete ruins.

Among the former, Van, Amid, now Diarbekr, Erevan,
Malatiyeh, Palu, and Manazghert might be mentioned; among
the latter, Armavir, Ardashad, Valarshabad, Dicranaghert, Ani
and others are mentioned. There are yet other cities, some of

them not of equal antiquity with some of the above named, but of great importance, both in the past and in the present time. These are Kars, Erzroom, or Erzerum, Moosh, Bitlis, and Karpert (Harpoot).

The ancient Armenia is now divided among three powers: The northern part, from Botoum on the Black Sea to Baker on the Caspian—the river Araxes being the boundary to near Mt. Ararat—belong to Russia; the southeastern course of the river of Araxes from near Mt. Ararat to Persia. The western from Mt. Ararat to the Black Sea and the Kizil-Irmak and the whole western part of Asia Minor, which is larger than the other two, is under the Turkish Empire, consequently some of the cities mentioned above are in the Russian provinces of Armenia, but the most of them are in Turkish Armenia.

The English traveler, Sandys, who visited the Turkish Empire over two centuries and a half ago, has described with truth and eloquence the unhappy condition of the regions subject to its destructive despotism in the following words:

These countries, once so glorious and famous for their happy estate, are now, through vice and ingratitude, become the most deplorable spectacles of extreme misery. The wild beasts of mankind have broken in upon them and rooted out all civility; and the pride of a stern and barbarous tyrant, possessing the thrones of ancient dominion, who aims only at the height of greatness and sensuality, hath reduced so great and goodly a part of the world to that lamentable distress and servitude under which it now faints and groans, those rich lands at this present time remain waste and overgrown with bushes, and receptacles of wild beasts, of thieves and murderers; large territories dispeopled or thinly inhabited: goodly cities made desolate, sumptuous buildings became ruins, glorious temples, either subverted or prostituted to impiety; true religion discountenanced and opposed; all nobility extinguished, no light of learning permitted, no virtue cherished; violence and rapine exulting over all, and leaving no security, save an abject mind and unlooked for poverty."

What an immense wealth yet lies in the entrails of Armenia; a ruler that loves the well-being of his subject, and loves to know both the condition of the country and of the people, instead of struggling for existence in extreme poverty would render both his government wealthy and his people happy, having in possession such a country as Armenia and other parts of the empire. But Turkish rulers have been destitute in prudence and have gloried in cruelty, deceitfulness and exaction. Had the long expected and delusively-promised reforms of the Turkish government been fulfilled, then would we have unfolded this wealth to the world.

Several years ago, when the missionaries of the American Board were organizing the college for the education of the Armenian young people at Harpoot, now so bloodily famous, they named it Armenia college; but the present sultan forbade it on the ground that there was no longer an Armenia, and the use of the name would encourage the Armenians to revolt. The missionaries were forced to change the name to Euphrates college. If any Turkish subject uses the word of Armenia he is fined and imprisoned; if it is used in any book the book is confiscated and the author banished or killed. The study of Armenian history is forbidden to the Armenians; they must be kept in ignorance about their own land so that many of them do not know where Armenia was or what Armenia is. A letter directed to any person or place in Armenia will never reach its destination; for the Turkish postal authorities recognize no such address. There is still another cause for the widespread ignorance concerning Armenia. These are the unhappy effects of the Turkish Empire on these once so glorious and famous countries, and after two centuries and a half this description is still literally true.

CHAPTER II.

The primal origin of the Armenians will be found in the Scriptures of Genesis x, 3-10: from Togarmah. Among the Armenian writers, calling the people by the appellation of "Togarmah Doon, the house of Togarmah," as also by the prophet Ezekiel xxvii., 14, was and still is very common.

Togarmah, the son of Gomer, the son of Japheth, the son of Noah.

The prophet Ezekiel mentions this name twice, not as a mere name of the patriarch, but as a nation descended from him, and known by the appellation, "of the house of Togarmah." The prophet does this in connection with other names as representatives of different nations. The third son of Gomer is Togarmah; the people descending from him are call "the house of Togarmah," Ezekiel xxvii., 14, where they are named after Javan, Tubal and Meshech, as bringing horses and mules to the mart of Tyre; and xxxviii., 6, where it appears after Gomer as a component of the army of Gog.

Togarmah had a son named Haig or Haik, as the ancestor of the Armenians, and they call themselves "Haikian" or "Haigazian" from him; and the land of Armenia is called "Haiasdan" or "the land of Haik."

"Togarmah," the people thus designated, are mentioned by the prophet Ezekiel. In the former passage as trading in the fairs of Tyre with horses and mules; in the latter, as about to come with Gomer out at the north quarter against Palestine. Neither passage does much towards fixing a locality, but both agree with the hypothesis, which has the support alike of etymology and of national tradition, that the people intended are

SPIRIT OF ARMENIA.

DYNASTY OF ARMENIAN FLAGS.

HAIK.

the ancient inhabitants at Armenia. Grimm's view that Togarmah is composed of two elements, "Taka," which, in Sanskrit, is "tribe," or "race," and "Armah," (Armenia), may well be accepted. The Armenian tradition which derived the Haikian race from Torgom, as it can scarcely be a coincidence, must be regarded as having considerable value. Now, the existing Armenians, the legitimate descendants of those who occupied the country in the time of Ezekiel, speak a language which modern ethnologists pronounce to be decidedly Indo-European; and thus, so far, the modern science confirms the Scriptural account.

Haik, the son of Torgarmah, like the rest of the descendants of Noah, was in pursuit of a new location for himself and his posterity, and had descended with the multitude into the country of Shinar of Mesopotamia. Here the people, for fear of another destructive flood, attempted to build a high tower, "the Tower of Babel." Haik and his sons distinguished themselves by wisdom and virtue in the erection of this tower; but ambitious Belus for supremacy, yea even requiring homage to him image, became too repulsive to virtuous Haik and his sons. Haik therefore left the plains of Shinar with his large family and returned to the home of his nativity, the land of Ararat, in the vicinity of the lake of Van; or the plain of Moosh. Belus, on hearing that Haik had withdrawn from his authority, pursued him with a large force. Haik, when he heard that Belus was coming against him, mustered the male members of his family and those who were willingly under his authority, armed them as well as he was able and set out to meet the enemy. He charged his little army to attack that part of the enemy's force where Belus commanded in person, "for," said he, "if we succeed in discomfiting that part the victory is ours; should we, however, be unsuccessful in our attempt, let us never survive the misery and disgrace of a defeat, but rather perish, sword in hand, defending the best and dearest right of reasonable creatures—our liberty." Then did the brave leader move on with his force, and faced the invaders. After a bloody

conflict Belus fell by an arrow discharged at him by Haik.
The army of Belus, soon after this, was dispersed.

Haik was a powerful warrior, and the founder of the Armenian kingdom, which began 2350 B. C., and ended with
Levan VI., 1375 A. D., thus lasting 3.725 years, though with
intervals of extinction.   Their own kings did not always reign
in Armenia.   Sometimes other nations ruled over it by way of
compensation; sometimes the Armenians ruled over other nations.   The people never call themselves Armenians, or their
country Armenia; they use the name simply for the sake of
foreigners.   The Armenians, therefore, call themselves after his
name, "Haik," and the country "Hayasan."

Haik, following the manner of the ancient patriarchs,
founded towns and villages, and after a long life died in peace.
Whatever its origin, it is certain that the Armenians are a very
ancient nation, as ancient as the Assyrians or Persians. [I have
seen an article upon this question in the "Independent" of
March 5, 1896, which was written by Rev. James D. Barton,
D. D., secretary of the American Board.   I would like to ask
from the author the privilege of using that article as follows in
my pamphlet.—THE AUTHOR.]

According to Armenian histories, the first chief of the
Armenians was Haik, the son of Togarmah, the son of Gomer,
the son of Japheth, the son of Noah.   It is an interesting fact
that the Armenians to this day call themselves Haik, their language, "Haiaren," and their country, "Haiasdan."   "Armenia"
and "Armenian" are words which cannot be spelled with Armenian characters or easily pronounced by that people.   That
name was given them and their country by outside nations, because of the prowess of one of their kings, Aram, the seventh
from Haik.   Probably this people are the resultant of strong
Aryan tribes overrunning and conquering the country now
occupied by the Armenians, and which was then possessed by
primitive Turanian populations.   Subject to the vicissitudes of
conquest and invasion, the borders of Armenia have fluctu-
ated.   Lake Van has always been within the kingdom, and the

capital has usually remained during their highest prosperity at the city of Van. They have had a long line of kings of valor and renown. They were an independent nation, but with varying degrees of power, until A. D. 1375, when they became completely a subject people. Since that time their country has been under the government of Russia, Persia, or Turkey, far the larger portion being under Turkey. During the years of their greatest prosperity, from 600 B. C. to about 400 A. D., this nation played a prominent part in the wars of the Assyrians, Medes, Persians, Greeks and Romans.

There are, perhaps, from two and a half to three millions of Armenians in Turkey, Russia and Persia. In the absence of accurate records we must be content with a mere estimate, based upon observations and inadequate government returns. In an extended district they comprise a majority of the inhabitants. They are everywhere mingled with and surrounded by Kurds and Turks. The Armenians are forbidden to carry or possess arms, under severe penalties, where the other races are armed, many of them by the government. Armenian histories relate that soon after the resurrection of Christ, Abgar, the King of Armenia, with his court, accepted Christianity. This was short lived, however; but in the third century A. D., under the leadership of Gregory the Illuminator, the Armenian people as a nation became Christian. This was the first nation to adopt Christianity as a national religion. The church was called "Gregorian" by those outside, but "Loosavorchagan" by the Armenians, the word meaning, "Illuminator," the name given to Gregory. The Gregorians and Greeks worked in harmony in the great councils of the Church until 451. At the fourth Ecumenical Council, which met at Chalcedon that year, the Gregorian church separated from the Greek upon the so-called Monophysite doctrine, the former accepting and the latter rejecting it. Since then the Gregorian church has been distinctly and exclusively an Armenian national church.

The organization and control of the church is essentially Episcopal. The spiritual head is a catholicos; but in addition to him there is a patriarch, whose office bears largely upon the political side of the national life, as related to the Ottoman government. There are three of the former, residing in order of their importance at Echmiazin, in Russia; at Aghtamar, on an island in Lake Van; and at Sis, in Cilicia, each with his own diocese. There are two of the patriarchs, residing at Constantinople and Jerusalem. There are nine grades of Armenian clergy. The Bible was translated into their language in the middle of the fifth century. Owing to a change in the spoken tongue, the Bible became a dead book to the people, although it was constantly read at their church services. As the priests scarcely ever understood the Scripture which they read, Christian doctrines were kept alive by oral teachings; but the restraint upon life which pure Christianity exercises was largely removed. They blindly accept the Bible as the word of God. They have many large and fine churches, some of which are several hundred years old. This nation has suffered great persecutions for its faith during the last eleven centuries; but with wonderful patience and endurance has clung to the old beliefs and forms of worship.

Mission work was begun among them for the purpose of introducing into the church the Bible in the spoken language of the people, in order that its teachings might reform the church and the nation. The Armenian nature is essentially religious. Born into the church, its customs, traditions and teachings have large influence over the life. Although much of their teaching and many of their customs are based upon mere traditions, and are not in accord with the enlightened, educated Christianity of the west, nevertheless, the fact that during the last few months thousands among them have deliberately chosen death, with terrible torture, to life and Islam shows that among them there exists much essential Christian faith. It must not be overlooked that the old church has been greatly enlightened and elevated by the mission schools and colleges planted in their country, and the evangelistic work carried on among them. They, too, in imitation of the evangelical branch of their nation, have organized schools, accepted the Bible in the spoken language, and introduced into their church worship many of the methods of Christian instruction used by the Christian church all over the world.

The Armenians' greatest enemy outside of Islam, is their incompatibility of character. They cannot agree among themselves. "Haik voch miapan" ("Armenians cannot agree") is one of their many proverbs. This is their national weakness. Owing to this fact, which led to internal jealousies and bickerings and strife during the period of their most successful national life, they were weakened, then disrupted, and finally completely subjugated. This characteristic has constantly appeared in the management of their ecclesiastical affairs, and the Turks, in order to control them, have made great use of this weakness, playing one party off against another. The source of this national weakness lies in their jealousy of imagined or actual rivals. Suspicious of each other, and jealous of competition, the race has been broken up into factions, which has rendered impossible anything like a national growth or unity, and has made it easy for the ruling Turk to keep them in complete subjection. Many times the Armenians themselves have been the most effective instrument in the hands of their diplomatic rulers in checking national progress. Owing to this fact, if for no other reason, a plan for a general revolution upon the part of the Armenians could lead only to exposure and failure. The most intelligent have from the first fully understood this, and have deprecated any agitation which must necessarily end in disaster. The advocates of revolution have almost invariably been men of narrow views and no leadership in the nation at large, who have, outside of Turkey, organized rival societies to collect money from credulous Armenians to the credit of their own personal bank account, and for the injury of their protesting people in Turkey. This same characteristic would make it impossible to-day for the Armenians to be self-governing.

The Armenians are the most intelligent of all the peoples of eastern Turkey. In western Turkey their only rivals are the

Greeks. They far outclass their Mohammedan rulers in the desire for general and liberal education, and in their ability to attain to genuine scholarship. During the last twenty years few institutions of higher education in the United States and in England have failed to have Armenians among their pupils, and the rank which they have usually taken is most creditable to the race.

The popularity of Euphrates College, in Horput, and of Central Turkey College, at Aintab, whose students are almost exclusively Armenians, as well as Anatolia College, at Marsovan, and Robert College, at Constantinople, which have many Armenians among their students, taken together with the fact that large sums are paid each year by the people for the education of their sons and daughters, all prove that in addition to the ability to advance mentally there is a strong desire upon the part of the Armenians for general enlightenment. Bi-lingual from childhood, and many of them tri-lingual, they learn languages easily. Their general tendency is to prefer metaphysical studies, being inclined rather to the speculative in their manner of thought. They have taken readily to the idea of female education, and the three colleges for girls in Turkey are among her most popular evangelical institutions. These are largely patronized by the Armenians. This nation has produced many well-known scholars, which fact, taken together with the general high standard of scholarship among her students, and the eager desire prevalent among the people for a liberal education, shows that the race, intellectually, compares favorably with the most favored nations of the world.

The Armenians are the farmers, artisans, tradesmen, and bankers of eastern Turkey. They have strong commercial instincts and mature ability, and being industrious withal have made much progress in all these lines. In spite of the heavy restrictions placed upon them by the Turkish government, in the form of general regulations and excessive taxes, in some parts of Turkey the leading business operations are largely in their hands. In some setions of the villages of Harput and

Diarbekir, twenty-five years ago, the land was owned almost entirely by Moslems, but rented and farmed by the Armenians. At that time the Armenians were not permitted to possess, to any extent, the soil. Lack of industry upon the part of the Mohammedans, and the acquirement of property upon the part of the Armenians, largely by emigration to the United States, have led the Turks to sell their ancient estates to Armenians, who are supplied with funds from their friends who are working in this country. The careful management of the property thus acquired led to the advancement of the proprietor-farmer, while the one from whom the land was purchased was left without an income.

While the Turks in many of the principal cities where Armenians dwell own most of the shops, the renters are largely Armenians. An intelligent Turkish governor once told the writer that if the Armenians should suddenly emigrate or be expelled from eastern Turkey, the Moslem would necessarily follow soon, as there was not enough commercial enterprise and ability, coupled with industry, in the population to meet the absolute needs of the people.

The Armenian, while industrious and naturally inclined to follow in the footsteps of his father, takes very readily to a new trade. When emigrating to foreign countries, he easily adapts himself to his new surroundings, and does creditable service in almost any line of work. This adaptability, together with a tendency to hold on to a line once begun, has given a stable character to the nation.

The Armenian is domestic in his habits and aspirations, and not military. In the early history of the race we do not find much writing of their conquests. They did not go outside of their borders, as a general thing, to conquer their neighbors. While not lacking in physical courage and prowess in war when called to defend their country against invasion, they did not seek to conquer. Sometimes in driving back an aggressive foe they carried the war into his territory, and levied upon it for injuries received. Yet it never seems to have been their ambition to be a great nation, ruling over conquered races. Their chief ambition appears to have been to possess in quiet their beloved fatherland, "hairenik," where they might worship God according to the demands of their own national church. To-day they have no desire of conquest or ambition to rule. Their greatest wish is to be permitted to enjoy without fear the blessing of their simple domestic life, together with the privileges of worship and education, and the opportunity to possess in peace the fruits of their frugal industry. The Armenian loves his children, and is most closely attached to his home. When he emigrates, it is only for the purpose of trade and gain. His heart's affection centres in the old home, to which he, if unprevented, will return to rejoin his loved ones. In all his native land the city or village of his birth is *the* spot on earth.

The Armenians are most simple and frugal in their manner of life. Uncomplaining and generally cheerful, they continue their occupations, following in the footsteps of their fathers without desire for change. The son of the carpenter is a carpenter, content with the adze and saw; and the shoemaker sticks to his last without a thought of being anything else so long as that trade serves him. The home life is patriarchal, the father ruling the household, and the sons bringing their wives to the paternal roof. In the event of the death of the father, the eldest son takes his place at the head of the family. The aged are held in high esteem, and their counsel sought and honored. The women occupy inferior positions, the nation copying many customs in regard to them from the Turks among whom they live. They are not an immoral race, but are inclined to drink wine, which is a cheap product of their country.

Thus we have a race old in national history when Alexander invaded the East, and with its star of empire turning toward decline when the Cæsars were at the height of their power; a nation not mingling in marriage with men and women of another faith, with blood now as pure in its descent from the undiscovered ancestors of nearly three decades of centuries ago as the Hebrews stand unmixed with Gentile blood; with a language, a literature, a national church, distinctively its own; and yet a nation without a country, without a government, without a protector or a friend in all God's world. This is not because it has sinned, but because it has been terribly sinned against; not because of its intellectual or moral or physical weakness, but because it has little to offer in return for the service which the common brotherhood of man among nations should prompt the Christian nations of the world to render.

THE STORY OF ARMENIAN DYNASTIES.

The First: The Haigazian, from 2350 to 328 B. C.

The Armenian dynasties are divided into four special branches or periods. The first is the Haigazian dynasty. This dynasty began 2,350 years before Christ, and ended in the time of Alexander the Great, 328 B. C. No other recorded dynasty has so long an unbroken succession. As already mentioned, Haig was the founder of the Armenian kingdom. He can scarcely be called a King, because in his time there was not a great Armenian nation. It was rather a tribe, and Haig was chief or governor. His position was like that of Abraham, what would now be called a sheikh; and like Abraham he was a worshiper of the true God.

Haig's son Armen succeeded his father, and greatly enlarged the kingdom. He subdued a large district northeast of Mount Ararat, and built a city and town of hewn stones there, near the banks of the river Araxes. He named the city after himself Armanir, and made it the capital of the government. It is most likely the name Armenia comes from him. Some recent foreign writers have the impudence to say that there was no such King, but that his name was made up to account for that of Armenia; but the same records which tell us of Haig tell us of his son. After Armen we find his son, Armaiss, was the successor of his father Armen, or Armenag. The son of Aramais was Amassia, who, soon after the decease of his father, took the lead of the government. Our historians tell us that it was Amassia who gave the name Masis, after himself, to that magnificent and huge mountain (Mount Ararat, so called). Harmah mounted the throne of his father Amassia after the latter's departure from this life. Aram, or Armanag, about 2000 B. C., the son and successor of Harmah towers among the monarchs of the first period of the Armenian history. He was, like King David, a great warrior and conqueror. One of the notable Kings is Aram, the seventh in succession, and the greatest of Armenian conquerors. He raised and drilled an army of 50,000 men, whose efficiency and his own military skill and energy are proved by his invading and conquering Media. He then invaded Assyria, and conquered a part of that country. Next, he marched westward, and subjugated some of the eastern portion of Asia Minor, inhabited by the Greeks. The latter, Cappadocia, along the Halys or Kizil-Irmak, Aram named the Hayasdan, translated by the Romans as "Armenia Minor," which, oddly enough, in later times became Greater Armenia, or Armenia proper. After the long and glorious reign of Aram, the country slowly came into a subordinate condition to the Assyrian empire, though the Kings of the Haikian dynasiy continued to rule over Armenia; but they were very much overshadowed when the Assyrian empire was at the zenith of her glory.

It, however, should be understood that Armenia was not completely subjugated; for every ruler of a district was a King by himself, and on account of the inaccessibility of some districts an entire subjugation of a country like Armenia was an impossibility in those days. Tiglath-pileser I., the King of Assyria (1110-1090 B. C.) unconsciously confesses in his famous inscription, which contains the most of his great achievements, that some of these districts never knew subjugation.

The enormous growth of the Armenian kingdom under

Aram or Armanag, and its conquest of part of Assyria, excited the alarm of the Assyrian King Ninos. Not feeling strong enough to engage in open warfare with him, he thought to compass his destruction by winning his friendship, and then putting him out of the way; and as a first step he sent him a costly jeweled crown. The intrigue failed, however, and Aram lived to a great age, reigning fifty years.

Aram was succeeded by his son Ara, called "Ara the Beautiful." The fame of his beauty went abroad through the world. The Assyrian Queen, Semiramis, was so enchanted by the sight of his person that she fell madly in love, and proposed marriage to him, but Aram refused her. This military Amazon was not to be balked so. She resolved to marry him by force, and came with a great army to Armenia to capture the prize; but he was killed in the war, and she took possession of the country, with which she was so charmed that she decided to remain. She removed the capital of the enlarged Assyrian kingdom to the lovely shores of Lake Van, erecting a palace there for herself, and buildings on the eastern side of a city named "Shamiramagerd" (built by Semiramis). Many years later a King of the Haigazian dynasty, whose name was Van, rebuilt it and called it after himself. This was the present city of Van.

The next great interesting event was in 710 B. C., when Sennacherib of Assyria was assassinated by his two sons, Adramelich and Sharezer, who escaped into Armenia. The King of Armenia at this time was Sgayorty, which means "son of giant." He received the sons of Sennacherib with great kindness; they married Armenian women, and remained in the country till their death. Their descendants were great Armenian princes, bearing the titles Prince Arziroonian and Prince Kinoonian.

It has already been said that the Assyrian influence, civilization and culture had characterized this period, moulded the customs of the people, and wrought changes in the names of some places and persons. It has been inferred by some historians and scholars from these changes that the Kings and the people of Ararat, or Armenia, were not Aryans, and do not belong to the Indo-European race or family. But they, unfortunately for them, have no better argument to support their hypothesis than two or three names found in the Behistum inscription. The unhappiest aspect of their passion is this: One of the two scholars mentions those names as an argument to prove the existence still of these non-Aryan* people and language, and the other adduces the same names as evidence of the Aryans making their appearance at that period, or just a little before that time.

Armenia comes ti view again in connection with Biblical history in the capture at Jerusalem by Nebuchadnezzar, 600 B. C., and the deportation of the Judean people. The Armenian King, Hurachia, was one of his allies in the siege, and on returning to Armenia carried with him a Hebrew prince named Shampad. This was a very intelligent man, and made himself greatly loved and esteemed by the Armenians—a sort of Daniel or Joseph. He, too, married an Armenian noblewoman, and his descendants became the very foremost of the noble families and ecclesiastical functionaries of the country, crowning the Kings on occasion. They were called Parkradoonias princes, and at last one of them founded the third dynasty of Armenian Kings, the pakradoonian. Though the nation is Aryan, there is noble Hebrew (Semitic) blood mixed with it.

Perhaps the most interesting past of the Haigazian dynasty comes just before the end, the time of Dikran or Tigranes I. In him both wisdom and valor were combined to an eminent degree. As soon as he succeeded his father, Yerevant, he instituted great reforms to improve the state of the country. He not only enlarged it by conquest, but he greatly improved public education and morals, removed obstructions to international commerce, introduced navigation on the lakes and rivers,

---

*In the Behistum inscription we have three Armenian names, Dadarshish, Drakha and Hanitn, must be the same with Khaldita of the first quotation, for he is the father of Arakpa; both, therefore, must be either Aryans or non Aryans.

encouraged cultivations; trade flourished, every acre of ground was tilled, the country was alive with energy and hope. This vigor and prosperity aroused the envy of Ashdahag, King of Media. He resolved to kill Dikran, and, to throw him off his guard, married his sister, Princess Dikranooee. A plot to murder Dikran was then set on foot. The princess learned of it, warned her brother, whom she loved, and ran away. Dikran collected an army, made a rapid march to Media, surprised and slew Ashdahag, and brought back a vast amount of spoils in captives and goods. He built a fine city on the bank of the Tigris, and called it Dikranagerd, "the city of Dikran." It was afterwards the residence of the sister who had saved his life. It is now called by the Turks Diarbekr.

The most important political achievement of his life was assisting Cyrus in the capture of Babylon, 538 B. C. The two monarchs were very friendly, and Dikran's Armenian army was a chief factor in the conquest. In Jeremiah's prophecy of the capture about a century before it occurred, he mentions the Armenian kingdom as one of the actors, "the kingdoms of Ararat, Minni and Ashkenaz." (Jer. li., 27.)

After Dikran's death his son, Vahakn, or Vahi, succeeded him; he was considered a god by the people, and worshiped as such through a monument after his death. Thus far the people had mostly worshiped the one true God, but from this time they relapsed into heathenism for a while, on account of the influences pressing on them from outside. The last King of the Haigazian dynasty was Vahi, or Vahakn. When Alexander the Great invaded Persia, Vahe went to Darius' help with 40,000 infantry and 7,000 cavalry. But Alexander conquered first Darius and then Vahi (323 B. C.), and annexed both Persia and Armenia. From this time the country of Armenia was governed by the Macedonian rulers until the defeat of Antiochus the Great by the Romans. At this time Armenia recovered her independence, which did not, however, last very long. Thus came to an end the first Armenian dynasty, after an existence of 1,922 years.

THE STORY OF ARMENIAN DYNASTIES. (CONTINUED.)

The Second: The Arshagoonian, from 150 B. C. to 428 A. D.

This dynasty began not far from 150 B. C., close to the time when Carthage was utterly destroyed and Greece was finally subjugated. It ended 428 A. D., about half a century before the extinction of the western Roman empire, and about the time Genseric and his Vandals conquered Africa. It is by far the most famous of the Armenian royal houses, for it embraces the very heart of the classic times with which all educated people are familiar. It brings us perpetually in contact with the most brilliant and best known of classic names. It is sprinkled with names towering up familiar and powerful, even among the Greek and Roman magnates, and in spite of political ups and downs it covers a time of immense expansion for the Armenian people, of a firmly rooted growth in numbers, wealth and consciousness of national unity, which has enabled the nation to survive and keep its united being through many centuries of dismemberment, impoverishment, massacre and attempts at outright extermination again and again. More than all, it covers the time of Jesus Christ and the conversion of Armenia to his religion, first of all the nations of the earth, as by its history and traditions it ought to have been. During the time between the disappearance of the line of Haig and the rise of the line of Arshag, Armenia was not by any means wholly without Kings of its own, but it was mostly a dependency. The rise of the Arsacidæ or Arshag dynasty of Parthia was a complete overthrow of the Macedonian influence in the East. Arsaces, the Parthian King, appointed his brother Valarsaces King over Armenia, and these two countries, governed by one reigning family, were in full sympathy with each other and in firm alliance for a time, and a worthy antagonist and opponent of the Romans, who were pushing eastward over the territories once subdued by the Macedonian prince, Alexander the Great.

Among the successors of Valarsaces of Arsacidæ or Arshag

DIKRAN II.

dynasty of Armenia, Tigranes the Great, or the second, immortalized himself, not only in the history of Armenia, but also in universal history. His name was the glory of his people, as it was also a terror to his enemies. He extended his dominions from the Caucasian·mountains to the Mesopotamian plains, and from the Caspian Sea to the Mediterranean, including Media, Atropatene, Assyria proper, Cilicia, Syria, and Phœnicia. He built a new capital city of an immense size, and called after his name, Tigranaghert* (built by Tigranes).

After these conquests he called himself "King of Kings" (that is, emperor, king with other kings under him), which title the Parthian Kings had claimed theretofore. He would probably have ended by mastering and restoring the unity of the old Seleucia kingdom in its widest extent, the whole heart of western Asia, had he not in an evil hour been induced by that reckless old fighter, his father-in-law, Mithradates of Pontus, to join him in war against the Romans. Tigranes' own son had quarreled with him, and taken refuge with the King of Parthia, whose daughter he married, and now offered to guide his father-in-law into Armenia if he would invade it as the ally of the Romans. This was done, and Tigranes the Elder had to fly to the mountains; but the Parthian King grew tired of the siege of rock castles, and went home, leaving his son-in-law to carry on operations with part of the army. The great Armenian King at once broke loose, and annihilated the forces of his son, who fled to Pompey, just invading Armenia with the Roman army. Even the great Tigranes was no match for Rome, and had to surrender. Pompey was not harsh with him, but left him Armenia (except Sophene and Gordyene, which were made into a kingdom for his son) and his Parthian conquests, even going so far as to send a Roman division to wrest these from the Parthian King, who had reconquered them on Tigranes' defeat, and restore them to the latter. On

---

*According to Strodo, twelve Greek cities were depopulated to furnish Tigranacerta with inhabitants (xl. 14, section 15). According to Appian, three hundred thousand Cappadocians were translated thither (Mithrid, page 216 C). Plutach speaks of the population as having been drawn from Cilicia, Cappadocin, Gordyene, Assyria, and Adiabent, (Lucull, 26), "Sixth Oriental Monarchy," by G. Rawlinson.

the departure of Pompey, the Parthians once more reclaimed
them, but a compromise was finally made. Phraates of Parthia, however, resumed once more the title of "King of Kings."
Tigranes remained the ally of the Romans till his death in 55
B. C., a reign of thirty-nine years, on the whole of great glory
and usefulness.

He was succeeded by his son, Artavasdes (Ardvash), who
inherited that most dreadful of legacies, a place between the
hammer and the anvil. For the next quarter of a century the
Romans and the steadily growing and consolidating power of
the Parthian empire were alternately irresistible in eastern Anatolia. It was impossible to avoid taking sides, for neutrality
meant invasion by one party or the other; and whichever side
he took he was sure to be punished for as soon as the other
came uppermost. If Artavasdes had been as dexterous as
Alexius Comninus himself he could hardly have escaped ruin;
that he kept his throne for over twenty years is proof that he
was not unworthy of his father. First came the invasion of
Parthia by Crassus. Artavasdes, faithful to his father's Roman
allegiance, asked him to make the invasion by way of Armenia,
and offered to help him. Crassus refused, but the Parthian
King, Orades, invaded Armenia. However, he made peace,
and betrothed his eldest son, Pacorus, to Artavasdes' daughter, just before news was brought him of the annihilation of
Crassus' army, guaranteed by Crassus' severed head and hand,
The civil wars of Rome for years to come broke the Roman
power, and the Parthians (with the good will of the inhabitants,
who detested the Roman pro-consuls), swept westward, compelled submission or alliance from all the countries to the Taurus, and even annexed all Syria for a time, just as, seven centuries later, the Syrians, from hate of the Byzantine governors,
gave up their cities to the Saracens. But the Roman power
once more rallied. The Parthians were driven out of Syria,
and Pacorus was killed. The aged Orades, under whom the
Parthian empire proper reached its pinnacle, died, leaving the
throne to one of those jealous, murderous despots so familiar

in eastern history, who made a general slaughter of his brothers, and even murdered his son to remove any possible leader of
a revolt, and Artavasdes once more returned to the Roman
alliance.   In the year 36 A. D., Mark Antony undertook the
task Crassus had so terribly failed in seventeen years before, of
striking at the heart of Parthia.   But this time the invasion was
by way of Armenia.   It was almost as frightful a disaster as the
former; a third of the army of 100,000 men was destroyed by
the enemy, 8,000 died of cold and storm in the Armenian
mountains.   The wounded died in enormous numbers; but
that Artavasdes let the army winter in his country, it would
have perished as completely as Crassus' did.   In spite of this,
the Romans, wanting a scapegoat, laid the whole blame on
Artavasdes, without a shadow of reason that can be shown.   It
was the last time for a century and a half that the Romans attacked Parthia.   In default of that plunder they resolved to
have Armenia, and a couple of years later, in the year 33 A. D.,
they seized Artavades by treachery and occupied the country.
The Parthians at once took up the cause of his son, Artaxa,
and made war on the Romans to seat him on the throne, and
when the Roman troops were withdrawn to help Anthony's cause,
which was lost in the battle of Actium, the Parthians overran
Armenia, and killed or massacred all the Romans in the country, and made their candidate King as Artaxa II.   This was in
30 B. C., and in the same year his father, Artavasdes, who had
been carried to Alexandria by Antony, was beheaded by Cleo-
patra.   But the very next year, the worthless tyrant, Phraates
of Parthia, was driven from the throne by a rebellion, and
Artaxa made peace with Rome.

The history of Artavasdes' reign is in essence the history
of the next four centuries, save that the results were incompar-
ably worse.

We have been dealing with a time at least of steady, single-
handed government, of able rulers, either inside or outside, of
some sort of ability to keep the civil structure of the country
from breaking to pieces; but even that disappears over long
periods in the early centuries of the Roman empire.

One great secret of Armenia's misery during these ages of woe—indeed, to a large extent during all the ages—lies in the fact that she is a borderland, a buffer between great states, and, indeed, between great natural divisions of climate and society. She is the boundary between semi-tropic central Asia and temperate eastern Europe, touching the land of the fig and the silk worm on the one side, and that of the apple and the mountain goat on the other; between Scythian steppes and Syrian deserts. In these earlier ages she was fought for between East, West and South—Parthia, Rome and a Syro-Egyptian power of some sort; in these days divided between East, West and North.

Had Armenia been smaller or more level she would have perished without a struggle, perhaps, rather, would never have existed; but her territory is so large and so defensible, that her history could have been predicted—final dismemberment between great states surrounding her, yet not without ages of desperate struggle. She was not large enough to be permanently the seat of empire; she was far too large for either rival to let pass wholly into the hands of the other. So she was pulled to pieces. But she wanted to control her own destiny, and made a long and heroic fight before being dismembered.

To write the history of the next few centuries would tire out all readers, and would not do any good. It was a long duel between Rome and Persia for the ownership of Armenia, in which the prosperity and happiness of their unhappy football nearly perished. Almost the whole foreign policy of Parthia was to control or to have a paramount influence in Armenia; almost the whole foreign policy of Rome in the East was to do the same thing.

For nearly a century following Artavasdes' deposition, though the Romans professed to govern the country, and the Parthians sometimes held it, and both sides repeatedly put kings on its throne, it was actually in a state of pure anarchy. Every great family, seeing it must depend on its own strength for preservation, extended its rule over as wide a district as would submit. Nearly two hundred houses acted with perfect independence of each other and of the nominal government, and some of them established principalities of considerable size.

After this, though the country was for century after century just the same shuttlecock between the rival states, the feudal anarchy was somewhat reduced, the turbulent nobility better held in check; but it was impossible that there should be really firm and orderly government when a king could not be secure of his throne for a year on one side or the other, and dared not render his powerful subjects disaffected by making them obey the laws.

We may be sure that the government was really an oligarchy, under the forms of a monarchy, and even the title, "King of Armenia," during this period must not be taken to mean too much. There were sometimes separate kings of Upper and Lower Armenia, one under Roman and one under Parthian influence. The independent princes often made head against both, and outlying principalities, like those of Osrhoene and Gordyene, probably got hold of more or less Armenian territory in the melee.

At this time the Prince Abgar, or Abgarus, or King Apkor, the son of Arsham, from the dynasty of Osrhoene, was the fifteenth king of the little kingdom of Armenia, or in northern Mesopotamia, whose capital was the flourishing city of Edessa, called Uorfa, which lay next he southern border of Armenia.

According to the Armenian church history, and also the great Christian father, Eusebius, the origin of Christianity in Armenia dates from the time of its King Abgar, who reigned at the beginning of the Christian era. He had his seat of government in the city of Edessa, and was tributary to the Romans.

Herod Antipas, the tetrarch of Judæa, was hostile to King Abgor, but was unable to injure him, except by exciting the Romans against him. He therefore accused him falsely to the Emperor Tiberius of rebellious projects. King Abgar, on being made acquainted with this accusation, hastened to send messengers to the Roman general, Marinus, then governor of Syria, Phœnicia and Palestine, for the purpose of vindicating himself; then, however, he had vindicated himself before the Roman Emperor, Tiberius.

After Abgor's death his son Anane succeeded him. This Anane apostatized, and tried to make his people do the same as before. He reopened the heathen temples, resumed the public worship of the idols, and ordered the sacred handkerchief removed from the city gate. But Adde, the bishop, walled up the latter. The King ordered the bishop to make a diadem for him, as he had for his father. The bishop refused to make one for a head that would not bow to Christ, and the King had the bishop's feet cut off while he was preaching, causing his death—the first Christian martyr on record. By a just retribution the savage king met his own death by a marble pillar in his palace falling on him and breaking his legs.

Meantime, Abgor's nephew, Sanadrug, had set up his standard in Shavarshan, or Ardaz, proclaiming himself King of Armenia—one of the countless chieftains who took advantage of Armenian anarchy to carve out principalities for themselves. On the death of Anane, he marched to Edessa, claiming it as his own inheritance. The people admitted him on his oath not to harm them, but once inside he massacred all the males of the house of Abgor.

THE STORY OF ARMENIAN DYNASTIES.

The Third: the Pakradoonian from 885 A. D. to 1045 A. D.

For a century after the Mohammedan conquest of Persia the fortunes of Armenia were apparently at their lowest ebb, and as a country it almost disappears from history. But by one of the compensations of nature, which provides that human force, like other force, cannot be extinguished, but if suppressed will find an outlet elsewhere, its people began a career of brilliancy and power unequaled in its history, and broadened from the role of a tormented buffer-state to that of the great Byzantine empire itself. The Saracen torrent flowed over Armenia's lowlands, and up to the base of its mountain fortresses, but never overcame them; for generations the contending forces battled together, surging back and forth, and filling the beautiful valleys with fire and blood. But Armenia proper was never added to the list of Saracen conquests, never made a part of the Mohammedan empire, or strengthened Mohammedanism, till four centuries later, through Byzantine greed and folly.

Internally it was all in feudal anarchy again, so far as concerned any one central focus of government. Even the Persian satraps had gone from the Persian side, and with them the half-control they had kept over the turbulent baronage. On the Roman side, from early in the seventh century to early in the eighth, the throne of Constantinople was filled with weak and unstable monarchs, fighting for Anatolia against the Saracens, and unable to exercise any effective control over Armenia, to which, indeed, they looked as a frontier defense against these very foes.

But let us not attach too harsh a meaning to "anarchy." There were a hundred rulers, it is true, great dukes and barons, each supreme in his own district; but because they held power by the sword against a savage enemy their subjects had to be a strong, independent race, with arms in their hands, which they would use against their chiefs, as well as the foreigners, if there was great oppression. In this fierce school Armenia learned the sternest lessons of self-help and discipline. With no interference from outsiders to fear, and no help from them to be got it became even more confirmed in its own independent, isolated ways, a world to itself, as it has been ever since. Its cultivators tilled their fields as they had done for so many centuries, and its scholars reach such books as they had, and wrote such as their own minds furnished. But vast numbers of its hardy sons took service in the Greek armies, and became the bone and sinew of the defence of Asia Minor against the caliphs. Not only so, but they rose by hundreds to the highest commands in the empire, both civil and military. They formed the "best society" in Constantinople itself, and to crown all, a score of emperors and empresses, in four different lines, including the most illustrious ones that ever sat on the throne, from Constantine down and who ruled the empire for two hundred and seventy-seven years, were Armenians. It is within the truth, and can be justified from the greatest of English historians, to say that for four centuries the Byzantine empire was not a Greek but an Armenian empire. Armenians by blood filled all the great offices of state, commanded the armies, occupied the throne for nearly three hundred years, and preserved the empire from external invasion and internal disintegration. It was the accession of an Armenian dynasty that turned it from a decaying power to one that expanded steadily for two centuries, from one falling into anarchy to one the glory of the world for scientific organization, and it was the final overthrow of Armenian influence that ruined the empire, being followed almost at once by the loss of half its territory and the richest part, and the breaking up of its system of civil administration. Everywhere in the time of Byzantine glory you find the list full of Armenian names. The appearance of "Bordas" as the name of generals or civil magnates is always proof of Armenian blood, and that name is monotonously common. It is the Greek form of "Varton," though now and then they make it "Bardones." One of the greatest conquerors in Byzantine history, John Kurkuas, was an Armenian, from a family which supplied three generations of statesmen and generals and two great emperors, and this is part of what the immortal historian of "Greece Under Foreign Domination," George Finlay, has to say:—

Let us note the Armenian sovereigns of the Byzantine empire. First, the great iconoclast house of Leo, the so-called Isaurian, the saviour and restorer of the empire, which reigned from 716 to 797. Leo considered himself an Armenian, and he ought to have known best. He married his daughter to an Armenian. He saved Constantinople from capture by the

Saracens, causing the destruction of the finest Mohammedan army ever gotten together; of its 180,000 men only 30,000 got back home, according to the Mohammedan historians.

Twenty-two years later another great Moslem army was annihilated by Leo, and for two centuries the Saracens scarcely troubled the empire again. But not only so, he remodeled the whole administration so effectively that no serious breakdown occurred for three centuries, and he put new life into the whole society, so that it began to outgrow its enemies, as well as out-fight them. After his able dynasty ended another Armenian, Leo V., reigned seven and a half years, from 813 to 820.

About half a century later began the Basilian dynasty, under which the laws were codified and Bulgaria destroyed.

Basil was born in Macedonia, but the name of his brother, Symbatias—Armenian Simpad—shows that he was of an Armenian family, the colonies of Armenians having spread all over the civilized world.

His line reigned without a break from 867 to 963, when the beautiful widow, Theophano, was pushed aside for sixteen years by another Armenian house. Nikephoras Phokas and his nephew, John Zimiskes, two of the ablest generals and states-men ever on the throne, descendants of a brother of the great commander, John Kurkuas, before spoken of; then Theophano's son, Basil II.—Boulgaroktanas, the Bulgarian Slayer, and the ultimate destroyer of Armenia as well—took the throne 979, and the dynasty continued till 1057, when it had run to dregs, and had just before finally ruined Armenia, and by so doing ruined the empire.

To go back to Armenia itself, the reason a feudal anarchy always ends in a military monarchy, no matter how able or self-willed every one of the separate chiefs may be, is that this very class most interested in perpetuating it grow weary of it. The stronger barons oppress and plunder the weaker, who are always superior in numbers and in united strength if they will act together. A small lord may like to be free from control by the King's officers, as well as a great one; but if he can only have that privilege by letting his overbearing neighbor be free from it too, and rob him, he finds it does not pay, and sighs for a law that will control everyone alike, and a strong ruler to enforce it. So if a chief in such a community comes to be known as having a hard hand, and letting no one be above the law but himself, the small landholders flock under his banner; he grows into a prince, and eventually some prince of such a family will make himself king, with the good will and help of all but a few great houses, who feel able to take care of themselves and desirous of taking care of others.

This happened in Armenia. In 743, a century after the battle of Nehavend, and four years after Leo's crushing defeat of the second great Saracen army, we find that a chief named Ashod, of the family of Pakrad, or Bagrat, claiming descent from the ancient Jews, had managed to win control over central and northern Armenia; how long it had been exercised or what it grew from no one knows. When Ashod is the first known founder of the Pakradoonian dynasty of Armenia, probably in 885, the two most interested powers, the Persian and Greek, were both favorable to this change, and no doubt both expected to benefit by it. Under these auspices a dynasty, the descendants of Sumbat and Pakrat, and hence of the direct line of Israel (see the Haigian dynasty in this book), took possession of the Armenian throne. During the period of wellnigh two hundred years of their troubled sway, the history of Armenia has little other interest save what attaches to a condition of incessant commotion and massacre, arising from the alternating oppressions of Persians and Greeks, as they saw it to be their advantage to intervene in her affairs. The effusive friendship of both eastern and western patrons had begun to visibly cool before a single generation of the new regime had passed away. Issuf, a creature of the Persian caliph, after carrying on hostilities against the Pakradoonian King, Sumbat I. (the second of the dynasty), seized him, and tortured him to death. This miscreant continued his invasions of Armenia in the reign of Sumbat's successor. Ashod II., "the Iron," gained his title from his

ASHOD.

stern military power. He beat back the Arabs, and gave the land peace for a considerable time. He left no son, and his brother Appas succeeded him, another brave and wise ruler, who brought back the Armenian captives held in bondage by the Saracens. He made the city of Kars his capital. He greatly improved the city, and built a beautiful cathedral there. After a reign of twenty-four years he died in peace, and his son succeeded him as Ashod III.

This was the glory of the line in prowess and generosity. He reminds one of Alfred the Great in England. He was the terror of his country's enemies; not one of them, Arab, Greek, or Persian, dared to invade Armenia, and they sent presents to conciliate his friendship. It was under him that the country became formally independent again. He filled it with fortified places. He gave all his personal income in charity, and established almshouses and state charities. He was so benevolent and so interested in the destitute that he was called "The Merciful." He ruled over Armenia twenty-six years, and was succeeded by his son, Simpad. This was neither a good man nor good ruler, but corrupt, cruel, and ambitious only for selfish purposes. He made the city of Ani, on the north side of Mount Ararat, the royal capital, built strong walls and lofty towers around it, and is said to have erected 1001 churches in it—which he might do, and still be a bad man. The extent of its still existing ruins of palaces, churches, towers, and castles testifies that it was one of the great cities of the world, like Babylon and Antioch.

For more than a century Armenia flourished and grew rich; then it disappeared once more under the hammer and anvil of Byzantine and Saracen, aided by internal disruption and the treachery of its great nobles, who hated the Kings for controlling their lawlessness. Let us take in just its situation. It included the heart of the Armenian highlands, but it had not the extent of old Armenia, several Armenian districts being independent of it, and either free or tributary to the Byzantine empire. Ani was its seat, but the district around Kars, fifty miles northwest, had split off into a separate principality, the boundary between the two being the Aros; on the east was Vaspaurakan, another princedom; on the west Sebate, another; on the north Iberia, and Abkhasia, or Abasgia, or Albania, the realms of the Georgians, and one or two others not quite certain. But all these were ruled by Armenian princes, mostly of the Pakradoonian house.

The Byzantines and Armenians were not long destined to fight their battles side by side. In 1022 the Emperor Basil II. compelled the Armenian King, Johannes Simpad, to sign a treaty, ceding at his death the city of Ani, with the province in which it stood, to the Greeks. Constantine IX. called upon Gaghik, the last of the Pakradoonian Kings, to ratify this treaty. On his refusal, Constantine, forming an alliance with the Saracen Emperor Tovin, laid siege to Ani. The treachery of the Armenian chiefs aided the project of the emperor. Gaghik surrendered, and, receiving a safe conduct, set out to Constantinople to plead his cause. Meantime, the city of Ani was captured by the Byzantine forces (1045). This fatal blow to the Pakradoonian monarchy, coming from the hand of a Christian power, destroyed not only an Armenian dynasty, but the only barrier to the advances of the Seljauk Turks. It was, therefore, in due time destined to recoil with direct results upon the head of the assailant.

Following close upon the surrender of Ani the Seljauk Turks made repeated incursions into Armenia. In the third of these incursions they captured the city of Arzen, and massacred in cold blood 140,000 people; the remnant they carried away into captivity. The native historian adds that the same cruelties were perpetrated by this barbarous horde on many other cities of Armenia. Ani, meantime, was occupied by 60,000 Greek troops, under the command of Camenas, and these were well pleased to look on with complacency at the sufferings of the Armenians.

In 1062, after the death of Togrue, his successor invaded Armenia and captured Ani.

We have now reached the close of our brief survey of the general character of the Bagradoonian dynasty. The termination of the chequered career of the exiled King Gaghik is tragic in no ordinary degree. Father Chamich gravely relates how the exiled King visited Marcus, the Metropolitan of Cæsarea, with a few attendants. He had heard that Marcus kept a huge dog, which, to show his contempt, he named "Armenian." Marcus made a show of giving the ex-king a cordial welcome, and prepared for him a feast on the evening of his arrival. Gaghik desired his host to call his large dog. The animal, on being brought in was saluted by his master by the name "Armenian." On a given signal, the attendants of Gaghik seized the dog and put him into a large bag. They forthwith threw the Metropolitan in beside him, and securely fastened the bag. The dog was then severely beaten, and so becoming furious, he worried his master to death. Falling into the hands of the Greeks, Gaghik was, in revenge, subjected to the most horrid cruelties, and after being put to death, his bloody corpse was suspended from the walls of Kigistra, to strike terror into his followers. So perished, says Chamich, Gaghik, in the fifty-fifth year of his age. He had been three years in possession of the throne of Armenia, and thirty-five years in exile. The same authority observes: "A want of prudence removed the crown from the Arsacidæ, and a melancholy want of unanimity caused the downfall of the Pakradoonians."

With the overthrow of the Pakradoonian dynasty the fortunes of Armenia sunk to a still lower ebb than ever they had done before. A portion of the conquered dominions was seized by the Greeks, while the Turks and Kurds did their best to establish a claim to the rest. At this stage took place a general movement into different provinces of the Turkish empire, particularly into the regions lying to the west and south of their ancient settlements. Only one or two native princes continued to maintain their independence. Of these, Rupen, related to the Pakradoonia, extended the limits of his dominions, and his successors advanced to Cilicia and Cappadocia, where they established what is known as the Rupenian kingdom and dynasty.

THE STORY OF ARMENIAN DYNASTIES. (CONTINUED.)

The Fourth: The Rupenian, from 1080 A. D. to 1375 A. D.

In the time of Rupen the patriarchate was weakened by divisions. Instead of one, the Armenian church set up four rival pontiffs, but the general voice was in favor of St. Gregory, to whose character and reforms we have already alluded. Around him and successive pontiffs gathered groups of studious and scholarly men, whose names and works are still held in honor. While Rupen and his successors styled themselves Kings, it was not until the time of Leo II. (1198) that the Rupenian kingdom was formally constituted and recognized by other powers. In that year Pope Celestinus III., at the instigation of the German Emperor (Henry VI.), sanctioned the coronation of Leo, and sent him a magnificent crown by the hand of Conrad, Archbishop of Maguntia. The Emperor sent him at the same time a splendid standard, having in the middle a lion rampant, in allusion to his name. This device was henceforth adopted by the Armenian Kings in lieu of the ancient design of the eagle, pigeon and dragon.*

But we have anticipated the grand event which, in some measure, renders memorable this era in the history of the Cilician kingdom of Armenia. This was its temporary connection with the Crusades. While the new sovereignty on the west of Asia Minor was struggling into and for existence, first with Greeks, and then again with Persians, a new enterprise was rousing to its inmost depths the heart of the nations of Christian Europe. This was the conception of a grand Crusade, whose object should be to wrest Palestine and Jerusalem, and Constantinople as well, from the grasp of the infidel.

It was true that at this stage the deliverance of Constantinople was only prospective, as it was not yet in the hands of the advancing foe. But it was easily seen that, with the Turkish camp already pitched on the eastern shore of the Bosphorus,

---

*Camich, vol. II, pp. 215.

THE ARMENIAN TOMBSTONE.

this could only be a question of time. Peter the Hermit, laden with the benediction of Urban II., and supported by a countless host of warriors, bearing on their breasts or shoulders the sign of the Red Cross, was now at Constantinople, on the way to deliver Jerusalem. Under the leadership of Godfrey of Bouillon this motley group had made its way to this, its first friendly resting-place and object of succor. Crossing into Asia Minor, it had found itself in the horrors of famine and pestilence. The Armenians, both of eastern and western Asia, sent abundant supplies, and by their seasonable services earned the gratitude of the leaders of the Crusade. The same friendly spirit was shown also in the case of the second Crusade. On the capture of Jerusalem in 1099 the leader of the first Crusade sent the Armenian prince, Constantine, valuable presents, created him a marquis, and conferred on him the honor of knighthood.

Amid the turmoil of Saracen conquest, in honor of the founder this new dynasty was styled the Rupenian dynasty, which lasted about three centuries. Meanwhile Malek Shah died, and the vast Seljukian empire was divided into various principalities. One of these principalities occupied a large portion of western Asia, bordering on the Greek empire, having for its capital the city of Nice.

It was during the reign of Constantine, the son and successor of Rupen I., that the immense army of the Crusades for the first time marched into western Asia, took Nice and various places, and laid siege to Antioch. But a terrible famine broke out in their camp. When the information of it reached Constantine and his chiefs, they sent an abundance of provisions to the army of the Crusaders.

The last dynasty of the Armenians in Cilicia was by no means in a favorable condition. While western Asia was in a fearful agitation, and in a tumultuous situation, the Seljukian, after losing their capital, Nice, made Iconium—which over ten centuries before had listened to the famous missionaries, Paul and Barnabas, tell the story of the Cross—their capital, and made it resound with the "ezzins" of the "muezzin" from the numerous minarets, and became a source of great trouble to the Armenians. The Greeks, inflamed with like hatred and prejudice as before, were more or less in constant conflict with them. The Armenians, over-exultant because of the presence of the Christian forces of the western nations in the east, were willing to enlist in aid of their cause by entering into an alliance with them. But the suspicions of some that these foreigners were anxious to bring the Armenian church or people under the control of the Pope of Rome were sustained by the facts, revealed in due time. Though their attempts proved unsuccessful, a schism originated in the church, which, with its detrimental effect upon the church and the people, still continues.

A new tremendous army of the Mongolians, under the command of Chinghis Khan, made its appearance in western Asia. They spread all over Persia, Armenia, and Asia Minor destruction, devastation, and death, committing wholesale massacre, consuming the cities and towns by fire, and carrying away hundreds and thousands into captivity. Armenia has been over and over inundated with the blood of her inhabitants, enriched with their carcasses scattered upon her face; her beautiful and bright sky was often rendered foggy and smoky on account of the conflagrations of her immense cities and numerous towns, kindled by the enemy; her beautiful sons and daughters were torn away from the bosoms of their parents, carried away as captives, and sold for slaves; her magnificent churches and monasteries were converted into mosques and "tekes." Yet the "House of Togarmah" marched on through these tremendous seas of oppression, persecution, cruelty, and injustice, from a remote antiquity to the end of the fourteenth century of our era, lifting up the old, centuries old, flag of liberty, torn to pieces and ready to fall into an irreparable dissolution.

No doubt the object of the Popes, who urged the western sovereigns to raise Crusades against the Mohammedans, and kept them engaged in this unsuccessful enterprise for a length of time, at the expense of an immense wealth and millions of human lives, was twofold—to exercise their sublunary power over these potentates, and to further their influence over other Christian nations in the east.

But they signally failed in their purpose. There came a time that the Popes had no influence over the Kings of Europe, and the Crusaders in the east rendered their names detestable forever, both to the Christians and non-Christians. "In 1204 (Christian era) the capital (Constantinople) was captured by the Crusaders, whose conduct fixed an indelible stain upon the name of the Franks throughout the east, especially as it is contrasted with that of the Mohammedans, who, a few years before, had conquered Jerusalem. When Saladin entered the latter city the Church of the Holy Sepulchre was respected, and the conquered Christians remained in possession of their property; no confiscations were made of the wealth of the non-combatants. But the vaunted chivalry of the papal church plundered a Christian city without remorse, desecrated its shrines, and maltreated its inhabitants, while the profane cry of "God will it!" was raised to excite each other to act the part of brigands and debauchees. Sacred plate, golden images of saints, and silver candelabra from the altars; bronze statues of heathen idols and heroes, precious works of Hellenic art; crowns, coronets, thrones, vessels of gold and silver; ornaments of diamonds, pearls, and precious stones from the imperial treasury and the palaces of the nobles; jewelry and precious metals from the shops of the goldsmiths; silks, velvets, and brocaded tissues from the warehouses of the merchants, together with coined money, were accumulated in vast heaps as spoils to be divided by the victors. A few of the crusading clergy endeavored to moderate the fury which the bigoted prejudices of the Latin church had instilled into the minds of the soldiery against the Greeks; but many priests were as forward as the most abandoned of the troops in robbing the temples of a kindred faith."*

---

*"The Turkish Empire," pp. 238, 239.

Our Saviour's words were literally fulfilled. With what measure the Greeks so often had measured and dealt with the Armenians it was meted to them by the hands of the Crusaders. Yet such a conduct of the Crusaders with the Christians, and undoubtedly a conduct ten times worse than this towards the Mohammedans, accounts for the determination and fury of the latter against the Christians. The reply of Melick Nasr, the Egyptian Sultan, to an application of the Armenian King, Leo II., for a treaty of peace was the following:—

"I will never make peace with you until you promise on oath not to hold any correspondence or communication with western nations."

Often did the Mohammedan powers imagine that the Armenians had again stirred up the western nations, that they were marching against them in greater force than ever before, and then they would attack the cities and towns of the Armenians and commit all manner of atrocities, thinking that this might be their last opportunity. The Armenian independence of Cilicia was surrounded by the Ottoman power on the west, constantly growing in strength and in numbers; on the east and north by the Mongolian invaders, under such leaders as Togrul Bey, Alp Arslan, Chinghis Khan, Tamerlane, and others, who deserve to be called the greatest warriors and the most cruel sons of the world; on the south by the Mohammedans of Egypt, under the reign of the Mameluke Sultans, who were no less formidable than the previous two, both in hatred and cruelty toward the Christians.

After the withdrawal of the western nations—or, rather, their being driven out from the east, in full satisfaction of their complete failure, either to maintain their position or ameliorate the oppressed condition of the Oriental Christians under the Mohammedans, the latter had but little difficulty in destroying the independnce of the Armenians in Cilicia. By various incursions of the Mohammedans of Egypt into Cilicia, the Armenians were reduced in strength and in numbers. Finally a vast army of the enemy marched against them. These mis-

LEON VII.

sionary soldiers of Mohammed, indeed brutes in character and nature, though clad in clayey garments of human forms, spread themselves all over the country. No city, town, or village; no building of any value, whether church, monastery, or dwelling, and no human being of any age or sex that fell into their hands was spared. They slaughtered every human being, and burned to ashes every building or razed it to the ground. In their execution of the unfortunate victims fallen into their hands they did not leave any mode untried. "The deceitful above all things and desperately wicked heart" of a depraved human creature could not have suggested any new method of torture that these Mohammedans did not devise and experiment upon their captives.

King Leo VI. and the garrison surrendered on the condition that their lives would be spared. The Egyptian general promised this on oath. Leo VI. was fettered, and, with his family, carried to Cairo in the eleventh year of his reign. (A. D. 1373). The King, Leo, and his family, after serving a period of imprisonment at Cairo, were freed by the mediation and valuable presents of the King of Spain from their imprisonment. Leo, with his Queen and daughter, went to Jerusalem. There he left them, at their own request, and then visited the European countries. On the 19th of November, A. D. 1393, he ended his mortal career at Paris. Leo, King of Armenia, was of small stature, but of intelligent expression and of well formed features. His body was carried to the tomb clothed in royal robes of white, according to the custom of Armenia, with an open crown upon his head and a golden sceptre in his hand. He lay in state upon a bier hung with white, and surrounded by the officers of his household, clothed all of them in white robes. He was buried by the high altar of the church of the Celestine. The following epitaph is on his monument, which still exists to-day:

"Here lies Leo. VI., the noble Lousinian Prince,
The King of Armenia,
Who died 1393 A. D., Nov. 23d, in Paris."

The enemy had rendered the country a complete desert, and it still remains so. The people also fell under the iron yoke of the Mohammedan power, and still suffer all the injustice and cruelties of such a government as that of Turkey, which has no excuse for its existence.

CATHERINE KORNARO, LAST QUEEN OF ARMENIA.

CHAPTER III.

From the overthrow of Leo VI., the last of the Rupenian dynasty, in 1375, the Armenian Monarchy ceased to exist. From that time forward even the semblance of civil autonomy disappeared. Whether, and when, it is destined to reappear, as the outcome of the present situation, is one of the questions which is still awaiting solution. The absorption of Armenia, now deprived of her kings, first by Persian and again by Turkish rulers, makes it no easy matter to trace the course of her chequered history.

How many thousands of their children were alienated from their paternal homes and home altars to adopt Mohammedanism, to swell the number of the Janissaries; how many thousands of families were compelled to exchange the religion of Christ, which is the religion of love and chastity, with the religion of Mohammed, which is the religion of sensualism and tyranny; how many thousands were massacred because they could not obey such an infernal behest, it is surely impossible to tell. But suffice it to say that these questions are not imaginary possibilities, but actualities performed by our fanatic Mohammedans, and instances are not wanting even at this present day.

While the expatriated Armenians were so cruelly treated by the Turks in the western and central part of Asia Minor, those in Armenia proper received one of the severest calamities ever inflicted upon men. The scourger of this infliction was the famous Mongolian savage and warrior, Lénk Timour, commonly called Tamerlane. He made himself the master of an empire extending from the walls of China to the shores of the Mediterranean, having Samarkand for his capital.

He marched with an immense army in 1387 against the Persians and subdued them within a short time, and he then fell upon the Armenians; from the city of Van to the city of Sibastia (Sivas), from the one end to the other of Armenia. No city, town or village escaped the notice of this rapacious potentate, but he reduced them to ruinous heaps and ashes; he slaughtered a great number of the inhabitants, sparing the youths as captives. The inhabitants of the latter city (Sivas) surrendered on his solemn promise that "no soldier of his will lift up the sword on them." He, however, was true to the letter, but not to the spirit of his promise. Four thousand soldiers were roasted to death, great multitudes were buried alive, and thousands of young and old whose hands and feet were tied, were thrown together and trampled under the feet of the horses.

The spot upon which this barbarous mode .of massacre took place, to this day bears the name of Sev-Hakher, signifying in the Armenian language the "Black plains."

He then attacked the Turks, who received a signal defeat, and Sultan Bayazid I. in vain attempted to effect his escape; he was captured, and he possibly died in captivity about 1402.

"For a few years Timour was the undisputed lord of Asia, master of the original seat of Ottomans, reigning in all the splendor of the ancient caliphs of Samarkand, till death removed him to the presence of that awful Being whose laws he had violated and whose creatures he had destroyed." He died in 1406 in his capital, Samarkand.

The magnificent city of Constantinople, after being the metropolis of a Christian nation over eleven centuries, fell into the hands of the barbarian Turks. In vain, and too late, did the Greeks realize their critical condition, and struggle against the angel of death. The capture of Constantinople by the Turks filled the European nations with consternation.

The following is from the letter of Pius II., the pope of Rome, who tried to raise a crusade against the Turks.

The Strait of Cadiz has been passed, and the passion of Mohammed penetrates even into Spain. . . In the other direction, where Europe extends eastward, the Christian religion has been swept away from all the shores.

The barbarian Turks, a people hated by God and man, issuing from the east of Scythia, have occupied Cappadocia, Poatus, Bethynia, Troas, Pisidia, Cilicia and all Asia Minor. Not yet content, counting on the weakness and dissensions of the Greeks, they have passed the Hellespont, and got possession of nearly all the Grecian cities of Attica, Bœotia, Phocis, Achaic, Macedonia and Trace.

Still, the royal city of Constantinople did remain the pillar and head of all East, the seat of patriarch and emperor, the sole dwelling place of Grecian wisdom. . . This, too, in our own day, while the Latins, divided among themselves, forsook the Greeks, has that cruel nation of Turks invaded and spoiled, triumphing over the city that once gave taxes to all the East.

Nor is their savage appetite yet satiated. The lord of that unrighteous people, who is rather to be called a dark brute than a king, a venomous dragon than emperor, he athirst for human blood, brings down huge forces upon Hungary. Here he harasses the Eperotes, and here the Albanians; and swelling in his own pride, boasts that he will abolish the most holy Gospel and all the law of Christ, and threatens Christians everywhere with chains, stripes, death and horrid torments.

Even the great reformer, immortal Luther, composed a once popular prayer, suited to the times, to be sung as a hymn in the churches; and Robert Wisdame, afterwards Archdeacon of Ely, appended a translation of it to the metrical version of the psalms, by Steinhold and Hopkins. It commences with the lines:

"Preserve us, Lord, by Thy dear word.
From Pope and Turk, defend us, Lord."

The cruelties of Tamerlane had already caused thousands of Armenian families to emigrate still westward; all these, and those dwelling in Cilicia. Cappadocia, Pontus, and Asia Minor, became subjects to the Ottoman Empire.

Sultan Mohammed II., the most remarkable, perhaps, of all the Sultans, stormed and took the city of Constantinople, which was henceforth to be the seat of the Ottoman Empire.

The siege and fall of Constantinople rank among the most imposing events in the transition from ancient to modern history. Constantine XI., the last of the Greek Cæsars, had appealed for help to the Christian powers of Europe—but in vain. The disputes between the Eastern and Western churches had rendered the prospect of the fall of the former a matter of indifference, if not an object of desire, to the papal see.

The spirit of the Crusades was also largely quenched, and so the citadel of Eastern Christendom, in its hour of supreme need, was left to its own unaided resources. We cannot rehearse the story of the fifty-three days' siege. The forces of the attack and the defence were in sad and suggestive contrast.

Around a city, whose Greek population the recent calamities had reduced to about 100,000 souls, with an enfeebled garrison, there gathered the 258,000 soldiers of the Turk, with 320 sail, including all kinds of craft.

The day fixed for the final onslaught, i. e., May 29, 1453, was set apart by the Sultan Mohammed II. as a religious festival. The preceding night witnessed a magnificent illumination of the Moslem camp and ships, transforming the harbor of the Golden Horn and its vicinity into a scene of splendor such as, perhaps, had never been witnessed before, or was ever to be witnessed again in the history of Oriental display.

The stated calls to prayer rose upon the still air without, while the pathetic cry of Kyrie eleison resounded within the doomed city.

The attack commenced in the early morning, and by midday Mohammed II. was riding in triumph into his new capital by the gate of St. Romanus. He rode past the dead body of the Greek emperor, buried beneath a heap of the slain,

ST. SOPHIA, OF CONSTANTINOPLE, NOW IN THE HANDS OF TURKS.

The grand old emperor, whose courage had supported his people through the horrors of the siege, had already taken his last sacrament in the church of St. Sophia, and bidden farewell to his household, ere he went forth cheerfully to sec- rifice his life in defence of the throne of the Cæsars. But the heroic effort was in vain.

The blow long pending had fallen; the Roman Empire was no more.

Sultan Mohammed II., who captured the city of Constan- tinople, established an Armenian patriarchate there in 1461, A. D.

The first patriarch was Havaguem, the Bishop of Broosa, with certain privileges, and as well as the representative, and the responsible one for his nation.

The first patriarch Havaguem was a friend of the Sultan Mohammed II. had two motives in this, first, to have an Ar- menian ecclesiastical centre in Constantinople for the nucleus of a strong Armenian settlement there, to play off against the Greeks from whom the city was taken and who might be dan- gerous, whereas the feud between Armenians and Greeks would make each weaken the other. Second, to have a hos- tage for the Armenians, responsible for their not breaking into revolt; not at all for the benefit of the Armenians, but for that of the Sultan. The same reason obtains to this day; if there was no patriarch their cause would be much better off. After the establishment of this patriarchate the Armenians had no more kings or princes; their political head was the patriarch. Even after the patriarchate was established they were no safer. They yielded to the Sultans, they became slaves to the Sultans, but the Persian Mohammedans were foes of the Turkish Mo- hammedans, and Armenia, as of old in Roman times, was the battleground.

After some bloody conflicts in Persia and Armenia by hostile claimants for supremacy over these countries, Shah Ismail had found the Suffavean dynasty of Persia in 1499. A. D. The Suffaveans claimed that Ali, the fourth caliph, would

have been the immediate successor of the prophet Mohammed
and the head of Islamism had Abubekr Omar, and Osman not
usurped themselves and seized his right. They, moreover,
claimed lineage from Ali and thus the lawful successors of
Mohammed. The Osmanli Sultans repudiated this right and
descent. This difference between the Mohammedan Turks
and Persians furnished these two Islam nations with an occasion of constant war and bloodshed. But alas! the noble land
of Ararat had to furnish them the battlefield, and the unfortunate "House of Togarmah" to suffer the doleful consequen-
ces of their sanguinary conflicts.

In the time of Sultan Ahmed and Shah Appas, the latter
a "magnificent barbarian," was one of the Shahs of Suffavean
dynasty, and he, preparing for war with the Turks, fearing
that he might be compelled to cede Armenia to the latter, he
gave orders to his army to immediately vacate as many cities
and towns as possible, and to burn them to ashes, and drive
the inhabitants into captivity. Within a short time many a
city and town lay in ruins, and the country was converted into
a fearful condition of desolation. Thousands sought refuge
in the mountains and caves. Some found a refuge but others
found only the enemy, and fourteen thousand families were
led into captivity.

This great host of captives was composed of the venerable
patriarch, bishops, priests, vartabeds, old men and women,
and children of all ages, mothers with their infants in their
arms, baptizing them with their tears; the gallant looking
young men and maidens. These all indiscriminately were
driven by the Persian soldiers to the bank of the Araxes, where
some rafts and galleys were in readiness to hasten their crossing the swift waters of the river. Many gallant husbands and
knightly brothers who were determined to protect their beautiful but unfortunate wives and sisters, even unto death, found
watery graves in the river Araxes from the hands of the brutally lustful soldiers and officers. Opposite Ispahan these captives were settled and built New Jula (some write Julpa).

The Jula proper in Armenia was destroyed by Shah Abbas. The contest between the Turks and Persians over Armenia lasted more than two centuries, beginning in 1512, A. D., by Sultan Selim I., till the early part of the last century. Hardly had they signed a treaty of peace when there was another power creeping down the Caucasus. Peter the Great of Russia was too great to miss the opportunity of taking a portion of that historic land at Ararat. His successors too, very faithful to the charge delivered to them by him, though faithless to their promises, did the same.

The Russians contended with the Persians over a portion of Armenia and other provinces belonging to the latter from 1772—1829. In this contest the Armenians rendered a signal service to the Russians and decided the victory for Russia. The promise of liberty for their heroic service and bravery made by the Russians was intended to be abject servitude and ignominious exile.

From 1813 to 1829, the Armenians appeared to think their emancipation at hand.

Russia stood in need of them to make a diversion against the Ottoman forces, and held out to them the hope of becoming an independent principality, under the protection of the Czar. Her promises were believed, and, in their devotion to their destined liberator, they withstood for more than six weeks an army of eighty thousand Persians who were marching against Russia, and prevented them from crossing their frontier, but these services reaped a poor reward, for not only were the Russians faithless to their promises, but they seized the opportunity of some trifling disturbance in the country to lay violent hands on the venerable Archbishop Narses, who was dragged in the first place to St. Petersburg, and afterwards banished to Bassarabia, whilst several of the Armenian chiefs were scattered in exile through foreign countries or carried off to Russia to be heard of no more.

Russia also wrested from the degenerate Turkish Empire at times, especially in 1878, after the Russo-Turkish war, a large territory and the important city of Kars of Armenia. As it has been already said, the unfortunate land of Ararat is now divided among these three empires, the Russian, Persian and Turkish, the largest portion of it being still under the rule of the latter.

From the above brief history given in a cursory manner it will be easily understood that the Armenians have been subjected to all kinds of cruelties. Owing to the calamitous wars, merciless persecutions, voluntary and involuntary exiles, and emigrations into different countries, they have been often justly compared to the Jews scattered like them all over the globe. The Armenians are met with in every commercial city throughout Europe and Asia, but the great majority of the nation still dwells in the land of Ararat and in the Turkish Empire. There are over two hundred thousand Armenians in the city of Constantinople, and as many in other cities of European Turkey and other European countries.

The number of Armenians in Asia Minor and Armenia proper under the Turkish rule does not fall below two millions and a half. The three or four vilayets (provinces) of Erzerum, Diarbekr, Harpoot, and Kurdistan contain many villages, peopled entirely by Armenians, and in these provinces, notwithstanding frequent emigration (owing to the atrocities of the Kurds and Turks) the Armenians preserve a numerical superiority over the Turkish and Turcoman races.

The Armenians live in their respective villages, towns and cities. In those cities and towns where they are not the only inhabitants, but there are other nationalties like the Turks and Greeks, the Armenians live in certain districts clustered by themselves, having a sufficient number of churches and schools attached to them for their religious and educational wants. The dwellings in the villages and towns in the interior are of primitive style, either being of unhewn stone entirely, or half of stone and half of sun-dried bricks with flat roofs; first large logs or beams laid crosswise and supported with strong pillars, then covered with roots and earth and dirt, with a thickness of two or three feet, and then hardened to prevent leaking. But sometimes, "through idleness of the hands the house droppeth through." (Ecclesiastes x. 18), Proverbs xix. 13, and xxvii. 15.)

The Armenians living in large towns and cities are engaged in various occupations of life. The following trades are almost exclusively in the hands of the Armenians in Asiatic and partly in European Turkey: Locksmithing, blacksmithing, coppersmithing, goldsmithing, watchmaking, shoemaking, tailoring, weaving, printing, dyeing, carpentry, masonry, architecture, etc.

And some are grocery, hardware, and all sorts of storekeepers, and some others are peddlers, traveling merchants, merchants, money brokers, (sarafs), bankers, lawyers and physicians. "The 'Armenian nation,'" says a writer, "is the life of Turkey." Another says, "They are a noble race, and have been called the Anglo-Saxons of the East. They are an active and enterprising class. Shrewd, industrious and persevering, they are the bankers of Constantinople, the artisans of Turkey, and the merchants of Western and Central Asia."

Hardly will it be necessary to adduce numerous statements of many European and American observers, some of whom know the Armenians far better than many an Armenian himself, but let us suffice with the following testimony of Rev. Dr. H. G. O. Dwight, one of the first missionaries of the American Board among the Armenians.

"The principal merchants are Armenians, and nearly all the great bankers of the (Turkish) governments; and whatever arts there are that require peculiar ingenuity and skill, they are almost sure to be in the hands of Armenians, in one word, they are the Anglo-Saxons of the East."

The above statements are made undoubtedly and comparatively of the modern Armenians, but in order that the reader might not be misled to lightly think of the Armenians of old as lacking the ingenuity, skill, and the spirit of enterprise we will cite also the statements from secular and sacred his-

tory to show that the ancient Armenians were not much behind the Anglo-Saxonism of the Armenians of the present
time.

Herodotus, the great historian, who lived in the fifth century before the Christian era, tells us that next to the marvel-
ous city of Babylon were the boats, constructed in Armenia
by the Armenian merchants in the following manner:—

"But the greatest wonder of all that I saw in the land,
after the city itself, I will now proceed to mention. The boats
which came down the river (Euphrates to Babylon are circular, and made of skin. The frames, which are of willow, are
cut in the country of the Armenians above Assyria, and on
these, which serve for hulls, a covering of skin is stretched
outside, and thus the boats are made, without either stem or
stern, uite round like a shield. They are then entirely filled
with straw, and their cargo is put on board, after which they
are suffered to float down the stream. Their chief freight is
wine, stored in casks made of the wood of the palm-tree.
They are managed by two men, who stand upright in them,
each plying an oar, one pulling and the other pushing. The
boats are of various sizes, some larger, some smaller; the
biggest reach as high as five thousand talents burthen. Each
vessel has a live ass on board; those of large size have more
than one. When they reach Babylon the cargo is landed and
offered for sale, after which the men break up their boats,
sell the straw and frames, and loading their asses with the
skins, set off on their way back to Armenia. The current is
too strong to allow a boat to return up-stream, for which reason they make their boats of skins rather than wood. On
their return to Armenia they build fresh boats for the next
voyage." *

The prophet Ezekiel, in his enumeration of the ancient
merchant nations who were engaged in mercantile pursuits
with the merchant nations of the Phœnicians in the marts of
the commercial city of Tyre, speaks of the Armenians under

---

*Rawlinson's Herodotus, book 1, page 194.

the popular appellation of "the house of Togarmah," "They of the house of Togarmah traded in thy fairs with horses and horsemen and mules." (Ezekiel xxvii., 14).

The descendants of Togarmah, on account of their industry, ingenuity, and intelligence, have accumulated great wealth, and demanded, yea extorted, from the indolent Turks high trusts in the government and its affairs; but by the jealousy, cruelty, and cupidity of the latter, many of them have been precipitated from their elevated state and prosperity into terrible misery, often ending only with execution, as the following and similar inscriptions on their tombstones and on the pages of history will abundantly prove:—

"The most remarkable circumstance is that those Armenians who have undergone execution have the modes of their death commemorated on their sepulchres by the effigies of men being hung, strangled or beheaded. In explanation it is stated that having become wealthy by their industry, they suffered as victims to the cupidity of former governments, not as criminals; and hence their ignominious death was really honorable to them and worthy of a memorial. An inscription on one of the tombs of this class is as follows:—

"You see my place of burial here in this verdant field.
I give my goods to the robbers,
My soul to the regions of death;
The world I leave to God,
And my blood I shed in the Holy Spirit.
You who meet my tomb,
Say for me
'Lord, I have sinned.'
1197." *

It was Sultan Mohammed II. who first appointed Bishop Havaguam, of Broussa, patriarch over the Armenians in his dominions in 1461. This custom of appointing of the patriarchs by the Sultans of Turkey continued for a long time. But it did not prove to be the proper way on account of the

---

*The Turkish Empire, page 261.

abuses of procuring the office, and unqualified persons often obtaining the appointment by the influence of their friends.

The nation, therefore, obtained the right of appointing their own patriarch from the Porte; this national appointment, however, had to be ratified by the Sultan of Turkey.

At two different times two more grants were received from the Porte, namely, to have two distinct councils, the one ecclesiastical and the other civil. The former was composed of fourteen clergymen, the latter of twenty members from the laity, and the members of these councils were also elected by universal suffrage; the patriarch was the chairman of both of those councils.

The Ecclesiastical Council has its sphere of action in religious matters and is the highest authority in the Turkish Empire. The Civil Council is the civil authority, and has four sub-councils under its supervision through which to operate, namely: Council of Revenue, Council of Expenditure, Judicatory Council, and Educational Council. These names indicate the sphere of their activity. This mode of operation or division of the work is carried out into the provinces of the Turkish Empire, wherever there are sufficient Armenians to justify the existence of these councils. And all the councils and sub-councils in the provinces and in the districts of the capital are amenable to the General Ecclesiastical and Civil Councils, and these councils are responsible to the patriarch and the patriarch to the Porte.

Although such grants have been made and privileges accorded and many other promises of reforms uttered and recorded by the Turkish government at various times to ameliorate the oppressed condition of the Armenians, yet most of these grants, privileges, and promises now have their existence only as dead letters.

It has been said before that the Armenians are now, more or less, scattered all over the globe, like the Jews. The condition of this in India is far better than that of those in Persia, Turkey and Russia. Being subject to a comparatively just and Christian government they enjoy all civil and religious privileges, consequently they are both wealthy and influential, and some hold important positions in the queen's government in India.

At Calcutta they have a bishop, churches, schools, and an Armenian press. They have better educational advantages, both in the English and the Armenian languages. The Armenians are also conversant with the language of the country, wherever they are found.

The Armenians in Persia, or under the Persian rule, have not a very desirable condition, from a religious and educational point of view. And those especially living in Western Persia, or Pers-Armenia, are also subject to all sorts of cruelties by the hands of the Kurds, with whom they unfortunately live.

The most of them, however, are at this time free from the present tribulation that their brethren are undergoing in the hands of "the unspeakable Turk." In the summer of 1890 many Armenians found refuge in Persia from the atrocities of the Kurds and Turks. The Shah of Persia is very anxious to get as many Armenians as possible into his kingdom, knowing the value of their industry, intelligence and useful occupations.

Russia having wrested from Persia and Turkey a large portion of Armenia in this century, there are now over one million Armenians in the Russian provinces of Armenia, beside a good number of those in the commercial cities of the same empire.

The financial condition of the Armenians in Russia might be pronounced pretty fair. "The Anglo-Saxons of the East" have proved their shrewdness in business and industry; in character there, too, and according to a recent writer, in the city of Titlis money is controlled by the Armenians. But from a religious and national point of view the Armenians in Russia are in a serious danger. The policy of the government is to Russianize other nations, both ethnically and ecclesiastically.

The Russian government took occasion of a trifling disturbance and issued an order to take possession of the Armenian schools, and this order was carried out by military force in 1885, while the late Catholicos has not yet succeeded to his predecessor's vacant post.

The properties, consisting in real estate of the monastery of Echmiadzin, where the seat of the Catholicos is, were seized upon by the government, and the monastery and its schools were supported by the governmental money for a few years, but this support was gradually reduced, so much so that now the inmates of the monastery can hardly live on it, and the monastery is not able to support any schools as it used to do before with the plenteous income from the numerous villages and farms.

The very country where the forefathers of the Armenians lived centuries before the Russian nation had any existence, or if any, it was in the embryonic state among the barbarous Scythians, and by the very bravery and lives of many Armenians this country was extorted from the Turks for Russia, and it is strange, but nevertheless a fact, that the Armenian cannot own land in his own country, because he is a subject of the Russian government.

In the summer of 1890, while the country of Armenia, under the Turkish rule, was in a turbulent condition, some Armenians crossed the boundary line and fled into an Armenian monastery in Russian Armenia for a refuge from the Kurds and Turks. Most naturally were they protected and cared for by the priests and monks in the monastery. This was a pretense for the government to demand, or rather order, the imprisonment, and afterwards the exile, of those clergymen who sympathized with their persecuted brethren and cared for them.

It will be a violation of our intention and the limits of brevity of this present work to dilate on this subject, to point out the unjust policy of the Russian government, and her constant effort to absorb the Armenian nation and church in her dominions by compulsive teaching of Russian language instead of the Armenian in the Armenian schools.

The Armenians have, unfortunately, learned cordially to hate the Turks on account of their cruelties for centuries. The Russians also are making themselves as detestable as the Turks, not only to the Armenians, but also to all other nations who love justice and delight in mercy.

The Armenians now number more than four million in different countries in the world, of whom, two million, five hundred thousand are in the Turkish Empire; one million, five hundred thousand are in Russian Armenia and other parts of the same empire; five hundred thousand are scattered through Persia, India, Burmah, Egypt and other parts of Asia; one hundred thousand are scattered through Europe and the United States; the total number of Armenians being four million, six hundred thousand on the globe.

Probably about one half of the population of Turkish Armenia now is Mohammedan, composed of Turks and Kurds. The former are mostly found in and near the large cities, such as Ezzingan, Baibourt, Erzerum and Van, and the plains along the northern part. The Kurds live in their mountain villages over the whole region. The term Kurdistan, which in this region the Turkish government is trying to substitute for the historical one Armenia, has no political or geographical propriety except as indicating the much larger area over which the Kurds are scattered. In this vague sense it applies to a stretch of mountainous country about fifteen hundred miles in length, starting between Erzingan and Malatiah, and sweeping east and south over in Persia as far as Karmanshah.

The number of the Kurds is very uncertain, neither the Sultan nor the Shah of Persia, ever attempted a census of them; and as they are very indifferent taxpayers, the revenue tables—wilfully distorted for political purposes— are quite unreliable.

From the estimates of British consular officers there appear to be about one and a half million Turkish Kurds, of whom about six hundred thousand are in the vilayets of Erzerum, Van and Bitlis, and the rest in the vilayets of Harpoot, Diarbekr, Mosul, and Bagdad. This is a very liberal estimate. There are also supposed to be about seven hundred and fifty thousand in Persia.

CHAPTER IV.

It is not possible to give specific information on the
original forms of the religion of the Armenian race. The
culture and civilization of the West had begun to penetrate
into Armenia with the victorious legions of the Greeks and
Romans. Another of the many deluges which have swept
over this unhappy land was showing tokens of subsidence,
and the ark was once more nearing a place of rest.

We have acknowledged from the book of Genesis, "And
Noah builded an altar unto the Lord" (Genesis ix., 20.)

The Bible, modern scholarship, and the Armenian tradition concur on the question that the ark of Noah rested "upon
the mountains of Ararat," or Armenia. Again, we learn from
the Bible that "God spake unto Noah, saying, "Go forth out
of the ark," and Noah came out of the ark and all those that
were with him, and he builded an altar unto the Lord, "and
offered burnt offerings on the altar." This fact will entitle
Armenia to claim to be the country where a true and pure
divine worship was first practised after the Deluge. The tradition of the Armenians coincides with the fact in stating that
the primitive religion of the people was simple and pure
monotheism, in form patriarchal, Noachian. This tradition
has for its support both the Bible and the science of religion.

Prof. Max Muller tells us that "religion is not a new invention. It is, if not as old as the world, at least as old as the
world we know. As soon, almost, as we know anything of
the thoughts and feelings of man, we find him in possession
of religion, or rather possessed by religion." Thus find we

Noah and his descendants in possession of or rather possessed by religion.

The Bible furnishes sufficient facts to assert that this pure monotheistic worship in its patriarchal form was perpetuated among the descendants of Noah, especially in the family of Shem. More than four centuries after the building of the first altar unto the Lord we find Abraham called out of his country and the people by Jehovah, to become the head of a nation through whom the knowledge of the only one true God should be perpetuated. God's calling Abraham out of his country and people was not to make him a true worshipper of Himself, but He said to him, "I will make of thee a great nation."

Another example of the true worshipper of God in the time of Abraham was Melchizedek (king of righteousness), "King of Salem (peace), who was the high priest of the most high God." (Genesis xiv., 18). Melchizedek was not only a monotheist, but also the priest of a Monotheistic faith. He reigned over his people and on whose behalf he officiated as the high priest of the most high God. Now, therefore, it ought to be admitted that not only solitary individuals like Abram and Melchizedek, but the people of the latter also were the true worshippers of God. Another example: Job, his family and his friends, they were also true worshippers of God. They belonged to the eastern nations, they might be from Armenia.

The Bible is not a universal history, were it so, well might we have expected it to mention other nations and their religious beliefs; though what little it incidentally gives, or states in regard to them is marvelously accurate.

The Armenian tradition that their primitive religion was pure monotheism, therefore, is neither incredible nor untenable, but on the contrary it is most probable and almost certain, supported by the analogy of the Bible.

The investigations of modern scholarship maintain the idea and render it almost a moral demonstration that the primitive religions of the ancient nations were of a Monotheistic type, if not a pure Monotheism, at least they were not very far from it. Prof. Max Muller, of Oxford, England, in his lectures on the "Origin and Growth of Religion," says that "The ancient Aryans felt from the beginning, aye, it may be, more in the beginning than afterwards, the presence of a Beyond, of an Infinite, of a Divine, or whatever else we may call it now; and they tried to grasp, and comprehend it, as we all do, by giving to it name after name." It is conceded by the scholars that the ancient Armenians were closely connected with the ancient Aryans, that they were Aryans and their legitimate descendants now speak a language which modern ethnologists decidedly pronounce to belong to the Aryans cr Indo-Germanic. Although we do not know when the separation of the Aryans took place, we can safely say that the above statement of Prof. Max Muller is also perfectly applicable to the ancient Armenians, yet we are not able to say how long such a purity of faith lasted in Armenia.

The human mind is capable of progress, but when it is left to itself is sure to retrograde and degenerate. This is verified in the case of almost all nations and in the history of all religions of the world.

"That religion is liable to corruption is surely seen again and again. In one sense the history of most religions might be called a slow corruption of their primitive purity." Divine aid, especially in religion, is therefore absolutely necessary for a true progress. Armenia left to herself fell into a gross form of idolatry.

Her fall must have been hastened, if not caused, by her idolatrous neighbors, the Babylonians and Assyrians. For the idolatry which we find in the early history of the Armenians is decidedly like that of Assyro-Babylonians. It is not the same religion adopted and practised by the Armenians, but it is modelled after the Assyrian.

Anterior to the cuneiform inscriptions of Armenia, the people must have had an idolatry similar to the Sabeism of Babylonia, which was afterwards shaped to the Assyrian style, with its distinctive character. One of the inscriptions furnishes us with a long list of the gods and the regulations for sacrifices daily to be offered to them.

There are, however, three other gods, which stood apart by themselves at the head of the Pantheon. These are Khaldis, Teisbas (the air god), and Adinis (the sun god). But Khaldis is the supreme god and the father of other gods; and in addition to these every tribe, city and fortress seem to have its respective god. Some other gods are Anis or Avis (the water god), Agas (the earth god), Dhuspuas (the god of Tosp, the ancient name of the city of Van), Selardis, (the moon god), Sardis, (the year god). The Armenians in this period, do not seem to have any goddess. Soris is found only once mentioned in the inscriptions and is translated, "queen," yet it is supposed to have been borrowed from the Assyrian, Istar. Whether all the other gods are the children of the supreme god Khaldis, or they are subordinate to him and separate from his numerous offsprings, it is not quite clear. The latter, however, is most likely the case, because the Khaldians (the children of Khaldis) and other gods have their separate offerings assigned to them according to their importance.

It has been said that the Armenian culture, civilization, and religion were very much influenced by the Assyrians while the latter were in the height of their power. From the following citation it will be seen a resemblance of the religions of these two nations and they might have also the same origin and the growth:—

"The rise of Semitic supremacy was marked by the reigns of Sargon I. and his son, Noram-Sin. The overthrow of Sargon's dynasty, however, was soon brought about through the conquest of Babylonia by Khammaragas, a Kossacon from the mountains of Elam. Before the Kossocan conquest the Babylonian system of religion was already complete. It emanated from the primitive Accadian population, though it was afterwards adopted and transformed by their Semitic successors. The sorcerer took the place of the priest, magical incantations the place of the ritual, and the innumerable spirits the place of gods.

By degrees, however, these earlier conceptions became modified, a priesthood began to establish itself; and as a necessary consequence some of the elemental spirits were raised to the rank of deities.

The old magical incantations, too, gave way to hymns in honor of the new gods, among whom the sun god was especially prominent, and these hymns came in time to form a collection similar to that of the Hindu Rig-Veda, and were accounted equally sacred. This process of religious development was assisted by the Semitic occupation of Babylonia. The Semites brought with them new theological conceptions. With them the sun god, in his two-fold aspect of benefactor and destroyer, was the supreme object of worship, all other deities being resolvable into phases or attributes of the supreme Baal. At his side stood his female double and reflection, the goddess of fertility, who was found again under various names and titles at the side of every other deity. The union of these Semitic religious conceptions with the developing creed of Accad produced a state religion, watched over and directed by a powerful priesthood, which continued more or less unaltered down to the days of Nebuchadnezzar and his successors.

It was this state-religion that was carried by Semitic Assyrians into their homes on the banks of the Tigris, where it underwent one or two modifications; in all essential respects, however, it remained unchanged.

With the rise of the Medo-Persian Empire a new religion rises from obscurity to prominence in Western Asia. This is the religion of Zoroaster. This was the religion with which Christianity had so nobly contended since the introduction of the latter into Armenia, until the former, in complete despair and as a vanquished foe, almost disappeared from existence. It is generally believed that Zoroaster was a real person and the founder of this religion, which is called after his name, Zoroastrianism. There is, however, a great uncertainty about the period of his earthly existence: some would make him a contemporary with Moses, and others with David and Solomon. It is very probable, however, that he lived even in a good deal later period than these Israelitish kings.

Zoroastrianism is a dualistic religion. It teaches that there are two uncreated beings, Ormazed, the supreme good, and Ahriman, the evil; and Ormazed created the earth, the heavens, and the man, and that man is created free. Ahriman is the evil and evil-doer, and in constant war with Ormazed; this world is their battle-field. There are inferior good spirits which are called genii, who are the instruments of Ormazed, but the fire alone was the personification of the son of Ormazed, and therefore an object of veneration and worship.

The abominable religion of the ancient Babylonians must have had a great influence even over the religion of Zoroaster, for we find that the Persians and Armenians had also similar gods, like Mithea, sungod, and Anahita, the goddess of water. The magi were the priests of Zoroastrianism, with a high priest of this order who was called in Armenian language Mogbed, (the head or the leader of magi). No doubt this was the religion of the Armenians for nearly nine centuries, from the end of the seventh century B. C., to the end of the third century of our era (or A. C.). Possibly there were some modifications and additions from the Grecian polytheism after the conquest of Alexander the Great.

ABGAR, THE FIRST CHRISTIAN KING ON THE EARTH.

CHAPTER V.

At the time of our Lord's birth, Armenia was divided into separate portions, called respectively Great and Little Armenia.

The latter district extended from the Gordyian Mountains to the Euphrates, and had as its capital the Greek city of Nieibis (or Niezib, in Turkish). Greek art and civilization had long exercised a great influence upon the whole of Syria and Mesopotamia; but the Roman and Greek writers seem to regard the Kingdom of Osroene or Osrhoene, as that of Armenia Minor was generally styled, as in large measure Syrian. As is well known, the Roman government claimed the suzerainty over Mesopotamia; and Arsham, who died King of Osrhoene in B. C. 3, and left his title to his son Abgar, was in reality little else than their deputy, holding his position like Herod the Great in Palestine, only by the favor of his emperial master.

Abgar, being devoted to the service of the heathen gods, refused to permit the image of Augustus to be erected in the temples of his dominions. Herod Antipas, learning this, laid a charge against him before the emperor, and accused him of disloyalty. Finding that all his efforts to clear himself were in vain and offended at the treatment accorded at Rome to the ambassadors he had sent to plead his cause, Abgar determined to revolt from the Roman yoke, and to cast in his lot with kindred family who then held the throne of Persia. With this object in view he removed the seat of rule the Nieibis to Edessa, and began to strongly fortify the latter city. Moses of Khorene tells us that the King

carried with him to his new capital the images of the gods
whom he worshipped and the religious archives stored up in
the temples at Nicibis. Just when Abgar thought everything
was ripe for rebellion, relying on the assistance of the Parthians, Arshavir, the Parthian King, died and left his kingdom
a prey to confusion and civil war. Abgar felt himself called
upon to restore order, and accordingly marched into Persia
and put an end to the strife which had there broken out
between the rival claimants to the vacant throne (A. D. 21).
This expedition, through God's good providence, was over-
ruled to the conversion of Abgar, and to the opening up of
both Armenia and Persia to the light of the Gospel. The
story is told by Eusebius and by the ancient Armenian historian, Moses of Khorene, who profess to have learnt it
from the archives of the kingdom of Osroene, written in
Syriac.

On his expedition to Persia, Abgar was struck with a very
severe illness, which some Armenian writers tell us was lep-
rosy, and which all the skill of his court physicians was power-
less to heal. While in vain that the Roman Emperor Tiberius
had been informed of his intended rebellion, and believing
that Abgar's expedition into Persia had been undertaken
mainly with the hope of entering into an alliance with that
empire, was about to inflict on him condign punishment. In
order to avert this, Abgar in the first place entered into an
alliance with Aretes, King of Arabia Nabataca, whose daughter
Herod Antipas had divorced, and sent a body of Armenian
troops to aid Aratos in his war against Herod. Herod's army
was defeated with great slaughter; but the Romans, hearing
of the trouble brewing in Armenia, Mesopotamia and Syria,
sent Marinus to Cæsarea as governor, with a large army, with
orders to restore order. Hearing of this, Abgar sent three
Armenian nobles of high rank to Marinus at Cæsarea, together
with a copy of the treaty he had made with Artoshes, the
new King of Persia, that the Romans might understand that
he was loyal in his allegiance to the Emperor, and had no
intention of rebelling.

The ambassadors were received with great honor by Marinus at Eleutheropolis, and succeeded in their efforts to prevent a breach between the Emperor and King Abgar. But their visit to Palestine had another and a far more important result, for there had heard the fame of Jesus of Nazareth, whose miracles of healing were then attracting great attention; of some of these they were enabled to become eye-witnesses themselves. On their return to Armenia, these nobles, remembering that their sovereign had completely failed to obtain healing by ordinary means, informed him of the miraculous power and the Messianic claims of Jesus.

The whole Eastern world was, as Suetonius informs us, at that time full of expectation that a great ruler would soon appear in Judea, and establish his dominion over the whole world. The coincidence between the Messianic prophecies and hopes of the Jews on the one hand, and the strange and only slightly less clear traditions of the advent of a great Deliverer preserved in the Zend Avesta of Persia and the Sibylline books of ancient Rome and represented to us by Virgil's glorious Fourth Eclogue, on the other, had doubtless turned towards Jerusalem the eyes of pious and truth-seeking men everywhere. The visit of the Persian Magi to the Infant at Bethlehem is only one indication of the extent of this expectant longing. It is not at all unlikely, therefore, that Abgar, on hearing the report of his messengers, was greatly stirred. At last the long-expected prince had appeared and not only so, but was actually healing in Galilee and Judea those afflicted with diseases which no human skill could cure. Abgar's bodily affliction naturally made him the more anxious to benefit at least by the healing power of our Saviour, and the news which his messengers brought him left no doubt of his willingness and ability to grant his request.

Abgar, therefore, wrote a letter to Christ, and sent it to Him to Jerusalem by the hands of his courier Ananias. Later Armenian accounts state that Ananias was also accompanied by an able portrait painter, who had received orders

from the King to request permission to paint Christ's picture
and bring it back with him to Edessa to Abgar, in case the
Saviour Himself declined to accede to the King's written
request that He would come and heal him of his illness.

The King also directed his messengers to offer sacrifices
to the true God in his temple at Jerusalem.

They reached the Holy City on the very day of Christ's
triumphal entry into Jerusalem, and endeavored to approach
Him in order to present the King's letter to Him. Not being
able to do so, however, they gave it to Philip, and asked him
to deliver it and to procure them an audience. This, we are
told, is the meaning of the incident recorded in the twelfth
chapter of St. John's Gospel (vv. 20-34), where certain Greeks,
who had come up to worship at the Feast of the Passover,
were presented to our Lord. Christ saw in them the representatives of the heathen world, then longingly looking for
some one to give them the light of life, and prophesied that
His crucifixion would draw all men unto Him (ver. 32). The
Armenian tradition that these "Greeks" were Abgar's messengers has nothing directly contrary to it in the use of the word
"Greeks" in the original, since this word is often used in
the New Testament to denote any who were not Jews.

The tradition is at least as old as Moses of Khorene (died
A. D. 487), who mentions it as an undisputed fact (Paton-
Hayots-Hat. ii. Kl. 29), and was probably believed long before
then, for in the ancient Armenian version of the New Testament made by St. Mesrap (died A. D. 441), the word Greeks
in this passage is translated merely "heathens."

Eusebius, and after him Moses of Khorene, gives a version of the letter which King Abgar is said to have addressed
to Christ on this occasion, and which Eusebius tells us was
still preserved in his own time in the library at Edessa (Uorfa
in Turkish). Although all modern critics rightly regard this
letter and our Lord's supposed reply to it as undoubtedly
spurious, it may be of interest to enter them both here in order
to complete the narrative. Abgar's letter ran as follows:

Abgar, Toporch of Edessa, to Jesus the good Saviour, who has appeared in Jerusalem, greeting:

"I have heard of Thee and Thy cures, which are being performed by Thee without drugs and medicines. For, as report says, Thou dost cause the blind to recover sight, the lame to walk, and Thou cleansest lepers, and drivest out unclean spirits and demons, and healest those tormented with long-continued sickness, and raisest the dead, and having heard all these things about Thee, I decided in my mind on one of two conclusions—either that Thou art God, and having come down from heaven Thou doest these things—or that, doing these things, Thou art the Son of God.

"Therefore, I now write and entreat of Thee to take the trouble to come to me, and to heal the disease which I have. For indeed I hear that the Jews are murmuring against Thee and wish to do Thee violence. I have a very small and noble city, which will suffice for us both." (Euseb. Eccl. Hist. i., 13; M. Khorene, Paton, Hayots, Hat. ii., Kl. 99).

When our Lord had this letter and saw Abgar's faith in Him, he directed Thomas to write a reply to it from His own dictation, in the following terms:

Blessed art thou, who hast believed in Me without having seen Me. For it is written concerning Me that those who have seen Me will not believe Me, and that those who have not seen Me shall themselves believe and live. But where thou didst write to Me to come to thee it is necessary that I should here accomplish all those things for which I was sent, and that, after having accomplished them, I should then be taken up to Him who sent Me; and when I am taken up, I shall send unto thee a certain one of My disciples, that he may heal thy sickness and give life to thee and to those that are with thee.

Having received this letter, Abgar's messengers entreated permission to paint a portrait of Christ, in accordance with their master's orders. The required permission was accorded them, but the painter's hand refused to perform its task in delineating Christ's divine features. Seeing this, the Saviour took a towel and applying it to His countenance, impressed upon it a marvellously correct picture* of Himself, and sent it to Abgar with the letter above quoted, intending thereby to relieve his sufferings and strengthen his faith. Abgar, on reading the letter and receiving the portrait, worshipped the letter, and took courage, looking hopefully for the fulfilment of Christ's promise to send him a teacher to instruct and heal him.

This story as here related bears distinct marks of a later age, and it has received much embellishment from later Armenian writers which is not to be met with in Moses of Khorene or in Eusebius. The story of the portrait and of the worship paid to it by Abgar could not have originated until the worship of pictures had been introduced into the church. The letters ascribed to Abgar and to Christ bear evident marks of a clumsy forgery. The account of the interview which Abgar's messengers had with our Lord is possibly but not probably true. On the other hand, it seems rash to reject the whole narrative (as many writers do) as fabulous.

It may, perhaps, be better to hold that a certain substratum or residum of fact underlies the tale. It is certainly neither impossible nor improbable, taking into consideration all the circumstances of the case, that the fame of our Lord's miracles of healing may have reached Edessa, and that Abgar's illness may have led him to look longingly for the arrival in his country of a disciple of Christ able to heal him. This would prepare the way for a favorable reception being given to the earliest preachers of the Gospel on their arrival in Mesopotamia and Osraene, which must have taken place soon after the Ascension.

After that Jesus was received up, says the old Syriac document quoted by Eusebius. Judas (who is also called Thomas) sent up to him (Abgar) as an apostle Thaddeus, one of the

---

* See Appendix.

THADDAEUS AND BARTHOLOMEW.

seventy. He coming dwelt with Tobias, the son of Tobias, and when news was heard concerning him, it was told to Abgar, saying: "An apostle of Jesus has come hither, according as He wrote unto thee." Thaddeus accordingly began in the power of God to heal every sickness and every disease, so that all men did marvel. But when Abgar heard of the might and wonderful works which he did, and how he healed, he suspected that this was he of whom Jesus had written, saying: "When I am taken up, I shall send unto thee a certain one of My disciples, who shall heal thy sickness."

Having, therefore, called for Tobias, with whom abode, he said, "I have heard that a certain mighty man has come and has abode in thy house; bring him unto me." And Tobias came unto Thaddeus, and said to him: "Abgar the Toporch called for me and bade me bring thee to him, in order that thou mightest heal his sickness." And Thaddeus said, "I go up, since I have been sent unto him with might." Tobias, therefore, having risen early on the morrow, and taking Thaddeus with him, came to Abgar. And when he came suddenly upon his entrance the King's nobles also being present and standing there, a great sight was manifested to Abgar in the countenance of the apostle, Thaddeus. And when Abgar saw this he worshipped Thaddeus. Astonishment also fell upon all those that stood by. For they did not see the sight, which appeared to Abgar only. And he asked Thaddeus, "Art thou in truth a disciple of Jesus the son of God, who said unto me, 'I shall send to thee a certain one of my disciples, who shall heal thee and give thee life?'" And Thaddeus said, "since thou hast firmly believed in Him who sent me, therefore was I sent unto thee. And again, if thou believest in Him, according as thou believest the desires of thine heart shall be granted thee." And Abgar said unto him, "I believe in Him so much that I desired to take a force and destroy the Jews who crucified Him, only that I was hindered from doing so by the empire of the Romans." And Thaddeus said, "Our Lord Jesus hath fulfilled the will of His Father, and having

fulfilled it He was received up unto His Father." Abgar saith
to him, "I also have believed in Him and in His Father." And
Thaddeus saith, "I therefore lay my hand upon thee in His
name." And when he had done this, he was immediately healed of the sickness and the disease which
he had. And Abgar marvelled that, according as he
had heard Jesus, so had he received in reality from His
disciple Thaddeus, who had healed him without drugs and
medicines. And not only so, but Abdus also, the son of
Abgar, who had the gout. For the latter also, coming forward, fell at his feet. And Thaddeus, having prayed, took him
by the hand, and healed him. Many others also of their fellow citizens did the same Thaddeus heal, doing wondrous and
great things, and preaching the Word of God. But after
these things Abgar said, "Thou, O Thaddeus, by the power of
God doest these things, and we ourselves marvel at thee. But
beside these things I entreat of thee to narrate to me concerning the advent of Jesus, how it took place, and concerning His
power, and by what power He used to do these things of
which we have heard." And Thaddeus said, "I shall be silent
for the present, since I was sent to preach the Word. But on
the morrow assemble unto me all thy citizens, and unto them
I shall preach the Word of God, and I shall tell them about
the advent of Jesus, how it took place and about His mission,
and why He was sent forth by the Father, and concerning the
might of His works, and the mysteries which He proclaimed
in the world, and by what power He did these things, and
concerning His new proclamation, and concerning His love-
liness and humiliation, and how He humbled Himself and
died, and how He lessened His divine nature, and was crucified, and descended into Hades, and rent in twain the middle
wall or partition which had not been rent from eternity, and
raised the dead. For having descended alone, He
raised up many with Him unto His Father, and then
in this way He ascended." Abgar accordingly gave
orders that early on the morrow all his citizens should

come together and should hear the preaching of Thaddeus, and after these things he commanded to give him gold and treasure. But Thaddeus would not accept it, saying, "If we have left our own, how shall we accept the things of others?" These things were done 1865 years ago.

Eusebius adds that the result of Thaddeus' work at Edessa was the conversion of those that were healed and their admission into the number of Christ's disciples, and states that, in consequence of this, the whole of the people of Edessa had remained Christians even up to his own time (Eccl. Hist. ii. 1). This, however, is incorrect; though many were Christians in Eusebius' days.

Armenian writers inform us that Thaddeus, having thus converted Abgar and his people, baptized them, and then proceeded to erect a large church in the city of Edessa. He also consecrated as bishop of the city a pious convert named Addê, a silkmaker, who had previously been employed to make a royal tiara for Abgar. After his conversion, Abgar, filled with zeal for the Gospel, wrote letters to the Emperor Tiberius and to the King of Syria, and to Artashês, King of Persia, inviting them to receive the Gospel and accept Christ, as their Lord and Saviour.

Three years after his conversion Abgar died, and was buried in Edessa (A. D. 35).

His widow Helenê, was also an earnest Christian.* When some years later banished from Edessa by Sanatrouk, she went to her native city, Haran, and there ruled for a time. She is also said to have been queen of Adiabene. Somewhat later she went to Jerusalem, and Josephus tells us† that during the great famine in Claudius' time (Acts xi., 28), she bought a great quantity of corn in Egypt and, at enormous expense, had it carried to Jerusalem and distributed it to the poor. When she

---

*This is what Moses of Khorene says (Patur, Hayots, Hal. II., Kl 32), but Josephus calls her queen of Adiabene, and gives quite a different account of her, saying that she became a Jewess, (Aut. xx., 2).

†(Jos. Aut. xx., 2).

died, a noble tomb was erected to her memory in the suburbs of the Holy City, in memorial of her beneficence.

After founding the Christian Church in Edessa, Thaddeus went to Armenia proper, to the district Artoz or Shavorshan, which was at that time ruled over by Sanatrouk, Abgar's sister's son. The latter received him kindly, and gave him every opportunity of preaching the Gospel to the people.

As a result of this it is said that Sanatrouk and his daughter Sandoukht, together with not a few nobles and very many of the common people, were converted and received baptism. Thaddeus consecrated one of his converts named Zacharias, bishop, and it is said that the latter afterward carried the Gospel to the Alvanions, a tribe living on the shores of the Caspian Sea at the foot of the Caucasus Mountains.

Meanwhile strange things were happening at Edessa itself. The Christians at that city are said to have carried the Gospel into Persia, and the friendship and alliance which existed between Artoshes, King of Persia, and Abgar renders this very probable. But on Abgar's death, his son, who is called by different writers Ananias, Anane, Ananann, and Anan, ascended the throne at Osraene, and at once apostatized and restored the worship of the heathen gods, especially that of Beal, the great tutelary deity of the city. The temples, which had been closed by Abgar, were reopened, and a certain amount of persecution was begun against the Christians. One instance of this in particular is related.

Ananias ordered Bishop Addê, who had made a tiara for Abgar before Thaddeus' arrival in Edessa, to return to his old trade and make one for him also. Addê refused, saying, "My hands shall make a tiara for no head which does not bow down to the dust in honor of Christ." Enraged at this message, Ananias sent the executioner to cut off both the bishop's feet.

This was done as he was seated at worship in the church, and resulted in his speedy death.

Meanwhile Senatrouk was extending his power in Armenia, and was plotting to make himself master of the throne of Asraene. Great confusion and disorder followed, but was ended by Ananias' death (A. D. 38), after a reign of only four years. It is said that his death occurred in the following manner:

Ananias was having the royal palace in Edessa rebuilt with great magnificence. One day, while standing on the pavement below, surveying the work, a huge marble column fell from the upper story upon the King, striking him to the earth and crushing his legs so severely that he died of the shock. His Christian subjects saw in this event a just judgment upon him for the murder of their good bishop Addê, and remarked upon the noteworthy circumstance that the King had been smitten upon precisely the same part of the body where Addê had by his orders been struck by the executioner's sword.

Immediately on the news reaching him that Ananias was dead, Sanatrouk marched to take possession of Edessa. He seems to have already apostatized* from the Christian faith, and consequently the Christians at that city at first opposed his entrance. But Sanatrouk reassured them by binding himself with an oath to permit them the free exercise of their religion. On taking possession of Edessa, Sanatrouk slew all Abgar's remaining sons, and banished his daughter and his widow, Helenê, to the latter's native city, Haran, though he left her the title of Queen Mesopotamia.

We have already the rest of the history of this lady. Having thus removed all rivals from his path, Sanatrouk felt free to govern according to his own pleasure. He rebuilt in the most splendid manner the city of Nisibis, which had been destroyed by an earthquake, and set up in the public square there a statue of himself with a single drachma in his outstretched hand, implying that he had expended all the rest of his treasures in the work of rebuilding the city.

---

*Through fear of the Armenian nobles, who were still heathens, according to Moses of Khorene.

But Sanatrouk is famous, or rather infamous, for deeds of a different kind also. In direct contradistinction to his oath, he began a most cruel persecution of the Christians in which he spared neither sex nor age throughout his dominions. Among others that fell victims to the tyrant's fury was Thaddaeus himself. This apostolic man, hearing of Sanatrouk's apostacy, returned from Cappadocia, whither he had gone to preach the Gospel.

On his way to Mesopotamia, it is said, he met five ambassadors sent from Rome to Sanatrouk's court. One of these was a noble and well-born man named Chrysos. Hearing the Gospel message from Thaddaeus, they accepted it and were baptized. Chrysos himself was ordained presbyter. These men, in the ardor of their new-found faith, sold all that they had and gave to the poor, and then devoted themselves to preaching Christ crucified to the people of Armenia. They seemed to have formed a body of itinerant preachers from among their converts, who lived among the mountains and who, from the Armenian translation of their original leader's name, were called Voskeaukh, the "Golden Ones." These men for some years continued their work in Armenia.

Hearing of their conversions, Sanatrouk summoned Thaddaeus to his presence in Shavarshan, where he then happened to be. On the arrival of the apostle, he was martyred with many other devoted Christians, including Sanatrouk's own daughter, Sandaukht, the first of a noble band of Armenian women who have not feared to lay down their lives for their faith (A. D. 48). Tradition relates that miracles of healing were wrought at Sandaukht's tomb, and that this led to the conversion of many others, not a few of whom wore the martyr's crown.

So in all ages and in all lands has the blood of martyrs been the seed of the Church of God.

Later legends add that Bartholomew also came to Armenia in A. D. 50, bringing with him a picture of the Virgin Mary.

He is said to have preached in Lower Armenia, and to have made many converts, including Sanatrouk's sister Thakauhr (Queen) and the generalissimo of his army.

Sanatrouk's fury was not appeased by these fresh proofs of the power of the Gospel, which he hated with a renegade's hatred. He put his sister to death, scourged Bartholomew, and then crucified him in the city of Arevbanus, where his tomb was long after an object of veneration. Armenian superstition or patriotism claims that the apostle Jude also labored in the country, died and was buried at Urmia. The bones of St. Thomas, the apostle of Parthia and India, were brought from the latter country (where he had been martyred), and interred in Armenia. St. Enstathius, one of our Lord's seventy disciples, was martyred in the province of Sinnikh, and buried at a place still called Stathew or Sather. Elisha, one of Thaddeus' disciples, accompanied by a little band of these devoted followers, preached, we are told, in Upper Armenia, and then passed on to labor among the Albanians.

He was instrumental in bringing a very large number of these people to a knowledge of the truth, and finally died in the plain of Arghann. Sanatrauk the persecutor reigned for thirty-four years, and having seen the failure of his attempt to crush the infant Christian Church in his dominions, was at last accidentally killed by an arrow while hunting (A. D. 65).

Dr. Philip Schaff says: "It is now impossible to decide how much truth there may be in the somewhat mythical stories of correspondence between Christ and Abgarus, and the missionary activity and martyrdom of Thaddeus, Bartholomew, Simon of Cana, and Judas Lebbeus. But it is certain that Christianity was introduced very early in Armenia." How much or how little of this account of the first preaching of the Gospel in Armenia is true must perhaps forever remain unknown. What we have narrated above is the story as told by Armenian writers for the most part, and believed by them to be correct.

After this time, Christianity spread in Armenia as it did

in other parts of the Greek Empire; rapidly in the cities, where intelligence was quick and new ideas were welcomed; slowly in the country districts, where people did not readily change. Its first result everywhere was not so much to make people believe in it as to make them disbelieve in Paganism; for every person who actually came to believe in Christ, there were fifty who ceased to believe in Jupiter, or Bel, or Throth, Vanus, or Astarte.

There would be a flourishing Christian church in a great city when most of the people did not have any faith in any religion.

But everybody who had a family came gradually to think very well of a religion that gave them the power to teach children righteousness, and enforce it by the command of God, and the respectable classes became more and more Christian.

But the fact that till two or three centuries after Christ there was no general attempt on the part of the Pagan governments to put down the Christian by persecution, shows that not till then did they become so numerous as to frighten the government for fear they would before long have a majority; persecution means fear. The government let the Christians pretty much alone, except for little fits of anger now and then, till they were afraid the growth of the sect would overthrow themselves or bring on civil war.

The Christians had become well established in Armenia within a century or so after the death of Christ; but it was over a century and a half before they seemed an imminent menace to the ruling class. Then a furious persecution began, about the same time as that of Diocletian in the Roman Empire, and indeed, part of the same movement. Diocletian had set the persecuting King Tiridates on his throne, and Tiridates had passed his life from boyhood almost to old age in the Roman service, and had the same ideas as the Pagan Roman upper classes. Yet in the providence of God this same Tiridates made Christianity supreme in Armenia years before Constantine made it supreme in the Roman Empire, thus making

Armenia the first Christian nation. Might be our readers know that when Gregory the Illuminator, who was born (A. D. 257), the proclaimed of the message throughout Armenia, he found Christians everywhere, and a church which, though sorely persecuted and oppressed, had existed from apostolic times. He was, in fact, rather the restorer than the founder of the Armenian Church, which became the church of the whole nation half a century before the cross was emblazoned on the standard of Rome. The Armenians may justly claim to be the oldest Christian nation in the world.

The Father of Gregory, Prince Anak, was of the royal family of Arsacidæ of Parthia, whose reign was overthrown by Artaxerxes, the founder of the Sassanian dynasty of Persia. But the Armenian branch of Arsacidæ was still in full vigor in the person of Chosroes I., the King of Armenia, who had tried to restore the seized sceptre of Power to the deprived royal family of Arsacidæ of Parthia from the revolter, Artaxerxes, the Persian. In order that Artaxerxes might secure his reign he tried to subdue Armenia too. But, failing to do this manfully, he resorted to treachery. Anak, the relative of Chosroes I., was induced by Artaxerxes, with promises of large reward, to play the part of an assassin. It was so arranged that Anak would be chased out of Persia, being a member of the Arsacidæ dynasty, a dangerous person to the newly-established sovereignty of Persia. "Anak, with his wife, children, brother, and a train of attendants, pretended to take refuge in Armenia from the threatened vengeance of his sovereign, who caused his troops to pursue him, as a rebel and deserter, to the very borders of Armenia."* Anak was received by Chosroes I., who credulously listened to his story and sympathized with him. Anak committed the crime of assassination of the King, but the King lived long enough to request the complete destruction of the family of Anak, and Anak also had no time to effect his escape, and being seized upon, he

---

*The Seventh Oriental Monarchy, p. 51.

received the due recompense of an assassin. However, his son Gregory, who was only on infant, was saved by the faithfulness of his nurse, who took him and escaped into the city of Cæsarea, Cappadocia, where he was brought up in a Christian family with a thorough Christian education.

On the other hand, Artaxerxes obtained his object without paying for it, and hearing of the condition of affairs in Armenia, he immediately hastened thither with his army and took the people by surprise. He doomed the family of Arsacidæ to death, so as not to leave any to rival him for the throne. However, Tiridates, the son of Chosroes, escaped into the Roman province of Armenia, and then to Rome, where he received a military training, and his sister was hid in the stronghold of Ani.

Tiridates was welcomed by his people, who joined his army and drove out of the country their common enemy (A. D. 286).

The Gregory was brought up in Cæsarea as a Christian, and was well instructed in the Scriptures and in the Greek and Syriac languages. When he had grown up, he married a maiden named Mariam, daughter of an Armenian who bore the name of David. Both were Christians, and must naturally have told Gregory something of the deplorable heathenism of their native land and of the brave martyrs who had already been the first fruits of Armenia to Christ. Of this marriage two sons were born, the elder named Vethanes and the younger Arestakes.

Three years after their marriage, it is said, Gregory and his wife parted by mutual consent. She entered a nunnery at Cæsarea, taking her younger son with her. Gregory entrusted to guardians the training and education of the elder, and himself went to Rome to enter the service of the youthful Prince Tiridates (A. D. 280), hoping by faithful and devoted service in some measure to atone to Khasrov's son for the crime which Anax had committed, and of which and his own connection with the perpetrator Gregory had until very recently been kept in complete ignorance.

ST. GREGORY, THE ILLUMINATOR.

St. Gregory returned to Armenia and entered King Tiridates' service, whose "purpose being to win over to eternal life, through the Gospel of Christ, the son of him who had been slain by his father, and thus to make amends for his father's crime." Though he suffered many a torture and torment, and thirteen years' imprisonment in a pit, yet this noble Christian hero and apostle was determined "to win (the King) over to eternal life, through the Gospel of Christ." Finally, the King was converted and baptized by St. Gregory, and became himself a worthy champion of the truth, and the first honored King, who proclaimed throughout his dominions that henceforth the religion of Christ is the religion of Armenia. The Armenians have been nationally converted to Christianity, from the King to the servant; however, there were some, especially among the nobility, who with a heathenish tenacity held on to Zoroastrianism; but this was for a mercenary purpose, not from a real appreciation of Zoroastrianism; for St. Gregory, by his evangelistic spirit and labors, had laid a firm foundation for the religion of Christ in the land of Ararat. (A. D. 289.)

He was, by the request of the King, sent to Cæsarea, Cappadocia, to be ordained bishop over Armenia (A. D. 302).

The temples of the idols in every important city or town were pulled down and Christian churches in their stead were reared. The most splendid of all these churches was Etchmiadzin, "the descent of the only begotten," which was afterwards clustered about with other buildings and became a monastery and the seat of St. Gregory's successors to his prelatic chair to this day. This done, Gregory and Tiridates set about exterminating idolatry; they smashed the idols and demolished the temples, the new converts joyfully assisting them. The work of conversion went on rapidly, under the wonderful preaching of the Saint, and the zeal of the King; all the people converted were baptized by immersion.

In eight years the majority of the Armenian nation, many millions in number, had become Christians. That religion was

made the State creed of Armenia in 310, while the Council
of Nice, which did the same work for Rome, was not held till
(A. D. 325).

Gregory deserves every credit for this magnificent work;
but I cannot help wishing he had been less zealous in destroying the Pagan literature, which is a great loss to the
world. However, Christianity is worth it, if we could not
have it at a less price.

Schools, as well as churches and benevolent institutions,
were organized in great numbers under Christian auspices
during the next two or three centuries, and a brilliant band of
scholars and preachers went out from them, the equals of any
in their age and perhaps in any age.

During the long reign of Tiridates the church greatly
flourished. Indeed, did St. Gregory lay the foundation of the
religion of Christ upon the immovable rock of the Word of
God.

Both the noble founder and the valiant defender of that
divine faith, committed to their care by King Jesus, entered
their rest, after having seen the prosperous condition of the
church, and were succeeded by their sons. However, the
power of Armenia was unequal to the conflicting forces on
either side, though the descendants of Tiridates held the sceptre of Armenia nearly a century longer, but in a very enervated
state. Nevertheless the church of Armenia made a decided
advance within this period.

The rivalry between Rome and Persia grew fiercer than
ever with the introduction of Christianity, for new religious
hate was added to political ambition; and on the side of Persia the Armenian difficulties were doubled, for a considerable
part of the Armenians were still Zoroastrians, and sympathized
with the Persians against their own government, while many
of the Persians had become Christian, and opposed their
Pagan rulers. Thus the Persians felt that they had a civil
war on their hands as well as foreign wars, and persecuted
their Christians horribly.

DERTAD.

On the other hand, they had the hold of the Pagan part of the Armenians in invading or controlling that state; still again, the Armenian Christians now favored the Romans much more strongly than they had before, because Rome was now Christian; while on top of all were the great barons, almost independent of the nominal Kings, and who favored neither party, but wanted their feudal independence.

Yet the Roman control of the Kingship for what it was worth, lasted without a break for over half a century after the victory of Christianity, and over three-quarters of a century from the accession of Tiridates; which was due largely to the great ability of the Roman Emperors, Diocletian and Constantine, and the excellent administration and military organization they left, which saved the eastern provinces from Persia for over a quarter of a century after Constantine's death. Shahpur II. of Persia, won many victories, but he could not hold even the places he captured, and he gained no territory till the death of "Julian the Apostate" in his Persian campaign of 363. His weak and frightened successor Jovian surrendered a great section of the Eastern Roman territory, and still more disgracefully agreed that the Romans should not help their ally Arshog or (Arsaces), King of Armenia, against Shahpur. Armenia was at once invaded, but she felt her national existence at stake, and fought with desperation. Though Shahpur had the help of two apostate Armenian Princes, Mesurgan and Vahan, and other native traitors, who ravaged the country and fought their King because he was a Christian, Arshag held out four years, aided by his heroic though unprincipled wife Parantzem, and his able chief commander Vashag. Vagharshabad, Ardashad, Ervandshad, and many other cities were taken and destroyed; finally Arshag and Vashag were captured. Arshag's eyes were put out, and he was thrown into a Persian dungeon in Ecbatana; Vashag was flayed alive, and his skin stuffed and set near the King. Queen Parantzem still refused to surrender, and with 11,000 soldiers and 6,000 fugitive women held the fortress of Ardis fourteen months, till nearly all of them were dead from hunger or disease; then she opened the gates herself. Instead of honoring her, Shahpur, who was a worthy predecessor of the Turks, had her violated on a public platform by his soldiers, and then impaled (638). Meantime, her and Arshag's son, Bab (Papa), had escaped to Constantinople and asked the help of the co-Emperor Valens.

That Emperor hated to break the treaty, and involve Rome in a new Eastern war; but he could not suffer Persia to be strengthened by the possession of all Armenia, and the Roman statesmen had determined to end the long struggle over Armenia by dividing it between Persia and themselves. Bab was secretly helped by the Romans; he kept up a guerilla warfare in the mountains, and a large part of the Armenian people were prepared to welcome him back to his rightful throne. The Romans tried to keep within the letter of their treaty by not letting him assume the title of King. The Persians considered his support by Greek troops a breach of the treaty, none the less, and Valens alternately aided and disavowed him. The matter was not mended by the worthless character of Bab himself, who murdered his best friends on the least suspicion, and had the incredible baseness to hold a secret correspondence with Shahpur, the worse than murderer of his parents. Finally the Romans, convinced that he must be under their watch if they were to have any security of him, tolled him down to Cilicia, and prevented him from returning by guards of soldiers.

He made his escape, and professed his allegiance to the Romans as before; but Valens resolved to be rid of him, and had him murdered by Count Trojan, the Roman commander in the East.

Meantime a powerful Roman army under Count Trojan, and the chief Persian host, had actually camped opposite each other on the borders of Armenia (A. D. 371); but neither side wanted a general war just then,—Rome must have her hands free for the Goths, and Persia hers for the Mongols.

Finally, in 379 (A. D.), Shahpur died, and there was an instant and entire change in Persian policy toward Rome, and even toward Christianity for a while. His brother and successor, Ardosher, was an old man, and reigned but four years; his successor, Shahpur III., at once sent embassies to Rome, and made a treaty of peace (384). Finally, on the succession of Bahrom IV. (Kirman Shah), in 390, that monarch arranged a treaty of partition with Theodosine, the Roman Emperor, by which Armenia ceased to exist. The western portion became a Roman province, the then reigning sovereign, Arshog IV., was made governor to keep the people contented.

The eastern and much the larger section, was annexed to Persia, under the name of Persamenia; and to please the people, an Arsacid, Chasraes IV., was made governor, and the dynasty was continued in its rule over the Armenians till after the great Perso-Roman war of 421-2, and the persecution of Christians by Persia, which was the pretext of it.

The persecution and the war led to a movement for Armenian independence; after it was over, Bahram V. at Persia (Gor, the Wild Ass, "the mighty hunter"), put a mere vassal, Ardoshes IV., into the governorship; but the great Armenian barons would not give up the struggle, and this last of the Arshagaanian dynasty was removed in 428 and Persian governors substituted.

Thus ended the rule of the line of Arshag. It was a mighty race, and swarms with brilliant names, but in Persia it was justly displaced by one of better public policy; and in Armenia the position of the country was fatal to it.

CHAPTER VI.

Nierses the Great.—This was the great founder of Armenian scholarship. Nierses, the representative of Gregory's house, would most probably have been chosen to occupy the position, which might almost be said to be hereditary in the family of the Illuminator. He studied in the Greek schools of Cæsarea during boyhood, had he then been in Armenia. But he was resident at Constantinople, where he became famous for learning. He was married to a Greek princess of a distinguished house. And it may well be believed that the King was in no hurry to urge the return and appointment to the Archiepiscopal dignity of a man likely to be both strong and good, and therefore bound to oppose him in his evil conduct. Phoren occupied the patriarchal throne for only about two years, dying in A. D., 364. On his death it was resolved to elect Nierses a Catholicos, though he was still absent from the country. This was done, and the nobles sent an urgent message to him, begging him to return to his fatherland. Nierses acceded to their desire, and was consecrated at Cæsarea on his way to Armenia.

When he reached his native land, the nobles and people received him with great gladness (A. D., 365). He immediately set about the reformation of abuses which had crept into the church during recent times, endeavoring very successfully to restore the strict and healthy discipline which had been maintained under his great progenitor, and to abolish the laxity of morals and general disorganization which had of late prevailed. He also introduced many ecclesiastical improvements which he had seen in Constantinople. By the King's per-

NERSES THE GREAT.

MUSHEGH.

mission he called a great council or synod of all the bishops and many leading nobles, which met at Ashtishat in A. D. 365, the main object of which was the correction of abuses in the church. The chief of these which were condemned at the council were:

1. Marriages contracted between near relatives, among the nobles more especially, with the object of retaining property in the family.

2. The practice of indulging in excessive mourning for the dead, and in conduct unworthy of Christians.

3. The habit of expelling from the towns and villages all lepers and persons suffering from infectious diseases. Such unfortunates, besides the lame, the blind and hopeless incurables, were often left unaided to die of starvation.

He founded over two thousand schools and benevolent institutions as well as great numbers of churches. To put a stop to the latter practice, Nierses was successful in getting hospitals and suitable asylums built in every canton for the reception of these unfortunates. He also erected orphanages and places where widows and the poor might receive help, and succeeded in having taxes levied for their endowment. In certain places where they were most needed, he also built resthouses for travellers. He was a powerful and persuasive preacher, and a considerable writer, part of the church history being his. From these schools went forth a very brilliant band of scholars, preachers and orators, the equals of any in the world.

It was during his pontificate that the affairs of Arshag and Bab (or Pap) took place, and he was intimately connected with them till his death at the hands of the latter. Previous to the desertion of Armenia by the Romans in 363, they had quarrelled with Arshag, and sent an army to punish him; but on Nierses' intercession with Valens it was recalled and the saint obtained high favor with the emperor.

Arshag's conduct, however, grew too bad for endurance; he had his father and a relative named Kucuel (of Guel) killed,

and married Kuenel's wife, Parantzem (who afterwards met
such a horrible fate), though his own wife, Olympias, was still
alive, but bribed a priest named Mrjinnik to poison the queen
Olympias, which he did by mingling poison in the cup at
Holy Communion. Pharantzem, or Parantzem, thereupon became queen. Nierses, the Catholicos, finding admonition of
no avail, quitted Vagharshabad and went into a convent. But
Arshag, getting into fresh difficulties with the emperor and
his own rebellious vassals, besought the saint to assist him
once more, and once more Nierses complied. He first pacified
the turbulent nobility; then interceded with the Roman commander to such effect that the general withdrew his army and
went to Constantinople to justify himself to the emperor, taking a letter to him from Arshag, and hostages for the latter's
loyalty, and also inducing Nierses to accompany him. But
Valens was enraged at the withdrawal, would neither read the
letter nor see the saint, and ordered the hostages killed and
Nierses banished. The former sentence was revoked on the
general's intercession, but Nierses was shipped for his place
of exile. On the way a storm wrecked the vessel on a desert
island, but he and the crew were saved. It was winter, and
they could find no food but the roots of trees, but in a short
time the sea miraculously cast abundance of fish on shore, and
for eight months they never suffered for sustenance. At
the end of that time the saint was set free.

After the restoration of Bab to the land, though not the
acknowledged throne of his father, Nierses, the Catholicos,
convened an assembly of Armenian princes and ecclesiastical
heads, with the King, and show them all to mutual concord
and good behavior, to unite the land against the Persians, but
Bab, like so many Eastern potentates and indeed his father,
cared for nothing but to indulge his own passions, and would
have sold his country to Shahpur if he could have gotten his
price. Nierses earnestly remonstrated with him, but in vain.
Bab merely hated him for it, and finally had secretly poisoned
him (A. D., 383), in the village of Khakh in the province of

ST. SAHAG CATHOLICOS.

Eghueghiatz. Nierses, the Catholicos, had been pontiff eight years, but they were crowded with labors of immense variety and usefulness. He left one son (Isaac), who eventually became pontiff also.

MESROP. SAHAK (OR ISAAC) AND THE ARMENIAN BIBLE.

The great work of the conversion of Armenia to the Christian faith, begun by Gregory the Illuminator, had been left unfinished in at least one very important respect. Gregory had seen the desirability of rendering the church of Armenia as soon as possible independent of foreign missionaries, and had accordingly established schools for the education of the people, and for the training of indigenous clergy. But, as there was no Armenian literature worthy of the name at that time extant, and as no suitable alphabet capable of properly representing the sounds of the language had as yet been invented, he had not attempted to translate into the language of the people the scriptures and the service books used in divine worship. Greek and Syriac were carefully taught in the numerous schools established throughout the country by Gregory, and it became the practice to read the scriptures either in Greek or in Syriac—whichever language the officiating minister knew best—and to explain to the people in the vernacular the meaning of what they heard.

This was evidently only a temporary measure, and it worked well for a time. The schools turned out a considerable number of preachers and teachers able to expound to the people the meaning of the Greek and Syriac texts, and so the pressing need of an Armenian version was not so much felt. But during the troubles which followed on Tiridates' death the schools gradually lost both teachers and pupils. The new generation of clergy could indeed read the sacred texts, but they understood them less and less.

During the persecution under Meronzhan the study of Greek was, as we have already seen, entirely prohibited, and all Greek books which were found in the country were ruthlessly burnt. No serious attempt seems to have been made to interfere with the use of Syriac in worship; but the congregations accustomed to worship in Greek found their clergy in most instances quite unable to interpret to them the Syriac scriptures. The result was as ancient Armenian historians informs us, that the people left their churches uncomforted by the words of Life, which they had heard with their outward ears, but which they had been utterly unable to understand. Day by day this state of things grew worse and worse. Ignorance of the doctrines of Christianity spread rapidly, and there was great danger that the people would in consequence either lapse into their old heathen practices or at least be unable to withstand the efforts for their conversion to Magicianism made by the Persian court. This was the state of affairs which led to the invention of the Armenian alphabet still (with slight modifications) in use, and to the ultimate translation of the Holy Scriptures into that language.

This great work was accomplished by the Catholicos Sahak or Isaac in some measure, but more particularly by his famous associate and fellow-laborer, Mesrop Mashtats.

Mesrop was born in the village of Hatsik, in the canton of Taran. His father, Vartan, taught him a little Greek, and when still young he became a pupil of Nierses the Great, under whom he soon mastered Greek, Syriac and Persian. When he grew up he became for a time one of the court scribes, and found his knowledge useful in that capacity, for at that time the letters and edicts of Armenian kings were generally published in all three languages. He devoted himself to all secular studies, especially Greek, and became much respected by small and great, as his friend and biographer, Koriun, informs us. Wearying, however, of secular work, Mesrop soon left the court, and retiring to a hermitage with a few disciples, devoted himself to the practice of austerities and the preaching

MESROP, AS YOUNG PRIEST,

of the Gospel. He went especially to preach in those parts of the country, such as the canton of Gaghtha, where heathen practices still prevailed among the people, having never entirely ceased. With the favor and assistance of Sabith or Sabath, the chief of the district, Mesrop and his disciples were enabled to work a great reformation there, and the gods are said to have fled in a bodily form from them and to have retired into Media.

Being well acquainted with Syriac, Mesrop himself did not find it a very difficult task to translate orally to the people the passages of Scripture read to them in church, but the work was far more difficult for his disciples to perform. During the time that he spent in itinerating and preaching the Gospel in different parts of the country, Mesrop felt more and more how absolutely necessary it was for the people to have the Scriptures translated into and published in their native tongue. But before this could be done, it was necessary to invent an alphabet suited to the genius of the language. Owing to the number of sounds which Armenian possesses, neither the Greek nor the Syriac, nor even the pahlavi alphabet was at all suitable to write Armenian in. To the task of devising a really suitable alphabet and of having an Armenian version of Scriptures made, Mesrop now determined to devote all his energies.

Accordingly, leaving his hermitage, Mesrop came to Sahak, the Catholicos, and told him his plans (A. D., 397). This wise and good man showed the greatest possible interest in them, and gave Mesrop every encouragement to continue the efforts he had already begun to make with the object of devising an Armenian alphabet. Mesrop renewed his efforts, with fervent prayer to God for guidance.

About this time King Vramshapouh, who, at the request of the King of Persia, had visited Mesopotamia in order to arrange a dispute which had arisen in that country between himself and the Byzantine court met a Syrian presbyter named Abel, who informed him that a learned and pious

Syrian bishop, Daniel by name, had by him an alphabet which had formerly been used for writing Armenian. The King took no notice of this statement at the time, but did not forget it. By Mesrop's advice, Sahak got Vramshapouh to call a great council of the nobility and of the bishops and principal clergy of his realm, in order to decide what steps should be taken with the object of obtaining an Armenian literature. The council met at Vagharshapat in A. D., 402. The King himself was present and mentioned what he had heard about an Armenian alphabet. The council took the matter up most warmly, and entreated the King to send messengers to Mesopotamia at once to visit Abel and learn all he could tell them about the matter. This he did, and messengers obtained from Bishop Daniel a copy of the alphabet in question (which is said to have resembled the Greek) and information regarding the pronunciation of the letters composing it. Meanwhile the whole council, according to Lazarus phorpitsi, addressed a very earnest request to the Catholicos that he would complete the work begun by his great ancestor, Gregory, by taking immediate steps to have the Bible translated into Armenian from the Greek. Sahak most gladly undertook to have this great work carried out, for he saw that it was the desire of the whole nation, who deeply felt their need, and the almost utter uselessness of having the Scriptures read and divine service held in a language they could not understand.

A fitter person that Sahak to undertake such a work could hardly have been found. Setting aside his piety and zeal, Sahak's learning rendered him capable of the task. Born at Constantinople and educated there and at Cæsarea, Sahak knew Greek as perfectly as he knew his mother tongue. He had become Catholicos at the age of thirty-five, and the greater part of his life up to that time had been spent abroad. He had a very fair knowledge of Syriac, and was also well acquainted with Persian, at that time apparently the court language in Armenia. His energy was unbounded, and he was untiring in every good work.

He commanded the confidence of the people and was honored at court. Besides all this, he was an eloquent preacher and an able teacher, and had the rare talent of instilling into the minds of his disciples the zeal and earnestness that animated his own soul.

When Mesrop received the alphabet sent by Bishop Daniel, Sahak the Catholicos and he having carefully studied it, tried for two whole years to teach it in the schools, and use it for the development of an Armenian literature. But they found that it contained fourteen letters less than were actually needed to express the sounds of their native tongue. Mesrop had devoted a considerable amount of study to the conclusion that it was utter waste of time to continue to use this defective alphabet. Before, however, abandoning the attempt, he, with his assistants, John of Ekeghikh and Joseph Paghnatsi visited Bishop Daniel in Mesopotamia, and tried with his assistance to modify this alphabet so as to adapt it to the Armenian language. But the attempt failed.

While praying over the matter the right solution suddenly occurred to Mesrop. Koriun informs us that, "Not in sleep as a dream, nor in a vision while awake, but in the workshop of his heart he saw, manifested to the eyes of his spirit, the fingers of a right hand writing on a rock. The stone had a border line as of snow. It not only was manifested to him, but the exact figures of all the characters were collected together in his mind as a miracle.

Rising from prayer, he founded our written characters. At Samosata he and his assistants procured the aid of a Greek scribe named Ruffines, a disciple of Epiphanês, a hermit in Samos, who seems to have assisted him in improving and arranging the characters as far as possible in accordance with the order of the letters of the Greek alphabet. In fact, there can be no reasonable doubt that the Armenian characters are formed principally from the Greek, though some were apparently borrowed from the Avestic alphabet, and new letters —modifications of somewhat similar Greek ones—were introduced when needed to express sounds peculiar to Armenian. The alphabet thus formed was made symmetrical and harmonious, and it has ever since been used in Armenia. The date which Armenian historians assign for this invention is A. D., 406.

Immediately after this discovery, Mesrop with his two pupils, John and Joseph, set to work to translate the Bible from the Greek. He began with the Book of Proverbs, and then went on to translate the New Testament. How much of this work he accomplished at Samosata we do not know. . . . Koriun seems to imply that Mesrop translated the whole Bible, while Moses of Khorene attributes the work to him and the Catholicos Sahak and their disciples working together. It seems plain that the whole task cannot have been accomplished by Mesrop at that time for he returned to Armenia very soon, and we find the new invention warmly welcomed by King Vramshabad in 408, when he encouraged Mesrop and Sahak in their efforts to establish schools throughout the country, in which the new letters were taught.

The schools established at Vramshapouh was the most celebrated of these, and became in fact a sort of Alma Mater to all the rest.

The pupils there trained were dispersed throughout the country to found schools and train the most promising youths in the other cantons of Armenia.

They were also associated with Sahak and Mesrop in their translated work. Then began the Golden Age of Armenian literature.

The fifth century is known as the Age of Translators. These were divided into two groups. Among the "elder translators" are included Eznik Koghbatsi, who wrote a refutation of heresies. Koriun, the biographer of Mesrop, Joseph Paghnatsi and John Ekeghetsatsi, whom we have already mentioned, Joseph Vayots Tzorits and Leantius Vanandetsi. The "younger translators" were in most instances the pupils of the elder, and included Moses of Khorene, (the Herodotus of Armenian history), Eghishê (Elisha), who wrote a history of the great struggle which took place in the fifth century between the Persians and the Armenians under the Vardans, John Mando Kanni, Ghazar (Lazar) Phorpetsi the historian and others.

When Mesrop returned to Armenia he found that the Catholicos had already begun to translate the Bible from the Syriac. It had been his intention to make the Greek Septuagint the basis of his translation of the Old Testament, and to translate the New Testament from the original Greek. But a most careful search throughout the whole of Persian Armenia failed to discover a single manuscript of Holy Scriptures in Greek. Meranzhan's search for Greek books had been so thorough that he had burned every single copy in the country.

Nor were the Catholicos' messengers permitted to extend their search to that part of the country which, after Khasrove III.'s death, had again, in the reign of Theodosius II., been incorporated with the Byzantine empire. Even Mesrop's attempt to get permission to teach his alphabet to the people of that district were for the same considerable time successfully opposed by the Byzantine governors. Meranzhan's efforts had not been directed to the destruction of Syriac copies of the Bible; in fact, Syriac learning was encouraged by the Persians, while they sternly endeavored to repress the study of Greek. Hence Sahak had no difficulty in procuring copies of the Peshitto version of the Bible, and accordingly began to translate that into Armenian.

He first translated those portions of the Scriptures which were appointed to be read in the churches, and his version of these was published in A. D., 411.

The Catholicos now sent some of his own and Mesrop's most promising pupils to Greece and Syria to search for and translate all the most important books they could find, especially the works of the leading fathers of the church. Eznik and Joseph were sent to Edessa for this purpose.

When they had made many versions there from the Syriac,

they went to Constantinople in their eagerness to prosecute
the study of Greek. There obtaining possession of the Greek
originals of some of the works they already had in Syriac, they
carefully revised the versions of these books which they had
made at Edessa. They were joined at Constantinople by
Koriun and Leontes, who had been impelled to go thither by
their zeal for learning.

Shortly afterwards two others of their fellow students arrived, John and Arbzan, sent by Sahak to obtain authorized
copies of the Greek Bible for him, and these latter were also
directed to be present at the council of Ephesus in A. D. 431.
There they gave an account of the progress of the Gospel in
Armenia and of Mesrop's great invention.

On their return they took back with them copies of the
Greek Bible from the imperial library at Constantinople, which
must have been in accordance with those made by Eusebius at
Constantine the Great's command. They found Mesrop and
Sahak at Ashtishat, still busily engaged in translational work.

On the receipt of the Greek manuscripts, which his messengers had brought, Sahak was greatly puzzled by the numerous slight variations of reading to be found in the different Syriac and Greek copies of the Bible now in his hands.
It was partly for this reason, as well as with the object of securing the assistance of scholars thoroughly versed in Greek
learning, that he sent Moses of Khorene and others to study
philosophy, history and rhetoric at Alexandria. Others were
sent to Constantinople and other great educational centres.

On their return, after a period of about seven years, these
men devoted their energies to the enlightenment of their native land.

They do not seem, however, to have been of much assistance in the translation of the Bible, which was finished and
published in A. D. 456.

This was the second Armenian version, made this time by
Sahak and Mesrop, from the Greek. The receipt of the Greek
manuscripts brought from Byzantine had made Sahak resolve

to revise his version in accordance with the Greek. We might therefore suppose that he would have followed the Greek in all places where it differs from Peshitto Syriac text. But, however, the fact is to be accounted for—this is by no means the case. Certain passages show that the Syriac text was preferred to the Greek.

It will be sufficient to mention one illustration of this. In the last paragraph of St. Mathew's Gospel—which is read in the Baptismal service of the Armenian church—the passage "As (My) Father hath sent me, even so send I you;" is introduced at the end of the eighteenth verse, as in the Peshitto. It is repeated, however, in the Armenian version (as in the Greek text and the Peshitto) in its proper place, John xx., 21, Making allowances for such facts as these, which show a want of critical acumen—hardly to be wondered at in that age—on the part of the Armenian translators, the version made by Sahak, Mesrop and their coadjutors is a noble one, well deserving of the title of "queen of versions" which has been bestowed upon it. Its great defect is that the Old Testament was translated from the Septuagint and not direct from the original Hebrew. From the language of Moses of Khorene and other contemporary writers, it is clear that the Armenian Bible did not originally contain the Apocrypha. The expression they use is that the translators rendered into Armenian the twenty-two evident (acknowledged) books of the Old Testament. This, of course, means the books of the Hebrew canon, which were in ancient times reckoned as numbering twenty-two, the number of the letters in the Hebrew alphabet. The Old Testament Apocrypha is, however, now read in the Armenian church.

As far as we can learn from the somewhat varying accounts of contemporary Armenian historians, the whole of the Old Testament, except the proverbs of Soloman, was translated by Sahak, while Mesrop translated the proverbs and the New Testament. But the revision was shared in by both these great men as well as some of the most able of their disciples. It is needless to say what a boon to Armenia such a work was. The Armenian people were now able to understand the word of God read in their churches and circulated among them in every part of the country as quickly as scribes could multiply copies in sufficient numbers.

The Bible was everywhere eagerly studied, and one immediate result was a great deepening of the religious life of the people. The knowledge of the Gospel message and of the commandments of God spread everywhere, and Mesrop and Sahak were most diligent in the effort to enlighten the people in every canton of the country. We may form some idea of what then took place in Armenia by remembering the accounts which historians give us of the reception Luther's German Bible met with when it issued from the press. The Armenian Bible soon became the one great national book, and early Armenian historians have in most cases their whole style colored by their intimate acuaintance with Holy Scripture.

It has often been remarked, and with perfect truth, that it was to the invention of the Armenian alphabet, and the publication of Mesrop and Sahak's version of the Bible in that language that the nation owed not only its retention of Christianity during the terrible persecution that so quickly followed the fall of the Arsacidæ dynasty, but even its very existence. Had not the people been united by an intelligent knowledge, and a hearty acceptance of one faith and by the possession of a national literature, they could never have weathered the storms that in the fifth and following centuries beat with such fury upon Armenia. The breathing space afforded by Vramshabad's wise and peaceful reign, falling between these periods of trouble and discord, was giving by an all-wise and merciful providence to prevent the vessel of both church and nationality from dire and terrible shipwreck.

Besides the direct spiritual results of the translation of the Bible into the language of the people, (which were so great that Lazarus Pharpetsi says that in describing them he is warranted in using Isaiah's words, and stating that the whole land

MESROP, AS HIGH PRIEST.

of Armenia was thereby filled with the knowledge of the Lord as the waters cover the sea), it had also others less direct, but very important. One of these was that it reduced the language to a literary standard, and gave it order, fixity and permanence. From very early times many different dialects have prevailed in Armenia, but during the last few centuries of our narrative the dialect of the province of Ararat had come to the fore as the language of the court and of the central and leading district in the kingdom.

This was the dialect which was naturally adopted by the translators, and it became the literary language of the country. Even to the present time though no longer spoken, it is used in literature to a great extent and until very recently was the only written form of Armenian. The literary dialects of modern language, those of Ararat and Constantinople, are now extensively used, though the old literary dialect is still dignified with the title of Grapar, or written.

The literary impulse given to the leading minds of the nation by Mesraph's invention of the alphabet led to a great amount of other translational work, besides the composition of such books as Moses of Khorene's History of Armenia, Eznik's Refutation of Heresies, Elisha's History of the War of the Vartans, and other similar works of great value and interest. Not only were the old chronicles of the kingdom transcribed into the new alphabet, and thus preserved for some considerable time, but the works of all the Greek and Syrian Fathers that could possibly be obtained were translated into Armenian. A little later the works of Plato and Aristotle, of Homer and other classical writers were added to the list. We hardly know as yet at all fully what valuable writings have thus been preserved to us in Armenian libraries, but Tatian's Diatessaran and Eusebius chronicle are examples of the treasure still to be discovered by diligent search in this field of learning.

Armenian historians relate that to Mesrap is due the invention of the ecclesiastical alphabet in use in Georgia. The date they fix for this is A. D. 410.

BAROUYR OR BRAYERIOS.

We must not judge the ability and reputation of men
in their own ages solely by the familiarity of their names to
us: those that have come down to us are a mere handful, and
not by any means always the greatest of their time.

Much depends on chance—the preservation of certain
works, and the loss of others, or certain men happening to do
something dramatic. Great orators are especially likely to
be forgotten; they leave no written works of their own, and
not being in political life the common histories do not mention
them. The name of Barouyr is wholly unknown to this age;
but we have the testimony of a contemporary writer, Eunapius
of Sardis—not a countryman of his, and therefore free from all
suspicion of patriotic brag, and most unlikely to make out an
Armenian greater than he was—that he was the most wonderful orator of his time, famous all over the Roman world, and
greatly admired even by the emperors. He was one of those
men to whom all languages seem alike to come by nature, and
his oratory was as easy and as perfect in one as in the other;
in Latin or Greek as in his national Armenian. The only
comparison I can give in modern times is Louis Kossuth.

That Barouyr has not the fame of Cicero or Demosthenes,
Kossuth or Gladstone, is probably because under the circumstances of the time he could not engage in political life. Military service or high birth were about the only avenues.

I will quote in substance what Eunapius says of this brilliant orator, whom he probably knew all about, as our boys
know about Gladstone.

Barouyr, he was born in 347, and he was certainly alive
in the time of the Emperor Julian, who came to the throne in
361.

Barouyr lived to be ninety, and was beautiful even in old
age, having vigor of youth in his looks. He was eight feet
high. When a boy he left Armenia and went to Antioch,
the first of the Christians, and entered the school of oratory un-

der the celebrated Albianos, where he shortly became the foremost pupil. Thence he went to the Athens and studied under Julian, the greatest of the teachers of oratory there,—supporting himself by working meantimes, as he was very poor; in no long time he was recognized as the leading orator of Athens, and taught the art to the Athenians. The other teachers were so angry that they bribed the governor to banish him; but on the governor's removal some time after, he was permitted to return. The new governor instituted an oratorical competition: Whoever could deliver the best extempore oration on a subject to be given out on the spot, should receive great honors. Barouyr took part on condition that the auditors should take careful notes and should not cheer; but they were so fascinated that they broke both conditions, listening in rapture and applauding repeatedly. The governor offered him his chair and honored him as the greatest orator in Athens. Later the Emperor Constans was so struck with his wisdom and oratorical power that he called him first to Gaul and then to Rome, where he delivered his greatest orations and the Romans erected a bronze monument in his honor, inscribed "Regina Rerum Momoe Regi Eliquentioc." (Rome Queen of Affairs to the King of Eloquence). From Rome he returned to Athens, and taught there many years with great repute, up to the time of the Emperor Julian, who honored him and spoke as follows of him: "Barouyr was a flowing river of oratory, and in power and persuasiveness of speech was like Pericles." And I now add that with all this he was a thorough Christian man—not a priest, but a great Christian layman and teacher but not among his nation. He was mostly in foreign countries.

VARTAN, DEFENDER OF THE FAITH.

The Sassanian dynasty in Persia was a source, more or less, of perpetual misery and blood-shed in Armenia. As it has been said before, the Persians had two reasons for their cruel attitude towards Armenia. These causes were the existence of the Aroacide reign and Christianity in Armenia, while Zoroastrianism was revived in Persia under the Sassanian kings.

Christianity was a permanent cause or occasion for which Armenia has suffered and is still suffering indescribable miseries and innumerable cruelties. The Persians would imagine that as long as the Armenians are Christians they are in alliance with the Greeks, while, unfortunately and often, the Greeks were no longer in sympathy with them than the Persians.

Armenia about the middle of the fifth century had entirely lost her independence and was divided between the Greeks and the Persians, the eastern and the large part of the country being under the latter power.

Yesgerd II., the King of Persia, (A. D. 450), decreed thus: "All people and tongues throughout my domains must abandon their heresies, worship the sun, bring to him their offerings, and call him God; they shall feed the holy fire, and fulfill all the ordinances of Magi." Accordingly, Mihrnersh, the grand vizier of the Persian court, wrote a long letter to the Armenians, polemic in character, persuasive in style, and menacing in tone, the synod of the Armenian bishops he convened, who unanimously agreed to defend their religion at any cost, and at the same time it was decided upon answering the letter of the grand vizier in which they both refuted the charges made against Christianity, undauntedly defended their faith, showing the absurdity of Zoroastrianism, and concluded the epistle with these words: "From this belief no one can move us neither angels nor men, neither fire nor sword, nor water, nor any other horrid tortures, however they be called. All our goods and our possessions are before thee, dispose of them as thou wilt, and if thou only leavest us to our belief, we will here below choose no other lord in thy place, and in heaven have no other God but Jesus Christ, for there is no other God save only Him. But shouldst thou require something beyond this great testimony, behold our resolution: our bodies are in thy hands—do with them according to thy pleasure; tortures are thine, and patience ours; thou hast the sword, we the neck; we are nothing better than our forefathers who, for the sake of their faith, resigned their goods, possessions and life. Do thou, therefore, inquire of us nothing further concerning these things, for our belief originates not with men, we are not taught like children, but we are indissoluble, bound to God from whom nothing can detach us, neither now or hereafter, nor forever, nor for ever and ever."

As soon as this letter arrived at the Royal Court of Persia, King Yasgerd was enraged and summed the Armenia princes to immediately repair to His Majesty's presence. There in the presence of the King they manifested a great resolution in their faith, for which they were ignominiously treated and confined in prison. Having been threatened while in their confinement, they devised a scheme; they thought it was better, apparently, to comply with the demands of the King, but inwardly to remain true to their convictions and religion. God, who is able to bring good out of evil, indeed did so in this case. When it was made known to the King that the Armenian princes were willing to accept his terms, at once they were liberated and returned with distinctions to their homes, and a large army with over seven hundred magi were exultantly marching on to Armenia to raze to the ground every Christian church and school and disciple the people into the mysterious absurdities of Zoroastrianism.

No sooner had the news of the apostacy of the princes reached Armenia than the bishops, priests and the laity condemned the weakness and the folly of the princes.

When the princes returned to Armenia they found no one ready to listen to any explanation, but everywhere the people were ready to defend their religion at the cost of their lives. A large multitude made up of clergy and laity, among whom were many women, gathered for immediate action, for the enemy was marching on. Some of the princes could not endure the contempt of the people, nor the unrelenting remorse of consciences, so they were ready to expiate their folly at any cost.

Vartan Mamigonian is the most esteemed and beloved name in Armenian history. This noble man was a grandson of Sahak Catholicos. When Vartan Mamigonian was a little boy, he was so full of grace that the Pontiff Sahak adopted him as his son, and through this companionship of the aged ecclesiastic and the religious boy, the latter developed into a great spiritual light. In 421 he went to Constantinople with noble St. Mesrop, and was much loved and esteemed by the Emperor (Theodosius II.), and the court, then to Persia, where the King honored him and gave him the title of prince.

Vartan Mamigonian was a faithful servant of God and His Saviour. It was said of him that he was an honest, modest, wise, brave, true, pure, childlike and Christlike Christian commander, a great soldier of the Cross. He was a lamb in nature, but when he came to defend his religion he was a lion.

Prince Vartan, the Mamigonian, was unanimously appointed the commander-in-chief of the Armenians, against the Persians, and the multitude was formed into three divisions, intrusted to three princes: Vartan, Nershebuh and Vasag. The latter, however, proved treacherous and perfidious, and with his almost entire division sided with the Persians, and began to devastate the provinces, where he was stationed to encounter the foe. His treachery decided the fate of the Armenians. But brave Vartan and the rest were not dismayed, though they knew that they alone could not conquer an immense army of the enemy with a small force of their own. Yet they were not fighting for victory, but for their convictions and the religion of Christ.

Finally the forces were arrayed for battle on the banks of the Dughmood river, on the plains of Avaraye, near the present city of Van.

Prince Varton had 66,000 men, the Persians several times

VARTAN MAMIGONIAN.

as many. Before beginning war Vartan Mamigonian knelt down and prayed to God for help, and to Christ for his own salvation, then he made an address to his soldiers, in substance as follows:

"Soldiers, as Christians, we are averse to fighting, but to defend the Christian religion and our own freedom we have to fight. Surely our lives are not as valuable as Christ's, and if He was willing to die on the cross for us we ought to be willing to die in battle for Him. I have been," said he, "in many battles, and you also with me; we have sometimes bravely vanquished the foe; sometimes they vanquished us, but on all these occasions we thought only of worldly distinction, and we fought merely at the command of a mortal king. Behold, we have all many wounds and scars upon our persons, and great must have been our bravery to have won these great marks of honor. But useless and empty I deem these exploits whereby we have received these honorable marks, for they pass away. If, however, you have done such valiant deeds in obedience to a mortal ruler, how much more will you do then for our immortal King, who is Lord of life and death, and who judges every one according to his works.

"Now, therefore, I entreat you, my brave companions, and more so as you—albeit in bravery, worth, and inherited honors greater than I—have of your own free will and out of your love elected me your leader and chief, I entreat that my words may be favorably received by the high and the low. Fear not the numbers of the heathens; withdraw not your necks from the terrific sword of a mortal man in order that the Lord may give the victory into our hands, that we may annihilate their power and lift on high the standard of truth."

On the morning of the day of the battle the little army of the Holy League received the Holy Eucharist, and marched on with these words: "May our death be like to the death of the just, and may the shedding of our blood resemble the blood-shedding of the prophet. May God look in mercy on our voluntary self-offering, and may He not deliver the church into the hands of the heathens." Then, with his troops, he crossed the river fell on the enemy's centre, and scattered the huge army in rout, killing 3,544 men, besides nine great princes, and losing 1,036 of his men; but alas! one of these was himself, dying from a mortal wound not long after. Nevertheless he had won the victory he was striving for.

Yazygerd, the King of Persia, saw it was impossible to conquer the Armenians in a war for religion, and granted entire liberty to the Christians to believe and preach as they pleased. . . . .

PRINCE VAHAN MAMIGONIAN.

Christianity and Zoroastrianism had many a battle in the land of Ararat, until the latter, in total despair, was willing to submit to the former, on some amicable terms to be suggested by a brave son of Armenia, a worthy member of the house of Mamigoians. This valiant champion of truth was Vahan Mamigonian, whose uncle, Prince Vartan, led the Holy League in battle, and with the heroism and courage of the martyrs defended their religion and rights, and had sealed their testimony to the truth of Christianity by their blood in the previous battle.

The Persians, ofter their conquest of Armenia, destroyed many of the churches and schools. Many of the bishops and priests were captured. Some were martyred on the spot, others were carried to Persia and there executed. The patriarch, Joseph, in whose character and life shine forth piety, courage and devotion, was one of those carried to Persia. The Christians were persecuted with indescribable tortures and cruelties and Zoroastrianism inculcated among the Armenians, who in return most cordially hated both the religion of Zoroaster and its defenders, and were alert for an opportunity to drive out the usurpers as unwelcomed teachers of an unphilosophized reli-

PRINCE VAHAN MAMIGONIAN.

gion sprung out of Zoroaster's imagination. The northern
provinces of Armenia rebelled against the Persians. The latter,
therefore, attempted to subdue them. The Armenians availed
themselves of this ample occasion, armed themselves and urged
Vahan Mamigonian to take the lead of the army to clear out
of the country the troops of the enemy left there. The Persian
forces had received such terrible disastrous defeats in various
contests from the Armenians, under the command of Prince
Vahan Mamigonian, that when a new governor, Nikhor, was
appointed by Balos, the King of Persia (A. D. 485), he instead
of attacking Vahan, who held almost the whole of the country,
wished to come to an arrangement agreeable to the Armenians. Prince Vahan therefore proposed the following terms:

1. The existing fire-altars should be destroyed and no
others should be erected in Armenia.

2. The Armenians should be allowed the free and full
exercise of Christian religion, and no Armenians should be in
future tempted or bribed to declare themselves disciples of
Zoroaster.

3. If converts were, nevertheless, made from Christianity
to Zoroastrianism, places (of honor) should not be given to
them.

4. The Persian King should in person, and not by deputy, administer the affairs of Armenia.

These terms proposed by Prince Vahan, were favorably
accepted by Nikhor, and an edict of toleration was issued and
proclaimed that everyone should be at liberty to adhere to his
own religion, and that no one should be driven to apostatize.
Afterwards Vahan himself was appointed governor of Armenia by the King, and thus the church enjoyed a period of
tranquility from the persecutions.

ARMENIAN LITERATURE.

The Armenian schools and universities and their outpour
of great scholars and writers have already been spoken of,

but of course Armenian youths, eager for the best of the
world's learning, did not confine themselves to their own
country; they studied in Constantinople, Athens, Antioch,
Alexandria, and wherever great teachers were located,—all
zealous Christians, and the books they have left behind were
Christian literature, not works of mere enjoyment. A very
rich and valuable literature it is, too, in my judgment the most
so of any single body that exists; though much of it has perished in the recent destruction of everything Christian the
Turks can reach.

The fifth century is called the Golden Age of Armenian
literature. First in point of time as well as importance comes
the Armenian Bible. The furious opposition of the church in
the Middle Ages to letting the people have the Bible to read
in their own tongues seems perfectly ridiculous, when we remember that in the early Christian Church every people had
it in their own language, and it was thought to be the greatest
work for a heathen people that could be done, to translate
the Bible for them.

It was not thought needful then to keep the Word of
God in a strange tongue, so that the people could neither
read it for themselves nor understand it when it was read to
them.

There were probably some books of popular tales and
songs in Armenia before the fifth century, for we are told that
there was an Armenian alphabet to write them in as early as
the second, but if so they have all perished, and the alphabet
was doubtless a poor and meagre one. Armenian scholars
and writers read Greek or Latin books, and occassionally Hebrew or Syriac ones, and wrote in Greek or Latin themselves;
if it was necessary to write Armenian, as in letters, they made
the Greek, Syriac of Persian characters, which of course were
insufficient to give the Armenian sounds. They would have
got along with this, however, if it had not been for the eagerness of Christian enthusiasm which made them wish to give

the Bible to Armenia. It was to spread the Word of God, not to write books, that they were anxious.

St. Mesrop set to work and invented a very perfect alphabet of thirty-six letters, to which two have been added since. According to one of his disciples, having vainly sought help from the learned, he prayed to God, and received the new alphabet in a vision.

This was about 405. He and Sahag, the Pontiff, at once began to translate the New Testament and the Book of Proverbs from a poor Greek version, the best they had, with the assistance of two pupils, John and Joseph. This was finished in 406. Many years later they undertook the translation of the Old Testament; but as the Persians had destroyed all the Greek manuscripts, it was necessary to use a Syriac version. The same two assistants aided them; but being sent to the Council of Ephesus in 431, they brought back copies of the Greek Septuagint, and the old translation was at once dropped, and a new one put under way. But all found their knowledge of Greek too imperfect to rely on, and the pupils were sent to Alexandria and Athens to complete their education. On their return they seem to have brought a new Alexandrian version, and corrections were made from that, and the work completed, most likely about 435.

The Bible completed, they turned to other labors. The saints, Sahag and Mesrop, are said to have written six hundred books themselves, all in Christian theology and instruction; and the pupils from the schools St. Nierses and themselves had founded—the chief of their own were at Naravank, Ayri, and Vochkhoraz—wrote great numbers besides. The first original work of Sahag was one on pastoral theology, setting forth that the Church of Christ is the Bride of Christ, and the ministers must therefore be holy, pure, and obedient. He wrote many epistles to Kings and Emperors, all of whom reverenced and were greatly influenced by him.

He wrote a large part of the Armenian Church history,

composed many hymns, and translated many commentaries and theological works from the Greek.

Fortunately during this period the government of Armenia was very good, with the exception of one period of two years or so; even after its partition, for close on forty years it had practically self-government in internal affairs, and for another decade the Christians enjoyed full rights of worship. Bahram IV. at Persia (389-399), who helped divide it, was a monarch who loved peace above all things, both with foreign countries and his own people, his successor, Yazdegerd I. (399-420), went even further, employed the Catholicos or Pontiff on embassies to Constantinople, as mediator with his own brother, and made his son, Shahpur, governor of Persian Armenia, continuing the Arsacidæ dynasty. IIe was murdered by his nobles, instigated by the Zoroastrian priests, for being too tolerant to the Christians, and his successor, Bahram V., who got the throne by favor of the rebellious elements, tried to please them by persecuting the Christians. This involved him in a war with Rome, as I have said, and after a couple of years he made peace and gave toleration again. The turning of Persian Armenia into a satrapy in 428, but no fresh persecution was undertaken till that of Yasgerd II. in 439, ending in Vartan's revolt just detailed. Shahpur of Armenia was a Prince of great wisdom, generosity, and public spirit; he patronized men of learning, founded schools, made large grants from the treasury for scholarship, and sent scholars to all the great seats of learning to teach and acquire the languages, literature, and history of other nations, after which they wrote and translated hundreds of volumes. Among them were Tavit, Khosrohl, Mampre, and Zazer; a great historian, Eghishe, author of the life of Prince Vartan, and a great philosopher, Yeznic. These are only a few out of scores worthy of mention.

Dr. Philip Schaff says: "In spite of the unfavorable state of political and social affairs in Armenia, during this epoch, more than six hundred Greek and Syriac works were trans-

MOSES KHORENTZI.

lated within the forty years after the translation of the Bible, and as in many cases the original works have perished, while the translations have been preserved, the great importance of this whole literary activity is apparent. Among works which in this way have come down to us are several books by Philo-Alexandrinus, on providence, and reason, commentaries, etc.; the Chronicle of Eusebius, nearly complete; the Epistles of Ignatius, translated from a Syrian version; fifteen homilies by Severianus; the exegetical writings of Ephriam, Syros, previously completely unknown, and the historical books of the Old Testament, the Synoptical Gospels, the Parables of Jesus, and the fourteen Pauline Epistles; the Hexahemeran of Basil the Great; the Catechesis of Cyril of Jerusalem; several homilies by Chrysostom, etc. The period, however, was not characterized by translations only. Several of the disciples of Mesrop and Sahak left original works. Esnik wrote four books against heretics, printed at Venice in 1826, and translated into French by Le Vailliant de Florival, Paris, 1853. A biography of Mesrop by Koriun, homilies by Mambres, and various writings by the philosopher David, have been published; and the works of Moses Chorenensis, published in Venice in 1842, and again in 1864, have acquired a wide celebrity; his history of Armenia has been translated into French, Italian and Russian.

Sixth century: The leading authors in this century are Abraham Mamigonian, who wrote on the Council of Ephesus; and Bedross Sonnian, who wrote on the life of Christ. There are, however, many others of merit.

Seventh century: By far the greatest name in this century, and indeed the best known and most important name in Armenian literature altogether, is the writer who calls himself Moses Khorentzi, well known to all historical scholars as Moses of Chorene, author of the History of Armenia. For more than a thousand years, up to this century, indeed, this was practically the only source of Armenian history to the world; the other writers were inaccessible, and it is still very valuable, though not in just the way it was once thought to be. It preserves a vast amount of Armenian tradition, stories and ballads, and real history, which have perished except for this work, but he seems not to have had the Greek and Latin histories to draw from, and makes a great many mistakes. He gives a life of himself, and says he is writing in the fifth century, and knew Saints Sohag and Mesrop when he was young, but he really lived in the seventh, and wrote history about the year 640. But still he is a great writer, and one of Armenian's literary lights, and we do not need to claim for him anything more than he deserves.

Besides Moses, the chief authors were Gomidos, Yeze, Malassagha, Krikoradour, Hovhounes, Vertanes and Anania, They wrote chiefly religious books, but Anania Shiragatzi is the author of a valuable work on astronomy.

In eighth century, the leading authors were Hovhom Imossdosser, Sdepannoss Sonnotzi, and Lehamt Yeretz. They wrote hymns, books on oratory, etc. In ninth century, Zakaria Shaboah, Toama, and Kaur Ken, etc. In tenth century, the chief authors were Anania, Khosrov and Krikor Noregatzi. The latter wrote a prayer book in ninety-five chapters, which one of the missionaries of the American Board thinks the best in the world. He says that only Henry Beecher was able to offer such prayer as Krikor Naregatzi. In the eleventh century, the leading writers were Hovhannes, Krikor, and Aristaguss. In this century some of the best commentaries were written on the Bible. And the twelfth century the chief authors: Nerses Shnorhali, or Nerses Graceful, is the foremost of Armenian poets, and a thoroughly converted and consecrated man of God. His hymns were intensely spiritual, and the Armenians still chant them in their church. They are worthy to be translated into English, by Miss Alice Stone Blackwell, in Boston, Mass., as follows:

"O, wayspring sun of righteousness, shine forth with light for me;
Treasure of mercy, let my soul thy hidden riches see.
Thou before whom the thoughts of men lie open in thy sight,

NERSES SHNORHALI.

Unto my soul, now dark and dim, grant thoughts that shine with light.
O, Father, Son, and Holy Ghost, Almighty One in Three,
Care-taker of all creatures, have pity upon me!
Awake, O Lord, awake to help, with grace and power divine;
Awaken those who slumber now, Like Heaven's host to shine;
O Lord and Saviour, life-giver, unto the dead give life,
And raise up those that have grown weak and stumbled in the strife;
O skillful Pilot; Lamp of Light, that burneth bright and clear;
Strength and assurance grant to me, now hid away in fear.
O Thou that makest old things new, renew me and adorn;
Rejoice me with salvation, Lord, for which I only mourn.
Giver of Good, unto my sins bé Thy forgiveness given;
Lead Thy disciples, Heavenly King, unto the flocks of Heaven.
Defeat the evil husbandman that soweth tares and weeds;
Wither and kill in me the fruits of all his evil seeds;
O Lord, grant water to my eyes, that they may shed warm tears,
To cleanse and wash away the sin that in my soul appears;
On me, now hid in shadow deep, shine forth, O glory bright;
Sweet juice, quench thou my soul's keen thirst; show me the path of
    light.
Jesus, whose name is love, with love crush thou my stony heart;
Bedew my spirit with thy blood, and bid my griefs depart;
O Thou that even in fancy art so sweet, Lord Jesus Christ,
Grant that with Thy realty my soul may be sufficed;
When Thou shalt come again to earth, and all Thy glory see,
Upon that dread and awful day, O Christ, remember me.
Thou that redeemest men from sin, O Saviour, I implore,
Redeem him who now praiseth Thee, to praise Thee evermore.

This hymns the perfectly spiritual, and Armenians with
the pleasure and gladly still singing them in their church ceremonies in the every morning. (The Archbishop Nerses the
Graceful; born 1102, died 1172.) In this 12th century, Nerses
Lampranatzi, the greatest scholar ever born in Armenia, was a
distinguished commentator on the Old Testament, and wrote
many other books. Another is Yeremia.

In the thirteenth century, the leading authors: Krikor
Sguevratzi, Kevork Sguevratzi, Mukhitar Anetzi, Vanagan
Vartabed, Vartan Vartabed, etc. They wrote histories, commentaries, etc. As the Armenian dynasties ended in the fourteenth
century at Cilicia by the last King Leo VI., and after that pe-

riod have no important literature among the Armenian churches.

The Armenians, besides the language of country, wherever they may be found, speak their own tongue, which is a distinct language of itself, and belongs to the Indo-Germanic family of languages. There are, however, two Armenian languages, the ancient and modern. The former was the language of the pre-Christian era; and after the conversion of the nation to Christianity, and the translation of the Bible into it, it became the standard language of the literature. "In its syntactical structure the old Armenian resembles most nearly the classical Greek." Its close relation to the Sanskrit, ancient Persian, Greek, and Latin might be pointed out by numerous words commonly found in these and Armenian languages.

The modern Armenian language has been elevated to the dignity of a respectable language almost in this century by numerous original and translated works and periodicals published in various countries, especially by the translation of the Bible. The relation of this language to the ancient Armenian might be compared with that of the modern Greek to the ancient Greek language.

The Armenian literature of the pre-Christian era has not survived, excepting a few fragmentary songs, which lingered even until the time of Moses of Khorene, in whose history of Armenia they are preserved, and the inscriptions of the Kings of Van—if we admit with some—are "the oldest specimens of the Asiatic branch of the Indo-Germanic family."

Christianity brought with it into Armenia a great love for learning; Armenian youths flocked into the schools at Athens, Alexandria, and Constantinople. Most of them engaged themselves in translating many valuable works from the Greek and other languages into the Armenian. A recent writer speaks of these translators in this manner: Some of them obtained celebrity in their chosen pursuits. To this tendency we owe the preservation, in Amenian, of many works that have perished in their original languages."

The original works consist of theological and expository discourses, commentaries, histories, sacred songs, devotional works, etc. "The existing literature of the Armenians dates from the fourth century, and is essentially and exclusively Christian." This "literature is rich and continuous, uninterrupted through all the Middle Ages. It has furnished the philosophers, historians, theologians, and poets." The peculiar value of the Armenian literature is not realized as it should be, by European and American scholars; the language is well worth learning for what it can give the student. Not alone is the original work that comes from the first Christian nation specially valuable for its bearing on primitive Christianity, but the Armenian scholars translated great numbers of works from other languages, and these translations are preserved in Armenian monasteries when the originals have been irretrievably lost in the wars, and burnings, and devastations of other countries. Six hundred volumes of this old literature are known to exist now, two hundred in Europe, and four hundred in different places in Armenia.

"They (the Armenians) are a people of fine physical development, often of stature and powerful frame, industrious and peaceable, yet more jealous of their rights and liberties than any other Oriental race. They passionately cherish the memory of their fathers, and preserve the use of their national language, which belongs to the Indo-European family, and possess a literature of considerable importance."*

"These Armenians are a superb race of men; their costume, which is plain and noble, displays to advantage their athletic forms; their physiognomy is intelligent; they have florid complexions, black and blue eyes, and beards of lightish color. They are the Swiss of the East. Industrious, peaceable and regular in their habits, they resemble them also in calculation and love of gain. The women are lovely; their features are pure and delicate, and their serene expression

* "Bible Lands," page 367. By Van Lennep.

recalls the beauty of the women of the British Islands or of the peasants of Switzerland."*

In education the Armenians surpass all other nations of Western Asia, and many might even fairly be compared with the people of some Roman Catholic countries. But a great majority, safely may it be said, yet sit in the darkness of ignorance and superstition. This is a sad fact. But it is impossible to be otherwise, as long as the sceptre of power is in the hand of Islamism. "Islamism it is which palsies every effort to reform throughout the empire." "The conviction is inevitable, that until the power of Islamism is broken, the true reformation of this land is an impossibility." Islamism is a moral and photophobia; it dreads the light of civilization and Christianity.

As the religion of the Armenians, Christianity, though not in its simplicity and purity now as it was in the beginning, is infinitely superior to the religion of Mohammed, so the character of the Armenians, it might be said, is in the same proportion, superior to that of the Mohammedans, notwithstanding all the evil influences of the latter upon the former. The Armenians, moreover, lack the volatility of the Greek and the laxity of the Jews.

Before I finish this chapter I wish to say a few more words about the beginning of Christianity in Armenia.

Christianity was begun in Armenia, perhaps, as early as the days of the apostles, and had been mightily revived by Gregory the Illuminator. Armenia or the Armenians were now a Christian country, or people, with an independent and indigenous church and a Bible in their own language. She possessed a body of devout and learned clergy, full of energy and zeal. Her students went everywhere to seek knowledge and learning, and returned home to divide among her numerous congregations the mental and spiritual treasures they had won. Her people studied the Word of God, and grew in grace and in the knowledge of God. Christianity had routed and annihilated Paganism, and had struck her

* Lambertine," Voyage in Orient," volume ii., page 190.

INTERIOR OF ARMENIAN CHURCH.

roots deep down into the heart and conscience of the nation.
Like a noble tree on the mountain-top, buffeted by the storm
and yet unshaken from its post, the Armenian Church even
in near future, was to experience the tempests of persecution
and oppression, and yet by those very blasts be driven to strike
root more deeply still, as it were, into the very Rock of Ages,
and to stand firm during all future time as a proof of her
Master's protecting care in the very face of the gates of hell.

THE ARMENIAN CHURCH.

The Armenian Church was and still is a national,
independent and separate body as much as the Greek or the
Roman Catholic Church, and older than either of them; therefore the prosperity of the nation was also the prosperity of the
church. The nation had but little rest after her embrace
of Christianity. Christian Armenia during the first three
centuries of her existence made such a defence of her faith
against Zoroastrianism that the latter was completely par-
alyzed and no longer able to lift up the sword against the
followers of Christ.

But with the rise of Mohammedanism, a more formidable,
cruel, unjust, and inhuman enemy arose.

The Saracens or the Arabs, who were both the soldiers
and missionaries of Mohammedanism, literally panted after
the blood of the Christians as the hart panteth after the water
brooks.

Even these, after sucking all the blood that they could im-
bibe, fell off like swollen leeches and themselves were swal-
lowed up by the Seljukian, Tartar, and Mongolian Turks, who
surpassed even the Arabs in cruelty and deserved to be called
"the unspeakable Turk." The Greeks, with all their subtlety,
volatility, perfidy, intrigues, and intolerable bigotry, could
do no more than to cause some of the corruptions of their
church to creep into the Armenian Church. But this is not
all; for while the Armenians were driven into the mountain-

ous district of Cilicia, the land of the brave Apostle Paul, by the Mongolian and Tartar invaders, who spread desolation, destruction, and death wherever their feet touched the soil, there came with the appearance of the crusaders in the East a number of zealous missionaries of the Romish Church, who, instead of preaching and converting millions of Mohammedans to Christianity, tried to bring the Armenian Church into a subordination and jurisdiction of the Pope of Rome.

Though the missionaries of the Romish Church undoubtedly knew that their church excelled the Church of Armenia in corruption, in superstition, and nonscriptural claims and dogmas, yet they took advantage of the oppressed condition of the people and persistently disturbed their church. The overthrow of the political existence of the Armenians, according to some, is due to their intercourse with the Western nations, as we have seen. After this overthrow the Church of Armenia became both the custodian of the nation's existence and the defender of her independence.

The Armenians, owing to the frequent incursions, devastations, barbarous massacres, and being led captives in great numbers by the Saracens, afterwards by the Mongolian and Tartar hordes, were compelled to immigrate into safer districts and countries, especially after the overthrow of the independent dynasty in Cilicia.

When Constantinople was taken by the Turks, Sultan Mohammed II. appointed Bishop Hovaghim, of Brusa, the Patriarch over the Armenians then in Constantinople and in vicinity. This naturally also drew a good number of the Armenians from other parts, while nearly two centuries before this time Jerusalem was also made the seat of a Patriarch.

The seat of the Archbishop at Sis in Cilicia, Akhtamar, in the Island of Lake Van, and Etchmiadzin by bishops fearing the title of Catholicos. Some of the occupants of these seats were very much like some of the popes of Rome at the expense of honor, distinction, and well-being of their people they sought honor and distinction, but some others nobly

ARMENIAN CATHOLICOS IN CHURCH UNIFORM.

suffered privation, prosecution, exile, and martyrdom with their flock.

The Papal missionaries, under the order of the Unitors who had insidiously sown the seeds of dissension in the Armenian Church, took advantage of every calamity that befell the people, and afterwards being also augmented by the Jesuits and their sagacity, until they converted this dissension into a volcanic eruption about the beginning of the last century. Consequently thousands of the Armenians avowed their allegiance in spiritual matters to the Pope of Rome.

The Mohammedan conquerors always dealt with their Christian subjects with the utmost contempt, unmodified injustice, unabated cruelty, and relentless persecution. Undoubtedly did many of the people delude themselves with the idea that by uniting with the Romish Church they would enjoy protection through the influence of Romish France, then more influential in the East, for it is quite improbable that they could believe that the Romish Church was any better in simplicity and purity than the old Armenian Church.

The superiority of the educational institutions of the Jesuits to that of the Armenians was also an inducement then for some of the youths to flock into their schools. The monastery, founded by Makhitar, of Sebastia (now Sivas), about the beginning of the last century in St. Lazarus' Island, in Italy, and the literary pursuits of the Mekhetarits, who edited many old Armenian writings and translated from the Latin writers, always tinted with the Papal views, rendered great service to the Romish Church. Many a sad event is connected with this Papal movement which our space will not allow us to narrate; but suffice it to say that this movement resulted in the separation of about one hundred thousand Armenians from the Armenian Church (this separation took place in 1830), and it has now a standstill condition.

The following is from a French writer, Mr. A. Ubicini, who speaks of these sad events in detail: "Fortunately for the Catholics they found a powerful protector in De Feriol, the French ambassador, who obtained an order from the Porte, in 1783 for the deposition and banishment of the (Armenian) patriarch, Avedik. Exiled to Chios, he was clandestinely carried off during the passage, and conducted, some say, to Messina, others to Marseilles, and thence to the Island of St. Marguerite, where he died of martyrdom. There were strong grounds for suspecting the Jesuits established in Chios and at Galata of having contrived this plot in concert with the French ambassador."*

Often heard are such expressions as "Armenian Catholic Church," and many people think it simply a "branch" of the Great Eastern or Greek Church.

It would be just as sensible to consider the Greek a branch of the Armenian Church. Each of them represents a form of Church organization and body of doctrine which best satisfied the representatives of certain races or nations. The advantage of the Greek was that that race—or at least its speech and thought—happened to be dominant in the Roman Empire at the time Christianity won the battle, and so had the official backing of the Empire, and was able to outgrow and crush down the others. It was not any truer, any more the real church of Christ, than the Syrian or African, or Armenian. It was not the earliest, for the very first Christian Churches sprang from the Jews. It was not even the earliest great national church body, for the Armenian Church has that distinction.

The foundation of the Armenian Church by St. Gregory and Tiridates. That church has its own head—the Catholicos or Pontiff, who is no more a subordinate of either the Pope or the Greek Patriarch than the Grand Llama is or Dr. Parkhurst—and its own self-subsistent being.

As to the differences between them, in the first place the Armenian is a purely Trinitarian. There is no room for Unitarianism within its lines.

---

* "Letters on Turkey," volume ii., pages 250-7.

When Gregory the Illuminator was preaching his sermons on the hills and plains of Armenia, he laid the foundation of the national church in the Trinity. His first sermon
was on the Trinity, and his last sermon was on the Trinity,—
in all his sermons he asserted the Trinity—the Father, the Son,
and Holy Ghost; Jesus Christ being a perfect man and perfect
God; in His person we see God in man and man in God; a
perfect Emmanuel; God with us. We see in him that man
can be united with God. The only possible way of salvation
is through Jesus Christ. He is the Saviour of the world and
none else, and whosoever believeth in Him shall be saved.
This is the belief and the only belief of the Armenian Church.
Its members repeat the Apostolic Creed and the Lord's Prayer
every day in their church.

Secondly, the Armenian has never been a persecuting
church, and every other one of the great Christian churches
has been. The Armenian Church, as befits the first and most
Christlike of all the bodies that professed Christ before Luther's time, has always been the broadest, the most inclusive,
the most untechnical of churches. It fellowships with all
other churches. It demands only that men shall profess and
believe in its own church body. Its canons are conversion
and regeneration, purity, holiness, being born again from the
Holy Spirit and becoming Christlike. It holds that Christianity is brotherhood through Jesus Christ, and gives no
warrant for oppression or persecution, curses or anathemas.
But other churches hold that no one can be saved outside of
their own churches (the Greek and Catholic churches). The
Armenian Church has been repeatedly persecuted by both,
and has always protested against the principle of it, as well
as against the pretensions of the Popes to universal sway.

The next: That the Armenian contention is for freedom of will, freedom of conscience, freedom of worship, and
political freedom, is the cause of their being hated both by the
Mohammedans and by their so-called Christian neighbors.

The next one: As to theological questions the Armenian Church fathers did not pay much attention to them. Not because they were not able, because they were too able, and very far-sighted. They knew well that such questions can never be solved, no matter how many centuries pass away, no matter how great scholars the world produces; therefore they would not enter into the debate. And so every Armenian scholar has his own theology.

The Armenian Church has not a theology or any special official doctrine; and this is a very fortunate thing for the Armenians. They care more for righteousness of life than for particular beliefs about the way of getting it.

When there was a great controversy in the Council of Chalcedon, 451 A. D., about the nature of Christ, Armenians did not care about it. Some of the great theologians said Christ had two natures; some said he had only one nature; the Armenian bishops would not give any opinion. They believe in Christ as their Saviour, that is the essential thing; but whether He has two natures or one nature is not essential. Then came the controversy about the Holy Spirit. Whence does the Holy Spirit proceed? Some say from the Father and the Son, some simply from the Father. When the question came before the Armenian bishops they replied that they did not care whence he proceeded. They knew that they needed the Holy Spirit for guidance in spiritual life, for regeneration; they knew that the Holy Spirit was one of the persons in the Trinity; and that was enough for them.

The Armenian Church claims to be apostolic in its origin. Christianity being introduced into Armenia by the Apostles, and having survived the persecutions of heathenism during the first three centuries, finally subdued the entire nation about the end of the third century.

St. Gregory the Illuminator was sent to Cæsarea, Cappadocia, to be ordained Bishop of Armenia, A.D. 302. This custom of the ordination of the bishops of Armenia at Cæsarea lasted until the patriarchate of Nerses the Great (A. D. 363), one of the noblest and holiest bishops of the Armenian Church.

INTERIOR OF ARMENIAN CHURCH.

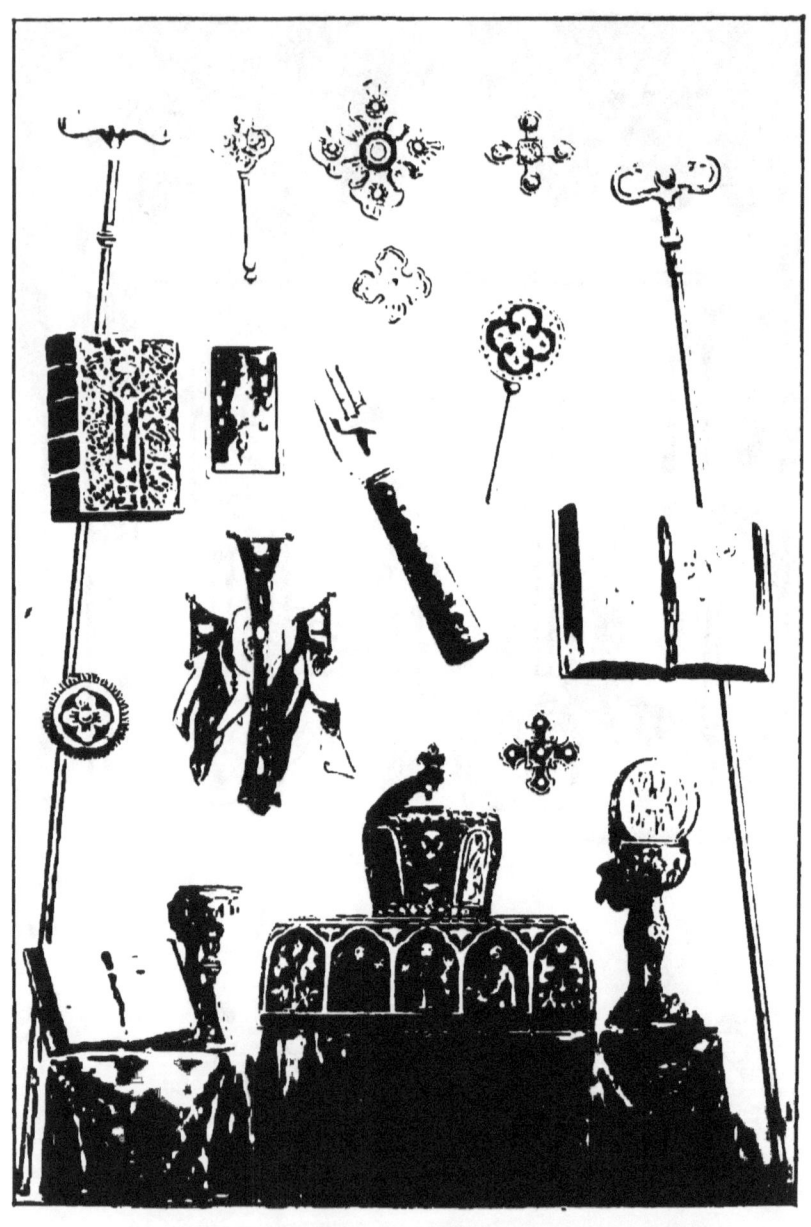

THE SCRIPTURES, SACRED VESSELS AND ORNAMENTS USED IN
ARMENIAN CHURCHES.

During the period of his patriarchate the clergy and the laity of the nation unanimously agreed to have their bishops ordained in Armenia by the Armenian bishops. It is evident, therefore, from the fact that there is no higher rank or order than that of a bishop or presbyter, which names are interchangeably used in the New Testament, as Vartabed (teacher), M. Muradian, of Jerusalem, correctly states in his recent "History of the Apostolic Church of Armenia."* Here it may be also interesting to add as a fact of history that St. Gregory and his immediate successors, his sons and grandsons, and for a length of several centuries, the bishops were married and the heads of families. Celibacy was not required of them, neither separation, but it was optional with them to choose either, or none.

"The election of the bishops, like that of all the Armenian clergy, takes place by universal suffrage;" the ordination, at Etchmiadzin, Akhtamar, or at Sis in Cilicia by the presiding bishop or Catholicos and his associates.

The priests or elders (yeretz) are chosen by the people from among themselves, who are expected to have a tolerable knowledge of the Bible and the liturgy of the church— some in former days knew very little of theirs—and are ordained by the bishops. The priests live with their families among the people and are occupied with their daily duties in the church services morning and evening; they perform also baptism for the infants, and marrying and burying the young and old.

"The Armenian clergy receive no stipends, and exact no contributions like those of the Greek Church: their revenues depend entirely on the voluntary contributions of the faithful. It is therefore rare to meet with a wealthy priest, though some few are in easy circumstances."†

With respect to morals also, though it is difficult to pronounce absolutely on the subject, the Armenian clergy appear

---

* See page 35 in the original.
† " Letters on Turkey," Vol. ii., pp. 285-286.

to be very superior to the Greek. The deacons are elected and ordained like the priest, and have no income whatever; they serve the church and assist the priests in the daily services of the church.

There is another class of clergy of the Armenian Church. Those forming this class are called Vartabeds, or doctors in theology. It is very probable that the very necessity of the case created this order. In the former days, after the conversion of the Armenian nation to Christianity, most of the literary men were of the clergy, and the monasteries became the seat of learning, and those who loved a literary life would retire to those places and pursue such a course. Asceticism of the East also must have played a good part in it.

They at first, most likely, voluntarily preferred celibacy, in order to devote their whole time to learning and teaching, and were ordained evangelists, to visit the churches and to preach the Gospel to the people, who were so often persecuted and oppressed by their enemies. But what was with them optional has become now a condition, for that order. Though "the Vartabeds form the most enlightened and learned portion of the Armenian clergy," and from them are the bishops elected and ordained, but unfortunately "they are restricted to celibacy."

The Armenian Church differs from that of Rome on the following points:

(I.) It denies the supremacy of the bishop of Rome.

(II.) It rejects the authority of the Council of Chalcedon as ecumenic.

(III.) It rejects the introduction of filioque into the creed, but admits that the Holy Spirit proceeds from the Father.

(IV.) It rejects the Romish doctrine of purgatory.

(V.) It rejects also indulgence.

(VI.) It does not withhold the Bible from the people, but encourages them to read it.

The orthodoxy of the Armenian Church would not have been questioned by some of the Western writers had they

A RETIRED ARMENIAN BISHOP.

drawn their information from the native authors, instead of drawing them from some later Greek and Latin writers. The following is a translation from a recent Armenian work, entitled, "The History of the Holy Apostolic Church of Armenia." The author is Vartabed M. Muradian, of St. James' Monastery at Jerusalem. It is sweet and comforting to discourse of the revealed truths of the Bible, which is the only foundation of undefiled doctrine, to which always have the Holy Church fathers trusted for the defense of faith.

"The Bible teaches concerning God two things: First, that God is one and there is no other God beside Him. Second, that divine nature is common to the Father, to the Son, and to the Holy Spirit, and these three persons have one Godhead. This is the faith of the Christians in harmony with the manifest word of the Bible. This trinity is the foundation of the Christian faith, and the three persons have one influence for our salvation, but in different ways of manifesting it; that is, the Father calls and causes us to approach His Son, whom be begat from eternity and prepared His coming. The Son came from heaven and was united with human nature that he might save us from sin and give eternal life to our souls. The Holy Spirit is our regenerator, who reestablished in us the likeness of God, making us receptive of the salvation offered of God.

"The Bible teaches that Christ, on account of His eternal generation from the Father, is called the Son of God, but for His incarnation in time, the Son of Man, brother of men, through whom we obtained the right to call God our Father, and for this reason the Church confesses in the personality of Christ two natures, divine and human, distinct and inseparable in their union. This mystery of incarnation is the great mystery of God's love for the world; and as much as this is incomprehensible and inconceivable by human intelligence, so much is it natural with divine love and omnipotent nature. In this great mystery was the salvation of mankind; for this the entire humanity waited, and therefore the law and the prophets in this mystery of incarnation were fulfilled. Because Christ, as the true Messiah, performed prophetic, priestly and kingly offices, and became for us true prophet, true priest and true King; teaching the doctrine of redemption, elucidating the past, the present, and the future of mankind, forgiving and reigning over us with a heavenly and spiritual kingdom.

"The Bible teaches that the Holy Spirit proceeds and flows from the Father, not as a common influence of God, but as a person of the Holy Trinity, infinite, eternal, a true God. But with respect to us, the Holy Spirit is the source of union of God to Man; the seal by which we are known as Christians; because without the Holy Spirit's dwelling in us, His help and guidance, we are only alive, for the Holy Spirit is co-worker with the Father and the Son for our salvation; and as the manifestation of God through Christ, to the world, is called redemption, so also the revelation of God through the Holy Spirit is denominated *regeneration* and sanctification.

"At this present day there is not a book like the Bible from which the intellectual world has been able to derive so much good for the real well being and progress of human society. There is not a book, and cannot be, that is translated into so many languages and is distributed so extensively as the Bible. Our immortal translators felt this great want, and they began the first step of the nation's enlightenment and progress by the translation and study of the Holy Scriptures, and this translation is so choice, with various praises bestowed upon it by the European scholars of the present century, who know the Armenian language, it is called the Queen of Versions. But we will be giving a still greater praise to our forefathers if we generalize the study of the Holy Scriptures among our people and rear the edifice of education upon that solid foundation of the Word of God."*

By no means should the reader think that the writer is

---

* " History of the Holy Apostolic Church of Armenia," pp. 171-121, 127-8.

AN ARMENIAN PRIEST IN CHURCH UNIFORM.

partial in not telling something of the superstitions, formalism and ignorance still in existence and practice among the Armenians and in their church. It has often been written and spoken, even with a great lack both of knowledge and charity. Had those writers on these subjects of the Armenian Church and people remembered that for almost fifteen centuries this church has been in constant conflict with Paganism, Zoroastrianism, Mohammedanism, and the evil influences of the corrupt Greek and Roman Churches, they would not have been so severe in their denunciations of that old relic of the ancient Christian Church.

Often were the bishops and priests in the battlefield with their flocks against the enemy of the Church. Often were they in chains, in imprisonment, in hostage, at the Pagan, Mohammedan, and so called Christian courts; often were they carried away into captivity and massacred by their captors. How could they give more attention than they did give to the education and enlightenment of their people, and to the purity of the Church? Even to-day the best intellects of the Armenian clergy, the lovers of the reform and purity of the Church and people, are in either exile or bondage by the Russian, Persian, and Ottoman Empires. These circumstances certainly will not justify the condition of the Armenian Church, but they ought to modify the severity of our judgment and fill us with a deeper sympathy, with a truer Christian love and activity for its reform, purity, and spiritual prosperity.

CHAPTER VII.

When the Congregational and Presbyterian churches in the United States were united for the work of evangelizing the world, one of the first things they did was to send Revs. Pliny Fisk, Levi Parsons, W. Goodell and Bird, that they may spread the Gospel throughout Turkey and reform the Christian people who were sitting in darkness. This was between 1819 and 1823.

These missionaries were landed and stationed at Beyrouth, Syria, for the purpose of evangelizing the Armenians in that city. In March and April, 1821, two of them went to Jerusalem, that they may preach the Gospel to the large multitude of Armenian pilgrims who flocked there at that time on account of their Easter.

Rev. Levi Parsons, one of the missionaries who went to Jerusalem, was an amiable, gentle, and sweet-natured man, and soon won the confidence and love of all who met him, especially of the notables in the Armenian church at Jerusalem. These men, after they found out Mr. Parsons' mission to Jerusalem, did not only consent to have the work of reformation begun in Jerusalem, but they also asked him to go to Constantinople, confer with the priests and notables of the church there, and begin the work of reformation.

This proposition Mr. Parsons gladly wrote to the missionaries in Beyrouth. But owing to their unfamiliarity with the Armenian language, Revs. Goodell and Bird thought it would be best not to start any mission in Jerusalem for the time being. They thought it would be expedient for them to undertake the

AN ARMENIAN MONK.

work only after the translation of the Bible in the Turkish language. But in the Providence of God a way was being prepared for them. For Bishop Dyonisius and Krikor Vartabed —the latter an Armenian bishop—being enlightened by the Gospel light, rendered the missionaries invaluable help to translate the Bible, both in Armeno-Turkish and Armenian vernacular. With the untiring efforts of these two prelates the Bible was printed in the vernacular, and was spread by them, in company with one of the missionaries, far and wide in Asia Minor. They went almost everywhere, and gave away Bibles. They came to my native town, which fact I, as a child, remember very distinctly.

At the close of this missionary tour, in 1826, Rev. W. Goodell, in company with two young Armenians, went to the island of Malta for the purpose of printing the Bible in the popular Armenian. They were there four years, and on their return the missionaries decided to make Constantinople a mission station, that they may start the work of reformation over there. In 1831 and '32 the American Board sent Revs. Elias Riggs, Dwight, Bliss and Cyrus Hamlin to work with Rev. W. Goodell. The first thing the missionaries did in Constantinople was to establish a school, educate the youth, print and publish Bibles and portions of Scriptures and religious tracts, thus to spread religious knowledge and enlightenment among the Armenians. To this some ignorant people opposed. But the chief men and especially the Armenian patriarchs were in hearty sympathy with the missionaries in regard to the reformation of their national church and the enlightenment of their youth.

But right here the Missionaries had another opposition. The Jesuit propagandists, who were in Constantinople to convert Armenians to Roman Catholicism, were jealous of the missionaries, and did all they could to frustrate all their labors in the way of evangelization.

In 1836 the Roman Catholic and Greek patriarchs tried very hard to influence the Armenian patriarch against the mis-

sionaries. In this they were successful. They now set to work
and enticed the Armenians away from the missionaries and
everything that savored of Protestantism. The result was that
the Armenian patriarch changed his friendly attitude toward
the missionaries, convened a general ecclesiastical meeting,
sent an encyclical to all the Armenian churches throughout the
Turkish empire, forbidding every Armenian from having anything to do with the missionaries, with the Protestant Bibles
and with the Protestant views. Anybody who opposed or disobeyed, any one who did not burn his Bible would be under
the ban and anathema of the church. But in the wonderful
providence of God thousands of the Bibles had already found
entrance to many an Armenian family.

The result of this official opposition by the church was the
general persecution of Protestant brethren and missionaries by
the common people and the burning of thousands of volumes
of the Scriptures. I myself was beaten and imprisoned
three times. I had to keep my Testament in my pocket
for three months, could not read it openly, but had to look for
secluded places to read the words of life.

This general and wide-spread persecution resulted in an
endless commotion. Everybody discussed the question. In
every house, street-corner and meeting-house the general topic
of discussion was the annihilation of Protestantism from Turkey. Although the missionaries and the brethren were very
patient in persecution and persevering in the good work they
had undertaken, time came when they could no more endure
the persecution. This was on July 1, 1846—the persecution
had lasted ten years, when the first evangelical Armenian
church was organized in Constantinople. This was also the
first Protestant church in Turkey.

From 1846 to '55 the new evangelical church was under
the anathema of the Armenian national church. As a result of
this ban all sorts of intercourse, intermarriage and trade with
the Protestants were prohibited to the Gregorian Armenians.
The brethren, a large part of whom belonged to the poorer

class, were often unable to earn their daily bread, for no Gregorian would hire a Protestant. Thus destitution, deprivation, ostracism and constant persecution were the natural outcome of the establishment of this new church.

It was right at this time that the wonderful Providence of God intervened in behalf of the brethren. In 1853 Crimean war broke out between Russia and Turkey, and naturally the brethren were the greatest sufferers among the rest of the people. But Dr. Cyrus Hamlin, with his natural ingenuity, generosity and capability, established flour mills to furnish loaves of bread to the Turkish army. This he did under a contract with the Turkish government. In his mills he employed as many Protestants as he could, and so almost all of them were able to support themselves for three years. The earnings of the mills were so great that Dr. Hamlin was able to build several churches and lay aside some amount of money for a further emergency. At the close of the Russo-Turkish war in 1856 a treaty was signed in Paris, according to which religious freedom was granted to all the Protestants and evangelical churches throughout Turkey. This was one of the numerous achievements of Rev. Dr. Cyrus Hamlin, whose name is so dear to every Armenian heart.

Ladies and gentlemen, you have seen by the foregoing brief description how the missionaries and the early brethren were persecuted and subjected to great sufferings. But when they saw the result of their labors they were exceedingly glad and forgot what they had suffered and gave thanks to the Lord of the Vineyard.

And now I want to call your attention to the outcome of the missionary labors and the work of evangelization during the past 51 years.

1. Educationally Turkey has advanced wonderfully.

Fifty or sixty years ago there was no school among the Armenians in Turkey, save a few monasteries and the websters' and dyers' shops, where but few boys could find their way to obtain a very meagre knowledge in reading and writing. As to the girls, there was not a place of education to be found for them, and so they were absolutely destitute of even the first rudiments of learning. But the missionaries' labors of the past fifty-one years have borne their abundant fruit. To-day we have 485 common schools for boys and girls among our Protestant brethren. Five hundred young men and women are teaching in these schools. The number of boys and girls in these schools is over 15,000. We have 23 boarding high schools for boys and seventeen for girls. We have four colleges for boys, in Constantinople, Aintab, Marsovan and Harpoot, in which educational institutions our young men are receiving the same same degree of education as young men in this country do in the American colleges.

We have four theological seminaries, which supply preachers and pastors for our churches. In all these educational institutions we have some 19,000—20,000 scholars in all.

To-day 80 per cent. of all evangelical brethren are able to read and write, and owing to the establishment of kindergartens, I have no doubt the rate of literacy will be 90 per cent. before long.

The annual contribution of the brethren for the work of evangelization is $15,000, which amount, being added to the allowance of the American Board, goes to help to enlighten and evangelize Armenians throughout Turkey. All these things, besides leaving their good impression and effect upon the other Christian churches, have also left a wholesome influence over the Turkish part of the population. The result was that in all the hamlets, villages, towns and cities throughout Turkey schools were established for children of both sexes, which spread light and knowledge everywhere. Thus you see Protestants besides owning these schools became the pioneers of education to their neighbors. Here we want to thank all the missionaries for their untiring labors in this respect and the Christian friends in this country who sent these missionaries.

2.   A wonderful religious reformation is another outcome of missionary labors.

Six years before the first evangelical church was established in Constantinople a theological seminary was established in Bebek, Constantinople, where twenty Armenian young men were educated for preaching. These young men were sent to different parts of Turkey after the establishment of the first church. In the year 1846 evangelical churches were established in Nicomedia, Adabazar and Trebizond. The persecutions were renewed. But the more the persecutions were strengthened the better the brethren were re-enforced and the more zealously they worked to spread the light of the Gospel. The number of the missionaries was augmented from time to time. They were stationed in the chief cities in the country. And now evangelical churches were being rapidly organized. Besides the cities I have already mentioned Erzeroum, Bitlis, Diarbekr, Harpoot, Marsovan, Aintab, Aleppo, Marash, Tarsus, Adana, Kessab, Killis, Antioch and many other cities, townships and villages had their evangelical churches.

In 1856 Abdul Mejid, the Sultan of Turkey, under the influence of the missionaries, issued an imperial edict, called Hatti Humayoun, by which religious freedom was granted to all Protestants. Thus the persecutions began to disappear and everybody was free to follow the way according to the dictation of his own conscience.

To-day American Board has 157 missionaries in Turkey, which number includes all the married, single, male and female missionaries. These are stationed in fifteen different cities, where they superintend the educational and evangelistic work. There are 110 organized evangelical churches, with a church membership of 12,000. In these churches there are seventy-four ordained ministers, 730 preachers and 130 assistants. The Gospel is preached at 203 different places to at least 35,000 souls every week.

Twenty-two thousand men, women and children receive religious instruction in Sunday Schools every Sabbath. The total number of Protestants throughout Turkey is 45,000. Their annual contribution for the preaching of the Gospel is

$48.000-$50.000, which is one-third of the sum the Board spends in Turkey. We have about thirty self-supporting churches, among which the churches at Aintab, Marash, Uorfa, Harpoot, Cæsarea, Marsovan, Adana, Tarsus and Kessab are noteworthy. We have many devoted, faithful and diligent native Christian workers.

Christian ladies and gentlemen, all the labor you have undertaken, all the money you have spent, all the time you have devoted and all the prayers you have offered at the throne of grace have not been in vain, but they have had their abundant fruit. You gave thousands and thousands of your dollars and sent your missionaries to Turkey. Great many of them have died on the field of labor, and caused you to mourn their loss. But over against these all you have had an abundant harvest, for which you have our unending thanks.

3. The institution of Young Men's Christian Associations has been beneficial to our churches in every way. Fifteen or twenty years ago our churches did not know anything about the organized labor of young Christians. But this important phase of Christian work has been introduced from this land to ours, and has created a new enthusiasm and activity in the church.

During the eleven years of my ministry from 1869 to 1880 the thought of how to lead young men to Christ greatly occupied my mind. As a result of my thoughts I used to bring together 30 or 40 of the young men in my church for prayer and conference, which proved to be a great help in the spiritual growth of those young men. As a result of these Christian labors in Marash we had a glorious spiritual awakening, which added thirty-seven young men to the membership of the church. I never knew at the time of the existance of the Young Men's Christian Association in this country, nor did any other preacher in Turkey.

Our beloved missionary, Rev. G. F. Montgomery, translated into our language an article on the work of Young Men's Christian Associations in America. This he showed me, which widened my knowledge and importance of the work. I brought the matter before my church in Marash, and fully explained to them the organization and the work of Young Men's Christian Associations. They took to the idea very favorably and we immediately formed an association composed of twenty members. This was in 1876. From that day to this many similar associations have been organized throughout our churches in Turkey, in cities, townships and villages.

The following are some of the lines of activity in which the members of these associations have proven themselves useful to the community among which they live. (1) Visitation of the sick. There are almost no hospitals in Turkey, and so all the poor patients of a parish are left entirely upon the care of such young men and such benevolent organizations. In this way the young men of the church have rendered invaluable service to the church, by visiting and comforting and providing medicine and food for poor sick people. (2) Visitation and helping of the poor. (3) Finding out the careless and cold and backslidden members of the church and bringing into the church people who would not otherwise go to church. (4) Home missionary work. These young men have sent teachers and preachers to many villages within their county, and in many cases, where the villages were near the cities, they have themselves visited and preached the words of life to the spiritually needy souls. (5) Every kind of humanitarian and Christian activity has been faithfully and efficiently performed by these young men. All these good works are the result of the devoted labors of these organizations of young men, who are the spiritual children of the missionaries you sent to us.

4. The American missionaries have further helped in the progress of the Armenians in that they have translated and published the Bible and many religious tracts. That the publishing of the Word of God in the vernacular is the chief means of the uplifting of a people is well known to you.

When the missionaries first came to Turkey the first thing they noticed in regard to the Armenian church was that the language of the Bible and all the ceremonies in the church was wholly different from the language of the common people. Consequently the people were left in utter darkness in regard to their religious and Christian duties. Besides the language of the church being wholly unintelligible to the average people, they did not possess the Bible or its portions, and even if one was fortunate enough to possess one, he was strictly forbidden by the priests to read it. The result was a general spiritual darkness.

As I have mentioned before, Rev. W. Goodell had the Bible published in the vernacular as early as 1826. But there was soon felt a necessity of a revised edition of the Bible. In this the British and American Bible Societies rallied to the assistance of the missionaries. Their labors have put the Bible within the reach of even the poorest. These societies, that have published the Word of God in more than 300 different languages, have also translated and published it in thirteen different languages now spoken in Turkey. These languages are: Common Armenian, Armeno-Turkish (Turkish language in Armenian characters), Armeno-Kurdish (Kurdish language in Armenian characters), Arabo-Turkish (Turkish language in Arabic characters, Persian, spoken Chaldee, modest Greek, Greco-Turkish (Turkish language in Greek characters) and Bulgarian. Although these have greatly helped all the different nationalities in the Turkish empire, but the Armenians have been immeasurably helped and benefited. The fruitage of the missionary labors among the Armenians is the most conspicuous among the rest. Although the Armenian church at first opposed the new translation of the Bible and burned hundreds and thousands of copies, still finally the Word found its way into almost every Armenian home and has since done its wonderful work in the hearts of men, for it is written, "The law of the Lord is perfect, converting the soul." "Thy word is a lamp unto my feet and a light unto my path." "Is not my word like as a fire? saith the Lord; and like unto a hammer that breaketh the rock in pieces?" "The gospel of Christ is the power of God unto salvation to every one that believeth."

A few anecdotes in connection with the first spread of the Gospel in Turkey are in order. I can say about myself that I was converted by the reading of the Bible.

In 1852, when I was seventeen years old, some strangers came to my native city of Alboostan. After stopping at an inn for a few days they left the city, but left behind in their room four copies of the Gospel. The inn belonged to a cousin of mine, so he presented one of them to me. I read this book stealthily and always kept it in my pocket, for fear I would be persecuted for reading it, and besides had I read it in public it might have been taken from me and thrown into the fire. For two years I kept reading my Gospel, which worked its inevitable result upon my heart. I was convicted of my sinfulness, repented of my sins and found forgiveness to my sins and peace to my disturbed soul. Thus the Bible is the only means of my conversion and the subsequent happiness and blessings of my life.

In 1869 I graduated from Marash Theological Seminary. In 1870 I was sent by Mr. Powers, the missionary at Antioch, to preach the Gospel at Beilan. I moved there with my family. No Protestant preacher had gone there before and there was not a single Protestant in the city. I labored there seven months. First two months of my residence there people would not speak to me, nor have anything to do with me. I used to take the Bible in hand and go to coffee-houses and even to liquor saloons to see if I could find anybody to talk with on spiritual matters, but was unsuccessful. Finally, one day when I was going on the streets, a venerable old man, by the name of Tiros Agha, called out to me by my name to his store and said to me he would be glad if I called at his house once in a while. Upon inquiry I found out the old gentleman possessed a copy of the Gospel, several copies of religious works and a copy of Young's Nights. He told me that many people came to his house almost every night and that if I called at his house sometimes and explained the truth to them he would be greatly obliged. This was what I was anxiously looking for, and beginning with that day I kept going to his house and expounding the word for three or four hours to a very attentive and inquiring gathering. For five months I continued this Bible Class work in that dear old man's house. He himself, already a good man, was wholly converted, and through him many people accepted Jesus Christ as their Saviour, until at the present time Beilan has an evangelical church with about 300 members. Thus I have seen the power of the Gospel upon myself and upon many others like myself. We Protestant Armenians never forget the unselfish and untiring devotion of Father Goodell in his great work of translating and publishing the Bible in our spoken language, who, like John in the Isle of Patmos, was confined on the island of Malta for three years and later ten years in Constantinople that he might bring the word of truth within the reach of all. His edition and translation of the Bible is held with great reverence in many an Armenian home, and I am proud to own a copy for my home use. Besides the thousands and thousands of copies of the Scriptures, 8,000,000 pages of religious tracts in twelve different languages are being yearly published by the missionaries. And so in the foregoing lines of Christian activity the work of the American missionaries has been very important for the Armenian nation.

BY JUDSON SMITH, D. D.,

Secretary of the American Board.

The first notice of an intended mission within the limits of the Turkish Empire appears in the Annual Report of the Board for 1819, nine years after the Board was organized. Missionaries of the Board were already at work in India and among the aboriginal tribes of America, and a mission to the Sandwich Islands was under contemplation. In this report the committee dwell upon the reasons for a special interest on the part of the Christian people in the re-establishment of pure Christianity in the historic regions honored by the earthly life of our Lord and traversed by his first disciples. Palestine was the region specially in mind, but the committee recognized the fact that the occupancy of a much wider field was included in the beginning of missionary work in Jerusalem, and the writer of this first report referred to "Smyrna, the provinces of Asia Minor, Armenia, Georgia and Persia, Mohammedan countries, in which, though there are many Jews and Christians, there is still a deplorable lack of Christian knowledge and of Christian life." Before this year had ended, the Rev. Levi Parsons and the Rev. Pliny Fisk were set apart to establish a mission at Jerusalem, and in the following year entered upon their labors, touching at Malta and taking up their residence at Smyrna for a time before they reached their destined field. From these labors, by a process of natural development, missionary work at first intended for Palestine, afterward set up in the Island of Malta and in Athens, came to take a firm and lasting hold upon the Turkish Empire.

In 1831 work was opened at Constantinople by Dr. Goodell, reënforced by Dr. Dwight in the following year, and thence gradually it was extended to Smyrna, Brûsa, Trebizond, Erzûm, Aintab, and so on throughout the entire district of Asiatic Turkey. The aim in the establishment of the original mission in Palestine and in these later stages of missionary work in Turkey, had respect to the entire population of the Empire; and this aim has never for a moment been abandoned or lost sight of, and remains to-day an unfulfilled but inspiring purpose. Actual missionary work, however, was restricted by the laws of the Empire to the Christian populations, chiefly the Armenians and the Greeks and to the Jews, and this has been the characteristic feature of the work of the Board in the Turkish Empire. An ancient but corrupted form of Christianity it has been sought to purify and bring back to a true acquaintance with the Gospels, a living faith in the Lord Jesus Christ, and a life molded in its spirit and aims by the Scriptures and by Him of whom they testify. It was not the intention of the missionaries to establish a separate Protestant community, but to assist, if possible, in a movement that should result in the reformation of the existing churches. The excommunication of the evangelicals from their own church and community by the Armenian Patriarch of Constantinople changed their plans and made necessary the organization of Protestant churches and of a Protestant community, which were at once formally recognized by the Turkish Government. This action took place in 1847 and introduced a change in the methods of missionary work but not a change of aim. It is a most happy circumstance of these later days, that the reformation of the Gregorian churches which was making such progress prior to the separation has reappeared, that these churches have in many instances come into most friendly relations to the neighboring Protestant churches, the true evangelical spirit has manifested itself with cheering results among the priests and people, and the original hope of the mission has begun to be realized on a wide scale in many parts of the Empire.

Originally the entire field of Turkey was regarded as one mission with its centre at Constantinople; but the practical difficulties of holding a yearly meeting of the mission at any one point, with other considerations, led to the division of the Empire into the four fields of the present time—the Western Turkey mission, embracing territorially the larger part, including as its stations Constantinople, Nicomedia, Brûsa, Smyrna, Marsovan, Cesarea, Sivas and Trebizond; the Central Turkey mission, lying to the south of the Taurus Mountains, and to the west of the Euphrates Valley, with its two principal stations at Aintab and Marash; the Eastern Turkey mission, including what lies between these two fields and the Russian and Persian borders, having for its stations Erzrûm, Harpoot, Mardin, Bitlis and Van; and the mission in European Turkey, of later origin, chiefly among Bulgarians, with its stations at Monastir, Philippopolis, Samokov and Salonica. From the beginning, work in behalf of the Greek Christians, found in certain parts of the Turkish Empire in considerable numbers, has constituted an integral and very interesting part of the whole enterprise, but has never constituted a distinct mission.

The languages employed in missionary work have been the Armenian, the Greek, the Turkish, the Bulgarian and in certain portions of the Central Turkey mission and of the Eastern Turkey mission the Arabic. The Bible translated into these languages, has been widely distributed, many text-books for school use have been provided, and a somewhat extended volume of Christian literature has been made available for the people by the efforts of the missionaries. The Bible House at Constantinople, one of the great centers of missionary activity and a right arm of the missionary work, sends out through all the Empire annually many millions of pages of the Scriptures and of other literature for the instruction and edification of the Christian people, as well as text-books for the mission schools.

The direct Christian work in these missions in Turkey has been most energetic, widespread and effectual, and many self-supporting, evangelical churches are found in the great centers in each of the missions. Education has been a marked feature of the work in these missions almost from the beginning, and nowhere else in the fields occupied by the Board have we to-day so many institutions of a high grade, so fully attended. Anatolia College at Marsovan, Central Turkey College at Aintab, and the Institute of Samokov, for men alone, the American College for girls at Scutari, and the Central Turkey Female College at Marash, for women alone, and Euphrates College at Harpoot, for both men and women, are all institutions doing a work of true college grade adjusted to the special conditions found in the Turkish Empire. Robert College on the Bosporus, though entirely independent of the missions, is a striking result of missionary labors and strongly re-enforces missionary influence. These colleges are re-enforced by twenty-six high schools for boys, nineteen boarding schools for girls, all thoroughly manned and attended by about 2,000 students, and by 350 common schools, with more than 16,000 pupils. At the head of all stand the five theological schools, in which men are trained directly for the native pastorate. It will suggest the breadth and fruitfulness of the work if attention is called to the 125 churches now in these missions, with 12,787 members with 100 native pastors, 128 other preachers and a total force of native laborers numbering 778. It is further evidence of the quality of these churches that last year they contributed for all purposes but little short of $68,000.

A work having the same origin with these missions, conducted by the Board for many years, achieving a like success, and now in the care of the Presbyterian Board of New York, is in progress in Syria, having its great educational center at Beirût. The Reformed Presbyterian Church of America sustains a small but successful medical and educational work at Mersin in Asia Minor. Work in behalf of the Jews in different parts of the Empire, at first included in the missions of the Board, is now in the care of missionaries from Great Britain; there is also an interesting work supported by the Society of Friends in this country carried on in different parts of Palestine. But, providentially, the great bulk of the missionary work in the Turkish Empire has devolved upon the American Board, and has at length reached nearly every principal city and village in European Turkey and in the territory from the Dardanelles and the Mediterranean eastward to the Russian border, and from the Black Sea southward to Syria and Arabia.

At no time has the work of the Board in Asiatic Turkey been in better condition or presented greater promise than within the last year. And it is upon the Armenian people, among whom this work has been so largely carried on, that a wild storm of massacre and pillage has fallen, sweeping the country from Trebizond southward into the valley of the Euphrates, westward to Marsovan and Cesarea and out to the Mediterranean Sea, covering the entire territory of the eastern and central missions and those parts of the Western Turkey mission that are adjacent. Thousands have been foully murdered, chiefly the leading business men, and hundreds of thousands of those dependent on them have been left utterly destitute; many a Protestant pastor and teacher has fallen in loyalty to his faith, and mission chapels and schools in great numbers have been burned to the ground. The stations where educational work centered have been especially assailed, and at Harpût and to some degree at Marash, the plant has been well-nigh swept out of existence, and the missionaries themselves exposed to deadly peril. Sympathy for the people, so broken and bleeding, is almost as widespread as Christianity and civilization, and generous gifts for their relief are steadily flowing to Constantinople. There is an additional reason why, for the American people, a peculiar interest should attach to the present situation in Turkey. Upon the uplifting and enlightenment of a noble portion of the people in the Turkish Empire American citizens have already expended more than $6,000,-000, have established there a mission plant worth to-day $1,500,000, are annually devoting to the further development of this work a sum exceeding $150,000, and have there as their representatives, distributed in small groups over the whole Empire, a band of 152 men and women, among the noblest and the best that our Christian homes and schools can produce. The bearing of these men and women in the midst of the terrible scenes of the last four months, their calmness when the people were filled with dread in view of the approaching scourge, their courage when death was all around them and even when it stared them in the face, their faith that out of all this tumult and distress will come the enlargement of God's kingdom in this land, their steadfast purpose to remain at their posts and share the troubles of their people and minister to their wants, proof against the natural shrinking of their own hearts, against the pleading of friends at home, against the persuasions even of those to whom they must look for protection—these things have won for them the meed of universal praise. The name *missionary* has gained a new definition by deeds like these, and instead of a term of reproach or ridicule, it has become almost a synonym of hero and heroine. And all this noble conduct has filled the Armenian nation with boundless love and gratitude, and has bound their hearts to the missionaries with hooks of steel. Henceforth this whole nation will be like wax in the hands of these their protectors and benefactors and personal friends. And even beyond the Armenian people, many and many of the Moslems are noting this high proof of the Christian faith, and are enshrining in their hearts' admiring love the names we cherish, and longing for a share of their faith.

But it is as teachers and exemplars of the Christian faith and life, not as political deliverers, that they have won their place; no political aim has ever been allowed to enter into this widespread and most effective Christian labor; and the missionary operations of the Board stand clear of all responsibility for the grave political disturbances which threaten the stability of the Empire. They have been loyal to the existing Government and have inculcated this duty upon their pupils; they have sought to make better men and better citizens of all those with whom they have had to do; and no truer friends of the Turkish Empire and of all its people than the American missionaries have lived within its borders these seventy years past. For the protection of themselves and of their legitimate enterprise within that territory guaranteed by treaty rights, and numerous precedents, and long continued usage, we may justly claim the utmost exertions of our own Government and the friendly regard of all mankind. It cannot be that upon this work, to which so many precious lives have been given, on which such treasures have been expended, on the successful maintenance of which such vast interests depend, ruin hopeless and universal is now to fall. May we not rather cherish the hope that this storm is for cleansing and purifying and shall endure but for a night, and that a day of brightness and glory is soon to dawn upon this great Empire.

Boston, Mass.

But alas! the result of their labor has been ruthlessly dealt with by the cruel Turks at the late massacres, 4,000 or 5,000 Protestants alone have been butchered, their personal property have been plundered and several thousands have taken refuge in the United States. I am one of of those suffering refugees, who with members of my family am in great difficulty. To-day there are in the United States more than 200 graduates of the American colleges in Turkey. Some of them are at work with various occupations, but the majority of them have no work to do. Ladies and gentlemen, these are the children of your missionaries. What are you going to do about them? They are now returned to you for help. If the Congregational Church does not take care of them, what denomination will. All the evangelical Armenians in this country are your foster children. Your missionaries, your prayers and your money brought them up. If you do not take care of them, I am afraid others will carry them off. But I myself cannot consent to it. After receiving so much blessing from them how can I turn against them and be ungrateful to them. For all we are to-day we owe to the Congregational Churches in this country.

CHAPTER VIII.

The events which have happened in Turkey during the last twenty years have drawn the special attention of the nations and governments of the whole of Europe, and have employed not only the skill of the diplomatists, but the pens of journalists every morning, and the evening newspapers have been examined for the purpose of learning the civilization or reformation of the Ottoman Empire.

The principal point considered in this contest has hitherto been the political, but people have entirely lost sight of its religion and moral aspects; still the oppressions and persecution of Christians can never be fully understood by those who may be born in a free land like you are, where there are no Turks, Kurds, Circassians, Georgians, Zaibacks and no Mohammedanism with its oppressions and persecutions to the Christians.

Therefore I propose to consider the religion and political causes that have ruined the population of Turkey entirely.

But the questions arise, Why the Sultan orders (during the last few years) the Turks, Kurds, or other followers to destroy the Christians, whereby more than one hundred thousand (100,000) of them have recently been killed and five hundred thousand have been rendered homeless and left to die of starvation among the streets and out in the mountains? and again why the Sultan ordered all who are willing to accept the Mohammedanism that have never been referred to with any sort of correctness by the newspapers or periodicals in their accounts of the dreadful oppressions taking place in Armenia, or all over Asia Minor?

1. The first cause of the horrors to the Armenians of Turkey is that chiefly of the Mohammedan religion.

Though the Islamism or Mohammedan religion is divided into a great many sects, but the moral precepts and laws of all are based upon the book of Koran. The book of Koran is not an apt instrument to keep pure the moral character of the population of the Turks; on the other hand it causes the opportunity for the greater corruption in moral respects, with that it nourishes in its followers a spirit of improving animosity and opposition to non-Mohammedan races and nationalities.

The following facts are the most interesting points which have attracted my attention:

A. The book of Koran teaches that the sinner having once performed his ablution and said his prayers, his sins should be forgiven. Ablution means that a man goes to a fountain of running water or takes some water from a jug and washes his head, ears, mouth, arms and feet, regarding that those sins were committed by those members and are washed away.

But a dying person who is unable to perform above religious duties can have the same forgiveness by raising his forefinger and with it confess that there is one God, and Mohammed is the true prophet; even then if the person is unable to do so he need only repeat the above confession in his mind, whose sins, having been instantly wiped away, he is made as white as snow.

B. The book of Koran, moreover, teaches that all Mohammedan people shall go to the seventh heaven any way, where all the sensual indulgences known on earth will await them; even others of a more degrading and bestial character. The language with which these ideas are clothed is so indelicate that it can hardly bear repeating in society.

Nobody who has not lived in Turkey can realize how hopeless, almost self-contradicting, it is to talk of "reforming" Turkey. It could not be reformed and be Mohammedan Turkey. The lack of reform or power of reform is just what makes it what it is. The root of evil is Mohammedanism itself; it is embodied social stagnation, corruption, ultimate ruin. Neither the Sultan nor the Turks can improve the state of the Empire, even if they wished. The usual "broad-minded" statements about Mohammed and his religion are simply elaborations of ignorance, made up out of men's own minds, and what they think must be true. It is customary for writers to talk in this fashion. Mohammedanism is a half-way house to Christianity. Mohammed converted the heathen Arabs to a belief in the true God. Mohammed established a great religion and a great empire, etc., etc. There is no truth in this, for all its plausible sound. Mohammedanism is not even on the road to Christianity; and Arabia, Asia Minor, and Palestine were all much better off before the Mohammedan conquest than after it. Buddhism and Brahmanism are better religions than Mohammedanism. The Chinese, the Japanese, the people of India are much more religious that the Turks. The Chinese Emperor and the Japanese Mikado are far better men than the Mohammedan Sultan. The heathen religions rear better men than Mohammedanism. The Mongols are more humane and sympathetic than the Turks. Heathenism at its worst, though a low form of religion, is really a form of religion; but Mohammedanism is not a religion at all.

Then what is it? It is a system of imposture and false pretense, and of lives of human lust and cruelty. Mohammed practiced all this, and his successors have done the same and taught the same ever since; and the system means just that now, and nothing else. There is neither love nor sympathy, manliness nor humanity in Mohammedanism. Can a system lacking all these be considered a religion? This is the substance of Mohammed's teaching: "Love your fellow believers, hate and slay all who refuse to accept your religion. Marry as many wives as you can afford; if you can afford but one, do not repine, for you shall have seven thousand to enjoy in Paradise."

The Mohammedan religion teaches that every believer after having died in that faith will be married to seventy thousand virgins in Paradise, so as they can enjoy all the happiness in gratifying the desires of flesh. In the book of Koran the picture of Paradise is drawn as such that all forms of pleasure and happiness as expected to be the outcome of jealousy and selfishness is to be found there, also not one faithful or one who believes in one God and confess Mohammed a true prophet of God, and those who bring Selavat will under any circumstances go to Hell, but will undoubtedly go to the Paradise as described in the book of Koran. If you conquer a country, show no mercy to the people unless they embrace Islam. If they refuse, either kill them or make slaves of them. What sort of reformers can you expect in Turkey, when the very religion that is to make people better inculcates such principles. If one does not know a language he cannot speak it; if he has not a principle he will not practice it. How can the Sultan, a vicious man to begin with, trained in a religion calculated to make a cruel and licentious animal even out of a decent man, reform anything? His very religion forbids it; he cares nothing for the religion when it stands in his way, but he will follow its injunction to please the Mohammedans, especially when they gratify and justify his worst passions. I shall be asked if the Mohammedans do not believe in one God, and the same God as the Christian, and if that does not make it a religion, and very near that of Christian. Yes, they do; and so do the devils. That is what Mohammedanism is—the religion of devils. Most of the Turkish conversation consists of oaths and smut. I do not mean among the common people—theirs is nothing else —but of the educated upper classes, their scholars, teachers, governors, and priests. I came in contact with them for years, and I hated to listen to them, their talk was so full of cursing and filth. You never see the fruits of the spirit in them; only the fruits of the flesh. They do not understand what spiritual life is; with them all is sense—eating and drinking, finery and lust—lust above all, everywhere and always—like cattle. They seem never able to forget sex and its uses. The whole Mohammedan system is designed to make the gratification of lust as easy and plentiful as possible short of a promiscuity that would lead to civil anarchy. A Mohammedan can divorce his wife any time, no matter how many children she or he has. He does not much care for his children: only he pleases by paying back her dower, and marry another to do likewise: every week, or day, if he sees fit, he can re-marry and re-divorce the first one as often as he pleases. It is like trading horses; as little sentiment or morality in one as the other, the slightest possible regulation of sheer animal desire.

There is, however, one form of divorce which is complete, and does not allow of re-marriage until another marriage has intervened; that is called the ieuchden docuza (meaning from three to nine divorce, from the terms the husband uses in doing it. He says to her, "I divorce you three to nine." Nobody knows what it means or meant. After this, if he wants his wife back, he must get somebody else to marry with her, and then he divorce her regularly; and as this is perilous, because the second husband after marrying her may take a notion to keep her, or any way keep her much longer that the first one relishes, or demand a large sum of money, the usual plan is to fix a very poor man, or a blind beggar (preferably blind, so that he canot see the wife, and be so charmed by her beauties that he will wish to keep her); get him to become the woman's husband for a few days, and then pay him something to divorce her, then the first can marry her again if he chooses. There are many more specimens of Mohammedan "purity" too shameful to write, and too shameful to read. I cannot soil the paper with them. But I must mention one more engine of corruption which lies at the very root of Mohammedanism itself, the pilgrimage to

Mecca, to the birthplace of Mohammed in Arabia. Once a year Mohammedan pilgrims from every quarter of the world go to Mecca to pay homage to their beloved prophet, averaging 200,000 to 500,000 a year. It is their duty to sacrifice. This is done on the hills which surround the great temple, the greatest mosque in the world. It is a square building, which covers several acres of land. Just in the cluster is the Holy Well, called Zamzem. Mohammedans believe that if they drink of that water, hell fire cannot burn them, and every pilgrim does so. Then they begin to die from cholera to the tune of fifty thousand a year or so, for the well is a mere cesspool. You see, after cutting the throats of the animals, they leave the filth and blood just as they are, for the Mohammedan religion does not allow the sacrifice to be touched. The sandy soil absorbs this putrid filth, which leaks into the well. But it is a great merit to die on the spot where Mohammed was born; one goes straight to heaven if he does. That is not the worst, however; they fill bottles with that water and carry it to their families and friends throughout the Turkish Empire, Persia and India, from which cholera is spread abroad over the world.

The pilgrims do not take their wives as far as the birthplace of Mohammed, but leave them half way, and on reaching Mecca they marry temporarily. About 20,000 prostitutes there make a business of being short-term wives of the pilgrims, getting $5 to $25 from each, and being his wife for anywhere from a day to a fortnight, so that each woman marries from fifty to a hundred pilgrims a year. This is not prostitution; it is religion—and Mohammedan "purity." Mecca is considered the most holy spot on earth by Mohammedans; but it is the most corrupt spot; it is a hell, and the Mohammedan Paradise is worse than Mecca.

The Mohammedan religion sets strict rules prohibiting the true freedom to female sex. While requiring them to perform all the other religious duties in mosques where men worship, there will not be one woman among them. As ex-

ception to this rule one might see an old woman, and that
to be over sixty years of age. Usually the female sex are
expected to perform their religious duties and do the act of
worshipping in the house.

Although the book of Koran accepts the object in
the formation of families (of family) to the generation of humanity, yet that pure object is ignored only through their
passion; they distinguish the difference between the unlawful
from lawful in this manner, that without ever having seen
each other, though the declaration of a few representative witnesses of the parties to be married that the marriage ceremonies are performed. It has taught that the wife of a married
man should not be seen by any other man; therefore each
Mohammedan woman is kept under the rules of namehram;
that is to say, the wife of a married man should not be seen
by any other men, and if any man come to the house or the
wife has to go out of the house, her head, face and the entire
body should be covered, and if it should be seen or understood that she has disobeyed this rule, is lawfully considered
divorced on the ground that she has been unfaithful to her
husband. Young girls also should not be seen by a man nor
should they talk to a man.

A married man enjoys privileges to such an extent that
he has full right to divorce a wife without any reason or excuse, even though he may have many children by that wife,
and can marry any other woman he may wish. A Mohammedan has the right to marry three more wives while he is married and living with the first wife.

Mohammedan women are not allowed the true liberty,
and they must be kept under the ruling of the hand. They
are treated like slaves; consequently, wishes a Mohammedan
husband can respect or show objection or trust his wife, nor
his wife can think the house in which she lives is her own nor
assured that she is to live with this husband until death; thus
there is on true family can be found among are supppressed.

It is better for a Mohammedan girl to be sold like a slave rather than to be the wife of a Mohammedan man.

This is one of the principal teachings of the book of Koran. There are other similar teachings of this book that deprive the female sex of their rights and liberty by the few examples here given of the true nature of Mohammedanism.

In one word, Mohammedans have no right to exist, politically, socially, or religiously. In the first they have wrought nothing but ruin; in the second nothing but corruption; in the third nothing but devilishness. They are working nothing else now in either of the three. They have never built up anything; they are pure destroyers. The day one becomes a Mohammedan he loses his intellect, his skill and his common sense. Mohammedanism is a poison, fatal to any good gifts or graces; it cultivates in him falsehood, cruelty and lust. It was sent by God for a curse to the Christians, as a punishment, just as the Philistines were sent to the people of Israel.

The book of Koran, moreover, teaches that all those who are not Mohammedans should be frequently invited to the true religion; that in case of complying with the invitation they should be well treated and receive every consideration; should they, however, perish in rejecting the true faith, all the possessions of the obstinates are declared to belong legally to the true believers, and here is the Fetua, or sacred sentence. "If the Gyver or Kaiffir (the blasphemer) does not renounce his blasphemy, his life should be taken away, and all his goods appropriated by the true believers." Although this is not the present practice of the Moslems, it has been the only rule for centuries past.

Therefore, by the few examples here given, the true nature of the Mohammedan religion may be clearly ascertained. That religion, as you may observe, gives many opportunities for the corruption of the morals of mankind, and with it endangers the morals and materials of humanity. One of the causes of deterioration of Christianity in the East is, and are apt to follow the bad example set before them. It is from this spirit the book of Koran, that the blood of many innocent persons has been shed in Turkey; it is from this spirit that children and delicate women have been ill-treated.

It has already been shown to be not a religion, but a system of falsehood, hatred, cruelty, lust, and sensuality. Of course these things combined can only result in corruption.

It would seem that Mohammed must have taken his inspiration from both the domestic and a bull. A rooster is a polygamist; he has his hens without limit. He claimed to have received a revelation from heaven directing him to take to himself any woman he pleased, no matter whether she was married and had a husband or not; that made no difference with Mohammed. He took any woman he wanted, and if her husband objected he was sure to be put to death. Mohammedans cannot differ from their prophet; they follow him; they strive to imitate him just as much as true Christians strive to follow and imitate Christ.

The Sultan grows more of a beast and more of a fiend as he grows older, and all the Mohammedans are of the same stripe. Armenian men and Armenian women alike dread the approach of an old Turk far more than of a young one. Unless one has witnessed a fight between bulls he can have little idea of Turkish warfare; no animal fight can approach it in ferocity or insatiability. When a bull conquers another, he never leaves him until he gores him to death; so when Mohammedans conquer a nation, be sure they will exterminate it. To them mercy means apostasy. To leave a man alive or a woman unravished is to be false to the precepts of Mohammed. They cannot help it; it is their religion; a religion for wild animals. Their priests go to the mosques and preach to them thus: "O, believers in Mohammed, love your fellow believers, but hate and kill all others; they are Giaours, heathen dogs, filthy hogs." To kill a Christian and to kill a hog is all the same to a Mohammedan; there is as little sin in one as the other. The priests of Mohammedan Khojas say:

SULTAN ABDUL HAMID II.

"Go ask them to accept our religion; if they do you must not harm them, but if they will not, kill them, for they have no right to live in a Mohammedan country; it is not only no sin, but a great virtue. The more Christians you kill the greater reward you will have from Allah (the God) and his prophet Mohammed."

The Turks are slaughtering Armenians to earn this reward. Of course if the men apostatize they are spared; but the Turk has no notion of losing the gratification of his lust on the women in that way. A woman who falls into their hands need not hope to keep her virtue on any terms, even by abjuring her religion. They violate her first, and force her to become a Mohammedan afterwards.

Let it be fully understood throughout the Christian world that the massacre is a religious demand. The Turks have to comply. As a Christian tries to be faithful to Christ and His teachings, so the Turks are trying to be faithful to their prophet and his. They go to the mosques and pray, "Allah, (O God), help us; strengthen our hands and sharpen our swords to kill the infidel Armenian." Then they come from the mosques and begin to kill, and plunder, and outrage, and commit every sort of indescribable atrocity on the peaceable and defenseless Armenian. And it will grow worse instead of better, since so-called Christian nations have given the Sultan public notice that they will not interfere with him. Do not be deceived by his lying reports. They did not kill the Turks; they never dreamed of such madness. This awful fate has fallen on them purely and simply for being Christian.

The second cause of the horrors to the Armenians of Turkey, is a despotic government.

According to the Koran, the Sultan of the Empire is also Khalif of the Mohammedan religious world. He cannot abdicate either office, if he would, without vacating the other by the same act.

In fact, herein lies the secret of the present Sultan's policy, which seems suicidal on general principles of government.

He has been lavish in the building and repairing of the mosques and the rooms of prayer meeting, and also in establishing Moslem schools throughout his dominions.

The Ottoman Government is a politico-religious system. This is the necessary constitution of any Mohammedan sovereign state, but the conception has special force and vitality in Turkey, whose sovereign claims to be the Mohammedan, and thus the Khalif of the Mohammedan world. The whole fabric of the Turkish Empire rests on a religious foundation; this religious foundation is not the general religious principle in man, but the particular form of religion established by Mohammed. The Sultan is a good conscientious Mohammedan. It is only fair to believe, even if he were not a sincere believer, he would still feel compelled to adopt the same course as a matter of internal political necessity. The Moslem population look to him as the defender of the faith, girded with the sword of the prophet. He feels it imperative at hazards to regain lost prestige over his fanatical subjects, especially in the South, where rumblings of discontent and disloyalty are ominous.

According to the book of the Koran, which is the basis and ultimate authority of Mohammedan law,—Code Napoleon, treaty stipulatoins, and Imperial Trades notwithstanding,—the whole non-Moslem population of Turkey are outlaws. The millions of ancient hereditary inhabitants, whether Greek, Armenian, Nestorian, Jacobite, Jew, or Syrian are considered aliens. Their legal status is that of prisoners of war, with corresponding rights and responsibilities. Not one of them is expected or even allowed to serve in the army. Non-Moslems, whose services are indispensable to the Government, are, in rare cases, put in civil offices, especially where integrity or ability can be found. It cannot be denied that the above is true in theory, and it is equally true that the theory is carried out so far as fear of intervention by Christian nations permits. So far as we can judge the Sultan is a sincere and honest Mohammedan, and regards himself as a true

Khalif—or successor of the prophet of Mohammed. He is the chief defender of the faith; under God the absolute arbiter of its destinies. He has undoubtedly done his best to reconcile the interests of the Khalifate with those of the Empire.

In one particular (the policy of the Sultan) is condemned by most enlightened Mohammedans, as strongly as by Christians. His attempt to concentrate the whole administration of the Empire in his own hands has led to the establishment of a dual government—that of the palace and the Porte. The whole machinery of a government exists at the Porte. There are ministers and fully organized departments; there is a council of ministers and a council of state. All business is supposed to pass through their hands, and the whole administration is supposed to be subordinate to them. All is, of course, subject to the supreme will of the Sultan, but his official advisers and his official agents are at the Porte.

The government of Turkey, under the supreme rule of the Sultan, is composed of the Sublime Porte and the council of state; under those there is the administration of the departments in the central government, and of the provinces throughout the Empire. There is, however, an informal, yet none the less powerful element, known sometimes as the privy council, or the palace party.

The Sublime Porte, which derives its name from the gate where the early Sultans held their audiences, and which enter the seraglio grounds near the Mosque of St. Sophia, corresponds very closely to the cabinets of other countries. Its officers are the Grand Vizier, the Sheikh-ul Islam, the Ministers of the Interior, of War, Evkaf, Public Instruction, Public Works, Foreign Affairs, Finance, Marine, Justice and the Civil List, and the President of the State. The Grand Vizier receives his appointment immediately from the Sultan, and makes up his own Cabinet, though with the Sultan's approval. He has no particular portfolio, but presides over the general Government, and his word is ordinarily all-powerful in any of the departments. The Sheikh-ul Islam also nominally receives his appointment direct from the Sultan, but in most cases is the choice of the Grand Vizier. He is not, as is so often supposed, the head of the Moslem religion, but is the representative in the Cabinet of the Ulima, the general body of teachers of Moslem law, having no very definite organization in themselves and yet exerting as a mass a very powerful influence over the Empire.

The Sheikh-ul Islam has comparatively little influence, except when there is a necessity for the interpretation of Moslem law in the conduct of the Government; then he becomes an important member. The other members of the Sublime Porte conduct their departments in much the same way as in the other Governments. Two only require special mention: The Department of Public Instruction is most important, including as it does the Board Censors, who have the right to pass upon the publication or importation of all literary matter, and can decree the suppression or confiscation of any newspaper or of any book which they think is derogatory to the interests of the Empire. The Department of Evkaf is peculiar to Turkish administration. It has to do with the care of the great amount of property vested in the mosques. Under Turkish law property which in other states would revert to the Government, reverts usually to the nearest mosque, and individuals as an act of piety frequently deed real estate or other property to the mosques, which thus have become immensely wealthy. This property may be purchased on condition of the payment of rent to the mosque or of an annuity to any persons specified in the deed by which the property is handed to the mosque. The income of this department has been somewhat reduced of late years by the seizure of a considerable portion of it by the Government. Under this same department comes also the care of the general expenses for Mohammedan worship, such as the pilgrimages to Mecca, the public reading of the Koran, etc. . .

In fact, however, there is another Government at the Palace of Yildiz, more powerful than the official Government, made up of chamberlains, moollahs, eunuchs, astrologers and nondescripts, and supported by the secret police, which spares no one from the Grand Vizier down. The general policy of the Empire is determined by this government and the most important questions of the state are often treated and decided, while the highest officials at the Porte are left in absolute ignorance of what is going on. It is needless to add that the Porte and the Palace are at sword's points, and block each other's movements as far as they can. . . .

The Sultan evidently believes that he is equally independent of all these governments, and decides all questions, great and small, for himself. In form he does so, but no man can act independently of all his sources of information, and of personal influence of his entourage; under the present system he makes himself responsible for every blunder and every iniquity committed in the Empire, but he has disgraced three distinguished Grand Viziers for telling him so, and seems to have no idea of the causes of the intense dissatisfaction with his government which prevails among his Mohammedan subjects. The Turks as well as the Christians also condemn the laws restricting personal freedom, which have increased in severity every year. In many ways these laws are more galling to the Turks than the Christians.

For administrative purposes the Empire is divided into vilayets, these again into mutassarifliks and kaimakamliks, and these again into mudirliks. The two highest grades are governed by Pashas appointed in Constantinople; the third grade or kaimakam receives his appointment ordinarily from Constantinople, but sometimes from the provincial superiors. The mudire are almost invariably local magistrates.

Associated with each one of those officials is a council, or mejliss, including prominent Turks. Turks are the head authority; tender their advice when it is desired to the Governor, and consult in general in regard to the interests of the communities.

There is another evil connected with this system which may lead to serious difficulties with foreign powers. All foreign relations are supposed to be managed through the Minister of Foreign Affairs or the Grand Vizier, but these officials have no power and but little influence; they can promise nothing and do nothing; but in all delicate diplomatic questions it is essential to treat with responsible agents, and to discuss them with such agents in a way in which it is impossible to treat with the Sovereign himself. The present system has been a serious injury to Turkey. It has roused the hostility of all the embassies and led them to feel and report to their governments that there is no use in trying to do anything to save the Empire; that it is hopelessly corrupt, and the sooner it comes to an end the better for the world. There is no longer any concerted action of Europe at Constantinople for the improvement of the condition of the people.

Over this whole administration presides the Sultan himself. His word is supreme in each department, and he can and frequently does override the decisions of his ministers. More than almost any of his predecessors in the line of Ottoman Sultans, Abdul Hamid II. takes personal cognizance of the most minute details of his Government. The interests not only of his palace and his capital, but of the most remote provinces come under his eye. His industry is proverbial, and to his ability all who know him personally bear cordial witness. He is however, by no means the absolute autocrat that he appears. He realizes very clearly his position between two contradictory and mutually repellant forces, the progress of the West and the conservatism of the East. If he antagonizes the former too much he runs the risk of losing his Empire; if he fails to keep in sympathy with the latter his Khaliphate is endangered. His position is one by no means to be envied, and no judgment of his can be just which does not take into account the peculiarities of that position.

If Sultan Abdul Hamid would come out of his palace, restore to the Porte its full responsibility, disband its secret

police, trust his Mohammedan subjects and do simple justice
to the Christian, his life would be far more secure than it is
to-day, with all precautions. His people and all the world
would recognize the great and noble qualities which they
now ignore, and welcome him as the wisest and best of all
the Sultans.

The sad pity of it is that he will never do it. It is too late.
The influence of the palace favorites is too strong. He will
appear in history not as the Sultan who saved the Empire, but
as the one who might have saved it and did not.

I might mention a thousand similar cases, all of them
traceable to this fatal spirit of the Koran. If such a despotic
Empire, or such a book of the Koran, be in the hands of the
Government, and if it should regard its subject races in the
same light as the Koran regards non-Mohammedans, how
can the populations living under it be reformed or improved
from within? All of you will of course agree with me in saying that it is impossible.

Now, this is the condition of the despotic Empire or Government, these are the principal causes of the internal ruin of
Turkey.

III. The third cause of the horrors of the Armenians in
Turkey: these are the products of the misrule and oppression
of the Government.

The rule of the Turkish Government is hopelessly and
remedilessly bad wherever that rule extends. For example:
The income of the Government is derived from customs, dues,
tithes, levied on all agricultural produce; from the sale of certain
articles, as salt, which are Government monopolies, and from
imports on pretty nearly everything, and from the capitation
and exemption taxes levied upon the Christian subjects. The
tithes are generally framed out, and by the misrule this gives
occasion for the greatest amount of oppression. There is
no regular system of collection, and when the treasury runs
low the Government sends out requisition to the interior
provinces. The money is then collected in whatever way is

feasible. There is no regularity in the payment of salaries. The Government is notoriously in arrears in regard to the payment of employees, being sometimes months, and even years, behind.

The statement that a month's salary is to be paid becomes a matter of comment in the public press and of general congratulation. The result is widespread corruption in all departments. The absence of salaries is made up for by the collection of fees; and every official from the lowest to the highest, through whose hands any money passes, is sure to keep as much of it as he thinks he can without incurring too severe wrath from his superior.

Throughout a large section of the fairest part of the earth's surface business enterprise, intellectual progress, to say nothing of religious freedom have long been dead. In the fair lands which border on the Mediterranean, lands which should be the garden spots of the earth, there is and has been for many generations, poverty, wretchedness and squalor, which can hardly be credited in lands that are better governed.

Naturally the character of the people has deteriorated, and a hopeless fatalism or cunning mendacity, which seeks to win by deceit what it cannot gain by fairer methods, have become characteristic of the people; in fact whether we consider the character of the people, the soil on which they live, the houses that cover them or the institutions by which they are misgoverned, we find that the trail of the Turk is over them all.

The traveler through Palestine cannot but be impressed by these facts; still more he who takes the overland journey across Asia Minor, where the Turk has had more full and undisputed sway.

He will find himself in a land of great natural resources, large possibilities; a land with a fertile soil, and exhaustless mines of precious metals; a land of rushing rivers and bold and rugged mountain scenery. When the Turk is deposed and some decent Government establishes its sway in Asia

Minor, we shall read of Cook's parties and Gaze's Tourists in the magnificent land of Taurus. The Cilician gates will be open to the traveler, though for many years they have been practically closed by the inefficient shiftlessness of a Government which taxes the people to death for roads which are never built, and bridges which are never constructed. Then the mines which, with their hidden treasures, have been sealed to all enterprise, will pour their wealth into the world's coffers. But now the Turk reasons with characteristic phlegm, that so long as the mines are undisturbed the wealth of the nation is intact, and he does not propose to allow outer barbarians to come in and open up mines and cart off his treasures of gold and silver. This is carrying the stocking-leg theory of finance to its absurdest limits. To be sure the traveler finds one feeble, struggling little railway on the Mediterranean coast of Turkey, from Mersin to Adana, a distance of about forty miles. It was built by foreign capital, however, and is managed by foreign enterprise, and has been hampered and taxed almost off the face of the earth by the ruling.

There is also a passable wagon road for Turkey for a few miles from Tarsus toward the Cilician gates, but this passable road soon runs into an almost impassable cart track. Though the camel path does not exactly run up a tree, it seems to loose itself when it gets to the most inaccessible portions of the Taurus Mountains, or at least is fit only for the sure-footed "ships of the desert" that continually traverse it with their swaying loads and their tinkling bells. The only bridges in many parts of the country are those built by the Romans, eighteen hundred years ago, so substantially and so scientifically that the war of the elements and the neglect of the Turkish Empire for twenty centuries has not been able to destroy them. It should be said that the road which starts from Tarsus comes to light here and there during the hundreds of miles which lie between the birthplace of St. Paul and the ancient city Angora, in old Galatea; but it as often gets lost again or is obstructed and rendered impassable by falling trees and descending boulders which no one has energy enough to move out of the way. And yet this road is the excuse for wringing tens of thousands of pounds every year out of the poverty-stricken inhabitants. To be sure, the money is not expended upon the road, and every year it is falling into a more utterly impassable condition; but, no matter, it furnishes an excuse for yearly taxes and for more misrule or misgovernment.

There are no hotels in that country, or inns even, of the humblest character, along this highway, which is the only artery between Constantinople and the same places of the Mediterranean ports; but there are stone huts called khans, in which men and bullocks and camels and asses may rest their wearied bodies in delightful promiscuity, while all are impartially attacked by other occupants that are not recorded in the census, and are not registered upon the books even of a Turk. For much of the distance along this highway every tree and shrub and root has been plucked up to furnish a little scanty fuel for the shivering inhabitants. The broad stretches of tableland, naturally so fertile, are so poorly tilled with the rude implements of the past, that only a scanty population can be maintained, and these at "a poor, dying rate," where millions might thrive under a good government.

The villages in the interior are for the most part built of sun-dried mud, though sometimes of stone, and are not clean and healthy. Very naturally, all enterprise and energy are killed out of such a people by hundreds of years of misrule and oppression. Why should a man strive to get on in the world, when he knows that he will only make himself, by his enterprise, the special prey of the oppressor? Why should he plant an orchard of superior fruit, when he knows that the tax-gatherer will get the best of it? Why should he try to improve his worldly condition in any way, when he knows that unless he can cover up his wealth and simulate poverty, he will but become the target for every corrupt and unscrupulous official? The land of Turkey has been picked bare; even the pin feathers of enterprise, if we may be excused the expression, have been singed off by a rapacious officialism during many generations.

Undoubtedly the rule of the Turk is hopelessly and remedilessly bad wherever that rule extends. The mildew and blight of his occupation are found wherever the star and crescent wave. Just as truly as in the olden days, destruction and desolation were left in the wake of the victorious "horsetails" of the triumphant Sultans, so now desolation and destruction are left in the retreating wake of the decadent and conquered Sultan.

The history of six hundred years teaches us that it is of little use to talk about mending the reign of the Turk. There is nothing left but to end it. To mend it is out of the question. To end it is the only hope for Moslem and Christian alike, who dwell within the Sultan's domains. And now these centuries of atrocious misrule and almost inconceivable corruption are crowned by the murder and the pillage and the wholesale massacres, which have caused the blood of civilization to run cold; outrages that will mark the years of 1895-96 with such blots as no other years have known for many centuries. Yet the civilized world allows the Great Powers, each disarmed against the Turk by their mutual jealousies, to look on supinely while the butchery in Armenia never ceases. Still the Queen's speech, read at the opening of Parliament in the year 1896, talks gingerly about the Sultan's promises to institute reforms, while very likely, at the very moment when her speech was read, the Sultan's hirelings were murdering Christians, pillaging their property and firing their villages.

What will our grandchildren think of the boasted civilization of the nineteenth century? How will the people of the happier age which is to come look back with shuddering horror, not only upon the deeds enacted in Turkey, but with scarcely less horror, upon the Christian nations who by reason of their insane jealousy of one another, permitted those atrocities, which they might have prevented.

Alas, that this century should be known not only as the century of invention and discovery, of the railway and the steamship, and the telegraph and the telephone, the century of religious progress and missionary enterprise, the century of the Sunday School and the young people's movements, but also the century stained with the deepest dye of Christian blood of which the great Christian powers can never wash their hands.

"The oppressive character of the Government of the Turkish Empire, with respect to the subject race," is a very clear declaration on the part of the editor of the Independent of the situation in the country known as the Turkish Empire. It is a character that is important; it is an actually existing Government that counts, and the mischievous results of that Government concern the civilized world to-day more in the relation to the "subject race," than the general reformation of that misrule itself.

The question is not so complicated as vast; not requiring so much skill in dealing with it as patient study to have a full comprehension of the main factors entering into it as potent influences.

As in a medical examination, so in this, euphony of diction is to be sacrificed to truth; and first, the "Government of the Turkish Empire," as it is to-day and has been for 500 years, is only Mohammedan domination with regard to the non-Mohammedan population of the country. Secondly, the "subject races" are only slave population and prisoners of war; and, thirdly, the essential character of that domination over those races has been a thorough and absolute system of oppression. In entering upon remarks regarding the character of that oppression, it might be necessary to point to the proofs of the above statements regarding the Government itself and the status of the "subject races." For that part, it is quite sufficient to point to the whole history of the Turkish Government through every step of its settled existence during 500 years. Not very keen insight is necessary, either, but only deliberate study and simple impartial judgment, to convince any intelligent mind of the justice of the charges.

The character of the oppression of the Turkish Government must be tried by the one test which stands higher than all theory and even logical inferences; by that test which has the stamp of the highest authority and comes with the power of a primâ facie evidence that compels conviction. "By their fruits ye shall know them." The timber of the oak is what tells, and we care not so much for the foliage or the acorn. The flower of the rosebush is enough to satisfy us regarding the result of the gardener's work: but from the orchard we expect fruit, and by its fruit we judge of the value of the husband-man's labor and of wisdom of his management. A Government is not for exhibition. It is not merely to make history. Before the judgment of God and man it is to stand and be judged by the fruit of its influences upon human life; its happiness, its comfort, its development—moral, physical and intellectual, judged by that standard.

1. The Government of the Turkish Empire, in its relation to the "subject races," is found to be radically and essentially oppressive. The Turkish Government is based upon the Mohammedan religion, the component elements of which are the sword and the Koran. While for half a century European diplomats have been deceiving themselves and the civilized world that the Koran could cease to be the law that regulated the movements of the sword, the events of the past year and a half have proved that the history of the Turkish Government has long ago demonstrated that the sword and the Koran are united so that nothing but the death of one or the other can put them asunder. If the Government of the Turkish Empire could be induced to recognize and permit the development of an "Ottoman Empire," after the type of civilized governments, where the equality of all citizens before the law is the basic principle, oppression in the Government might be treated as a disease; but as the Turkish Empire has always been, and is to-day a "Mohammedan Empire," oppres-

sion of the Christian and the "infidel" in it is a constitutional quality.

For those who have at heart, not only the fate of the Christian races in Turkey, but also the interests of civilization and Christendom at large, this must stand as the most important element in the case, namely, that the Government of the Turkish Empire, when true to itself, and standing upon the ground of its highest efficiency, is by nature destructive of those forces which make for righteousness in this world, and are the foundation of that which is counted by the Aryan races as the highest civilization.

All the other characteristics are the outcome of this one essential fact, and will be influenced by the remedy brought to bear upon this root of the evil itself.

2.   Turkish oppression is universal; it oppresses the "subject races," in all places and in all their relations.   The unalterable disabilities deny them justice in the courts, assuring immunity to the robber and the highwayman and the swindler, if he is only a Mohammedan.   The prosperity of the Christian races, merchant and artisan, dependent upon justice and protection, is thus reduced to a deplorable minimum; poverty is the highway open before every Christian community; but as taxation, unremitting, unlimited, and merciless, is also the law of the land, the instinct of self-preservation drives them on to labor incessantly in order to remedy the evil as far as possible.   In spite of the fertile soil and abundant natural resources, therefore, the "subject races" of the Turkish Empire are under the heel of a grinding oppression.

After centuries of honest, toilsome life, in sight of the golden dawn of the world's greatest century, and with the thunder of the chariot wheels of modern progress in their ears, the Christian "subjects" of the Sultan are there to-day without railroads or even highways, without any "improvements," ancient or modern, in science or art, agriculture or sanitation, with no police, and no fire alarms, no water works, and no house lighting or street lighting system, and as the shadows of evening descend, the entire land from east to west or Mt. Ararat to the Adriatic sinks into fitful slumber, under the black wings of a night of terror and insecurity that best enables weary souls to comprehend the felicity of a hereafter when "there shall be no night there."

The universality of the oppression is also assured by the fact that the Mohammedan of all conditions, however ignorant or dull in other respects, is remarkably well versed in this one doctrine, that he is lord and master, while the Christian is the slave; how he is to be reminded of his subordinate condition with every opportunity. An intelligent residence, of any length of time in Turkey, would convince one of this almost astounding fact. The Governor or the Pasha, as true Moslems, have never had scruples in denying justice to the Christian, in receiving bribes from defendant and plaintiff alike, in extending their protection to the murderers of men and the ravishers of women; but the barbarous Kurds on the mountains, as well as the beggar women in the streets of Constantinople, are just as conscious of their privilege in this direction as the watchful guardians of Turkish law in high places. On the hills of the Golden Horn, above Balat, on a sunny afternoon, a Protestant minister was out walking with a little girl and her brother. The girl was dressed after the fashion of Europeans, and to guard her eyes from the bright sunlight a green veil covered her face. There were Turkish villages around, and a group of Turkish women were passing by. Suddenly one of them sprang toward the little girl and snatched the veil from her head and tore it into shreds with ominous mutterings and imprecations. The veil was green, the sacred color of the Mohammedan religion, to be worn only by the highest clergy. How could the child of the accursed "Giaour" dare to go about under its shadow. Years afterward, far away on the jagged heights of Montenegro, a bridal party of Christians were attacked, as reported by the British consul, by a band of Turkish ruffians. They cut the bride into pieces, half killed the bridegroom, raised a funeral pyre, and burned the dead and dying under the rays of the setting sun. The bride had worn a green velvet jacket. Away on the mountains of Armenia the Kurdish chief, Genjo, upon the recovery of his son from a fatal malady, went out to seek a thank offering to the God of heaven, and the sacrifice he decided upon was the lives of seven Christian priests. Up and down through the length and breadth of the Turkish Empire, at the hands of millions of Mohammedans, universal oppression in every conceivable shape has been the law for the "subject races" of the Turkish Empire.

3. The oppression of the Turk is cumulative. Poverty and ignorance bring degradation, and degradation hardens human nature, cruelty becomes an instrument, and lust is there as the impelling power. Slowly, steadily, from village to city, from the cities to the capital of the Empire, the great tidal waves of cruel oppression have brought devastation through the centuries, and once and again the return current has dashed itself against the highlands of Armenia, as well as the habitations of other Christian races, and opened before the eyes of Christendom ghastly pictures of blood and destruction that to the mind of the uninitiated have appeared as accidental developments. The forces of this evil are there always, and are constantly accumulating their momentum. It is a farce to speak of inability to control fanaticism on the part of the Government or the Sultans of Turkey. It were just as reasonable to speak of the helplessness of the man to avert disaster who loosens a mighty boulder from the mountain heights above his village, or finds the entertainment of a summer day by carving a channel in the dam above the city. Sure enough, the ignorance of the Mohammedan disqualifies him from understanding the science of the correlation of forces in the Kingdom of the devil, but of their nature he is not ignorant, and glories in his liberty to set them moving in the midst of the Christian population of the Empire.

4. And, hence the greatest evil of the Turkish oppression is its far-reaching character. We must admit that there

are degrees of sin and evil; that there is a sin against the spirit which far outweighs many transgressions. The oppression of the Mohammedan Government by its universal, cumulative weight has crushed and is now crushing out those spiritual qualities which make the fiber of true human souls. No one who believes in the soul of man and its undying worth could fail to be appalled at the sight of the havoc that has been wrought upon the manhood of the people inhabiting Turkey in consequence of Mohammedan oppression. Degeneration and degradation lose their significance here. It is spiritual contagion; it is intellectual rottenness. From early childhood thousands of the Christian subjects of the Turkish Government, directly or indirectly in its employ, are led to seek promotion by qualifying to serve men whose business is theft and corruption. A Pasha or Governor in the interior seeks an accountant or a treasurer, not to render accurate accounts to the Minister of Finance, but to devise ways and means by which both the imperial treasury and the population of the district can be robbed in a manner that will be the least open to detection and the most profitable for the private treasury of the Pasha or the Governor himself. Thousands of the Christian youths of the land, naturally the most intelligent and capable among them, have been for centuries trained in a school of corruption and villainy, to oppress their own countrymen, as the servile tools of the corrupt officials of the Government. The most approved methods of fraud and bribery, of smuggling and wholesale deceit have, therefore, been at a high premium in the land known as the Turkish Empire, from the morning that the crescent waved over the walls of the city of Constantine. A lie is disreputable if it fails to deceive. It has the double reward of both remuneration and promotion to higher service if it prevails. How blessed the Christian under-secretaries of the Turkish Foreign Office, when they return with the trophies of the intellectual scalps of the astute diplomats whom Europe sends to Constantinople to fish for facts in the awful maelstrom of falsehoods of Turk-

ish diplomacy. It is a matter of surprise, indeed, that
there are men in high places of the Christian West who have
fallen into the habit of measuring the hideous injustice and
oppression of all the Christian races in Turkey, only in a
balance where houses, farms and bodies of men and women
can be weighed. We have been asked: "Oh, the condition of
the Christian in Turkey is surely not intolerable, except for
these occasional massacres, which European diplomacy ought
to prevent." And the answer is: "No, the disasters of fire and
sword are nothing compared to the frightful havoc of the
souls of men that has been brought with an iron hand and
a persistent, unrelenting compulsion upon the Christian races
in Turkey." Turkish Government, which is mainly nothing
but a colossal avalanche of corruption and sensuality, overwhelming the people of Turkey, cannot be justly qualified
by any definition that falls short of signifying an absolutely
unmitigated curse. I am reminded here of the sterling words
of the golden-tongued prophet, the noble Gladstone, who
stands towering above British mediocrity in these dark days
of ours: "This is strong language, gentlemen, but language
must be strong where the facts are strong." We are told that
the condition of the Christians in Turkey might be worse;
they might have been exterminated. It surely is in order to
ask here, Where is the justice of it, when there is help for
it? What right has Europe to attend to the balance of power
that is kept at the right level by piling high in the pan of the
scale, souls of men, both of Turk and Christian, laid low with
the contagion of corruption and the rottenness of all iniquity
combined, in order that they may serve as dead-weights? And
the iniquity of this condition and the awful responsibility at
the door of those who are responsible for it is enhanced by
the fact that the Christian "subject races" under the Government of the Turkish Empire have been striving and struggling through all these years of subjection for a higher manhood, nourished by the abundance of good works, and especially at the touch of Western civilization, have been aspir-

ing for their highest possibilities, as individual men and as nations.

This qualification of the oppression of the Turkish Government is especially justifiable and unavoidable because

5. An essential factor in the character of the oppression of the Turkish Government is its hopelessness. Some one wrote upon a prison wall the gamut of national degeneration. It went down from wealth and pride to war and poverty, and then started on a return tide of industry and prosperity back over the same path. If there is any correctness in this itinerary, it must have counted upon rapid transit not to give time for pride and poverty to leave an impression upon the soul of the nation.

The universal accumulation and all-pervading flood of Turkish oppression has torn up and borne down with it every single anchorage and mooring of virtue and manhood for the ship of state, so that no returning tide is ever possible for it. Action and reaction, with increasing rapidity, even through the past fifty years, have brought disastrous loss in all directions; so that Turkey has to-day less money, less manhood, less wisdom, less patriotism and confidence in itself. Only one power rises in the midst of universal degeneration, and that is the rampant spirit, desperate and malignant oppression.

In the midst of the colossal calamity of tens of thousands of innocent people murdered in cold blood, villages and cities laid in ashes, and hundreds and thousands of men, women and children on the verge of starvation and death from exposure to the cold blasts of a highland winter, civilized nations of the world stand appalled and appear to consider the difficulty of the situation as unsurmountable. But it is not so. First, there is the hope, if hope it may be called, in the principle that evil destroys itself, while the good rises strong with the power of self-propagation with every morning's sun.

The Turk is destroying himself. His government of oppression is as great a curse to himself as to the Christian; and Europe, in permitting and well-nigh supporting that oppression, has been as great a criminal against the Turk as against the Christian. What is wanted, therefore, for the Christian "subject races" in Turkey, languishing under the cruel yoke of this murderous oppression, is protection. If the Christian Governments of Europe are unwilling as yet to separate the sword and the Koran, they are surely in honor bound to extend the protection they so easily can extend to the Christian population in the Turkish Empire, and practically isolate the Mohammedan with his sword and his Koran. That is the efficient remedy of the situation, and one which, in the name of justice and humanity, honor and civilization, all believers in human rights can demand at the hands of those who have the power to apply it. Pure air and good soil are the best disinfectants. Before the swelling tide of Christian civilization, with its bracing atmosphere of justice and liberty, and the healthful soil of industry and continued well doing, the Mohammedan will be driven away as the floating clouds and the pestilential miasma are blown away before the breath of the mighty north wind, and nature blossoms into full life in the warm light of heaven.

IV. The fourth cause of the horrors to the Armenians of Turkey is the come-out through the present Sultan, or is produced with the hands of Sultan Hamid II.

The Mohammedan population in Turkey every year is decreasing. When the present Sultan captured the throne from his brother, Sultan Murad, the Turkish Government had 40,000,000 people; as soon as he girded the sword of Osman, he began the great battle with Russia, and after the Turko-Russian war he found himself with 18,000,000. Who are the losers. Roumania, Bulgaria, Servia, Montenegro, Bosnia, Herzegovina, a part of Macedonia, Cyprus and a part of Armenia—practically the whole of Europe was lost for Turkey, except Constantinople and the district Edirne or Adrianople.

Turkey is not an Empire any more, but it is a little Kingdom; rather a little feudal system, or, more accurately still, a little anarchy. If it were not for mutual European jealousy, the Sultan could not keep his anarchism. Yet many still think that the Ottoman Empire is a great one, a powerful Government. They look at the Sultan and his dominion through a magnifying glass. This shows ignorance. The Turks are decayed and are decaying. The sick man of Turkey is the dead man of Turkey, and ought to be buried; but the European powers do not bury him because there are precious stones and jewelry in the coffin; no matter how bad the corpse smells, they will endure it.

And the bad smell of the Sultan is killing hundreds of thousands of Christians; but the dead stays where it is, and may stay for some years; but the end will come before many have gone by. When I say that the days of the Sultan are numbered, and the brutal Turkish misrule will cease, many Armenians will rejoin "that the same has often been said long years since, though the Empire remains to-day, and seems likely to remain." The fact is, however, that during my or your own life more than half of it has gone to pieces, and the fragment which remains will go to pieces soon. Permit me to say that all former prophecies have been mistaken because those who made them have judged and misjudged the situation from an occidental standpoint; I judge it from that of a native. Who knows the realities as only a native can? What can an English ambassador or an American minister in Constantinople, staying perhaps two or three years, and entertained and decorated by the crafty Sultan, know about the internal state of Turkey? Having traveled through the country, lived and preached for years at a time, preached in different cities, including Constantinople, I can see signs of a break-up that a foreigner would not notice.

The reason the Turkish population does not increase is this: The army has to be made up of Mohammedans, partly because the Sultan does not put arms into the hands of Christians, for obvious reasons, since they have no motive to uphold and every motive to fight him, and partly because to be a soldier in Turkey is a holy service, the privilege of

Mohammedans alone. As there is a large standing army, nearly all the Mohammedan youths have to become soldiers. Their service begins when they are about twenty years old. The shortest term is five years; for many it is ten; and even after that there are many who cannot escape. If a young Mohammedan is not married at twenty, obviously he cannot marry until twenty-five anyway, and perhaps thirty—very late for a country population. If he is married, his wife is virtually a widow for from five to ten years. Now the reader can see my drift. With marriages so late, and husbands so long absent, Turkish families are small. They do not make good the deaths. And there is a still plainer cause: The soldiers being very poorly fed, and constant fighting going on, ninety per cent. die in the army, and so never have any families; the flower of the nation perishes barren. Those who survive and return are pale and sick, good for nothing, a burden to their families and to the nation. The Armenians have to support the Sultan's army, since they do not furnish it; but they rear families and are drowning out the Turk.

Another cause of decrease is the pilgrimage to Mecca, where Mohammed was born: On an everage, five hundred thousand pilgrims go there every year—of course not all from Turkey, but most of them—and every year about 50,000 or 100,000 of them die of cholera or some other disease before reaching home, from drinking the water of the Holy Well (Zemzorm Sooji), which is full of unholy foulness. Even those who live and return home take that water to their families, and many of the latter die too. Cholera is perpetual in Turkey, and it originates at Mecca. When I was in Adana, 600 at one time went on the pilgrimage, and only 50 of them returned to their home. It is a great virtue to die where Mohammed was born, or to drink that water and die, and they are going to him at a rapid rate. Just last year, when the English and Russian and French consuls at Jiddah, the seaport of Mecca, established a quarantine to detain those coming from Mecca, and bringing cholera, they were murdered by the Mohammedan Arabs, who said they were interfering with the sacred religion, and the Sultan had to pay the indemnity.

Another cause of decrease is the polygamy. People naturally think that marrying more than one wife should increase the number of children; but the facts emphatically prove the reverse. The polygamous Turks do not increase as fast as the Christians who have but one wife.

Hence the Mohammedans are fast decreasing in Turkey, and the Sultan is terrified, and hopes by killing a large part of the Christians and forcing the survivors to accept Mohammedanism, that their power of multiplication may be the boon of a Mohammedan people. Out of the 18,000,000 inhabitants of Turkey, 6,000,000 are native Christians, about 1,500,000 of them Armenians. This leaves only 12,000,000 for the whole Mohammedan population in the present Turkish dominion. The internal ruin of Turkey is made by massacres and forced conversions. That the Sultan has been planning this massacre ever since the Turko-Russian war is evidenced by the fact that after the war he encouraged or ordered a number of Mohammedan tribes—Circassians, Georgians, Kurds and Lazes —to emigrate from Russia to Armenia, confiscated masses of Christian property, and gave it to them, and directed them to reduce the number of Armenian Christians by any way they saw fit, giving them full license to do what they would with Armenians, without penalty. You know what that means with fierce tribes of human wild animals, cruel and foul, and he knew what it meant too, and intended it to mean that. Before his time the Christians far outnumbered the Mohammedans in Armenia proper; but under his "government"—his deliberate policy of extermination—great numbers fled the country, numbers were killed and their women made concubines to Mohammedans, and now the Mohammedans are more numerous in Armenia than the Armenian Christians. And if the Sultan is permitted to go on, he will kill a million more; the rest will be "converted." And then he will call the attention of European powers to this fact and say: "See here, you ask me to reform Armenia; Armenia is reformed. There is no Armenia; the people in that part of my Empire are all Mohammedans, and they are satisfied with my government. What do you want from me? What right have you to interfere with my country and religion?" That is the plan of the Sultan; but that is bad fortune for him; and still it is the real cause of the eternal ruin of Turkey. Because through his plan he has lost nearly 100,000 of noble Armenian people, and at the present time more than 500,000 of Armenian people have need only of bread. They have nothing in hand. And at the same time the Sultan has destroyed and burned many thousands of houses and shops and farms. And now he can not get the principal taxes which the Armenians pay to the government, because they have nothing. They are not able to pay the poll tax, $2 per head, including the new-born male baby, and tax on real estate, and land tax, and house tax, namely, 50 piasters on 1,000 of the value of the house; and Khamtchoori, namely, 5 piasters or 20 cents per head of sheep —one-eighth of the value of the sheep; and tithe of agricultural products. So that the Turkish Government has to-day less money, less manhood, less wisdom, less power, less patriotism and less confidence in itself, and has ruined itself.

V. The fifth cause of the horrors of the Armenians: It has come out with the Eastern question; or I say that it is the product of the Treaty of Berlin.

It is quite needless to remark that Turkey, instead of doing anything to improve the condition of the Armenians, has done much to make it worse during the past fifteen years. The question now arises, What have the powers signatory to the Berlin Treaty done to compel the Sublime Porte "to carry out the improvements and reforms" demanded in the sixty-first Article? And what steps has Great Britain taken in addition to discharge the additional obligation for the improvement of Armenia which she assumed by the so-called Cyprus Convention?

We find that in November, 1879, the English Government, seeing that matters throughout Asia Minor were really going from bad to worse, went the length of ordering an English squadron to the Archipelago for the purpose of a naval demonstration. The Turkish Government was greatly excited, and with a view to getting the order countermanded, made the fairest promises.

But England was not the only power aroused. On June 11, 1880, an Identical Vote of the Great Powers demanded the execution of the clauses of the Treaty of Berlin which had remained in suspense. On the conclusion of the Identical Vote a clear recognition is made of the fact that the interest of Europe, as well as that of the Ottoman Empire, requires the execution of the sixty-first Article of the Treaty of Berlin, and that the joint and incessant action of the Powers can alone bring about this result.

On July 5th the Turkish Foreign Minister sent a note in reply to the representatives of the Powers. "It is of great length and small real value, except as combining in a remarkable degree the distinguishing characteristics of modern Ottoman diplomacy, namely: First, great facility in assimilating the administrative and constitutional jargon of civilized countries; second, consummate cunning in concealing under deceptive appearances the barbarous reality of deeds and intentions; third, cool audacity in making promises which there is neither the power nor desire to make good; and finally, a paternal and oily tone, intended to create the impression that the Turkish Government is the victim of unjust prejudices and odious calumnies."

As soon as the reply of the Porte was received, Earl Granville sent copies to the British consuls in Asia Minor, inviting observation thereon. Eight detailed replies to this request are published in the Blue Book. They concur in a crushing condemnation of the Ottoman Government.

These conclusions, moderately and very diffusely expressed in diplomatic phraseology, are reflected in the collective Note which was sent on September 11, 1880, to the

Sublime Porte by the ambassadors of the Great Powers. On October 3d, without making the slightest references to censures which had been addressed to it, and even appearing completely to ignore the collective Note, the Porte, assuming a haughty tone, merely notified the Powers of what it intended to do.

In a circular of the 12th of January, 1881, Earl Granville tried again to induce the other five powers to join in further representations to the Sublime Porte on the subject. But the other powers seem to have thought that the diplomatic comedy had gone far enough, and sent evasive answers. Prince Bismarck expressed the opinion that there would be "serious inconvenience" in raising the Armenian question, and France hid behind Germany. Such action by the Powers had been anticipated by the British ambassador at Constantinople, Mr. Goschen, who had already written to Earl Granville. "If they (the Powers) refuse, or give only lukewarm support, the responsibility will not lie with Her Majesty's Government." The whole correspondence was simply a matter of form. I have condensed this outline of events since the Treaty of Berlin from Armenia, the Armenians, and the Treaties, following as far as possible the words of the writer, M. G. Rohlin-Jacquemyns, a high authority on International Law. From 1881 to the present time, almost without exception, England, on her part, has allowed no mention in her Blue Books of the manner in which her proteges and those of Europe have been treated. Her energies have seemed to be devoted to stifling the ever-increasing cry of despair from Armenia, instead of attempting her rescue or relief. The other powers are only less guilty in proportion as they have done less to perpetuate Ottoman misrule, and have made less pretence of sympathy and help for the oppressed. Freeman says of England: "By waging a war on behalf of the Turk; by signing a treaty which left the nations of southeastern Europe (and Asia Minor) at the mercy of the Turk; by propping up the wicked power of the Turk in many ways, we have done a great wrong to the nations which are under his yoke; and that wrong which we have ourselves done it is our duty to undo."

It is thus clearly seen that both the sixty-first Article of the Berlin Treaty, and the Cyprus Convention as well, have been of positively no value in securing for the Armenians any of the reforms which were therein recognized as imperatively called for and guaranteed. It is also clear that the condition of Armenia, and of Turkey as a whole, is even vastly worse and more hopeless than it was twenty years ago.

This condition I further maintain is in large measure directly attributable to those treaties themselves and to the attitude subsequently assumed by the Powers which signed them. It is said that the Armenians have brought trouble on themselves by stirring up the Turks. I ask what stirred the Armenians up? It was primarily the sixty-first Article of the Treaty of Berlin. Many a time has that precious paragraph been quoted to me in the wilds of Kurdistan by common Armenian artisans and ignorant villagers. They had welcomed it as a second evangel, and believed the word of England as they did the Gospel.

It was that Article which roused them from the torpor of centuries. There is another sequel to the Berlin Treaty and to the attitude of the Powers, namely: Its effect on the Turks themselves. The natural enmity and contempt of the Moslem rulers and population generally for the Christian subjects has been greatly increased by reason of the pressure which foreign powers have occasionally brought to bear on the Turks in order to procure relief for the Christian. To be sure, the only hope of such relief is from without. But the pressure should not be of a petty, nagging and galling nature. This is worse than nothing. What is needed is prompt, decisive and final action.

A recent writer wisely says that the Armenian question, if it ever be settled at all, must be taken out of the Turks' hands, whether he like it or not. . . . And we have an opportunity now, which may never come our way again, of settling a difficulty which if allowed to develop much longer, will prove more fruitful of mischief than any with which we have been confronted for a generation or more. Really it is the natural outcome of the horrible situation in Armenia since the Treaty of Berlin, and the disease is bound to grow more virulent and contagious until the European doctors apply vigorous and radical treatment to the "sick man." It is difficult to see how anything but a surgical operation can be helpful. The knife has frequently been used in the case of this incurable patient during the present century, and always with excellent results, as for instance in the case of Greece, Lebanon, Bulgaria, Bosnia, Herzegovina and Egypt. A situation in many respects parallel to that in Armenia existed until lately in Bosnia and Herzegovina. But the European powers never do that, though at the Treaty of Berlin they destroyed the nation of Armenia, and also the population of Turkey.

VI. The sixth cause of the horrors to the Armenians of Turkey. The Mohammedan population in Turkey decreased while the Christian increased. When the Sultan Abdool Hamid II. was enthroned Turkey had 40,000,000 population; as soon as he girded the sword of Osman, he began the battle with Russia; after the Turko-Russian war he found himself with 18,000,000, Roumania, Bulgaria, Servia, Montenegro, Bosnia, Herzegovina, a part of Macedonia, Cyprus and a part of Armenia. Practically the whole European part of Turkey except Constantinople and the district Edirna or Adrianople left.

Turkey is not an empire any more, but she is a small kingdom, rather a little feudal system or more accurately still a little Anarchy.,

If it was not for mutual European jealousy the Sultan could not keep his anarchism. Yet many think that the Ottoman Empire is a great one and powerful government.

They look at the Sultan and his dominion through a magnifying glass, which shows their ignorance.

The Turks were decayed, are decaying yet. Hence the Mohammedans are fast decreasing in Turkey and the Sultan is terrified but hopes by killing a large part of the Christians, he forces the survivors to accept his religion, that their power of multiplication may be the boon of a Mohammedan people.

Out of the 18,000,000 inhabitants of Turkey, 6,000,000 are native Christians, half of them are or rather were Armenians; which leaves only 12,000,000 Mohammedan population in the present Turkish dominions and she grows less, while the Christians grow more.

The Sultan, a few years ago, made the obtaining of a marriage certificate compulsory for Armenians, in order to decrease them, but the Turkish authorities found out that it would be almost impossible to notify them according to the order of their Sultan, because it would cost a great deal to establish the order; on the other hand, since many years there have been no marriages in Armenia. The authorities will not give certificates on any terms and prevent any more Christians being born. The daughters and young brides of the murdered thousands are made mothers, violated by the Turks and Kurds.

The Christians have been increasing, not only from within but from without, too. Europeans have begun to go wherever railroads go, hence another reason for massacre and forced conversion comes out by that way.

The Sultan has been planning this massacre ever since the Turko-Russian war is evidenced by the fact that after the war he encouraged or ordered a number of Mohammedan tribes—Circassians, Georgians, Kurds and Lazes—to immigrate from Russia to Armenia, confiscated masses of Christians' property and gave it to them; directed them to reduce the number of Armenian Christians by any way they could, at the revolt they should not be punished.

You know what it means with fierce tribes of human wild animals, cruel and fraud; he knew what it meant too and intended it to mean that. Before his time the Christians far

outnumbered the Mohammedans in Armenia proper, but under his government his deliberate policy of extermination,
great numbers of them fled from the country.   Many of them
were killed and their women made concubines to Mohammedans, for this reason they killed those who were between the
ages of 15 and 50.   Now the Mohammedans are more numerous in Armenia than the Armenians; if the Sultan is permitted
to go on he will kill a million more; the rest will be "converted," and then he will call the attention of the powers to
this fact, and say: "See here, you ask me to reform Armenia,
there are no more Armenians here, because the people in that
part of my empire are all Mohammedans and they are satisfied with my government.

"What do you want of me anyway?   What right have
you to interfere with my country and religion?" that is his
proper plan.

When the Berlin congress was held the Armenians were
the majority in his dominions; the congress decided on reform
for it so that Sultan accepted.   But he gave with the full intention of depopulating and converting it, and then telling the
powers there was no need of reform there.   He was doing
this a few years ago incessantly, and as remorselessly as a fiend.
Therefore you can understand the cause of the oppression and
the persecutions in Turkey.

VII.   The seventh cause of the horrors to the Armenians
of Turkey.   The Christian people are going to be rich and
educated, but Mohammedans generally are poor and ignorant.

The Turks have never cared for money or education.
They have always said, "Let the Christians make the money,
and we will take it from them whenever we choose.   We will
be the rulers, the soldiers, the police; we will have the sword
in our hands.   Then their property and their women too will
be ours at will, and we can force them to become Mohammedans."   Such being their reasoning, they took good of their
swords and their guns, which were furnished to them from

Europe and the United States. The Christian peoples believing that the great Christian powers would never permit the Turks to wreak their murderous and shameful will on them, did not risk the vengeance of the Turks by secretly buying weapons, nor train themselves in the use of arms. They trained their minds, got education, traveled in Europe and this United States, enlightened themselves in every way they could. They sharpened their intellects rather than their swords. They learned to make money also; they established all the business houses in Turkey, all the Turks that get employment in the cities get it from the Christian merchants. As far as Turkey has any finances, they are in the hands of Christians. Go where you will in Turkey, seaboard or interior, all the money and education belong to the Christians. Poverty and ignorance are the portion of the Turks. Ninety per cent of the Christians know how to read and write, while ninety per cent of the Turks do not. Sixty per cent of the Mohammedan property has been sold to the Christian peoples within twenty years. When I was in Turkey during the last twenty years, the Mohammedans were always selling and the Christians always buying. One day a Turk was going to sell his field to a Christian, and they went to the government office to make the transfer. The officer in charge said he could not transfer the property of a Mohammedan to a Christian. This was something new. "Why is that?" they asked. "The governor forbids it," said the officer. "He told him that hereafter it should not be done." Finally both went to the governor and asked him why he forbade it. The governor replied: "Of late the Christians have bought up the fields of the Mohammedans, till they own the greater part of them; if we let them go on they will own everything and the Mohammedans will be left without property. Therefore I forbid it. No Mohammedan shall hereafter sell any property to a Christian." He told the Turk he might sell his field to another Mohammedan, but not to a Christian. "All right," said the Turk, "I will sell it to you then at the same price, or may be a little

less. Will you buy it? because I need the money to support
my family." "I cannot buy it," said the governor. "I have
no money." "I know that," replied the Turk, "and not only
you, but all the other Mohammedans have no money either;
they are all poor. I cannot find any Turk who has the money
to buy my field, and I need money and I have to sell it to that
Christian." Finally the governor was forced to give permission and the Christian bought the field. This is only one case,
but it is typical. There are thousands of just such, and this
is another cause which aroused the jealousy of the Sultan and
his subordinates to order the massacre of the Christians and
the seizure of their property. The Sultan is just the same.
He is outwardly very pleasant, very gentlemanly, very humane. He will promise almost anything, but he will do nothing, and he calls his enraptured guests dogs and hogs behind
their backs. Who knows how many times he has called Lord
Salisbury, the German Emperor, or Russian Czar, who are
helping him to kill the Christian or Armenians, heathen dogs?
See the promises of the Sultan in 1878, in the Berlin Treaty,
Article 61 :—"The Sublime Porte undertakes to carry out without further delay the improvements and reforms demanded by
local requirements in the provinces inhabited by the Armenians, and to guarantee their security against Circassians
and Kurds. It will periodically make known the steps taken
to this effect to the powers, who will superintend their application." These promises were made eighteen or nineteen
years ago, and the reforms were to be made, "without further
delay." His reforms have consisted in ordering Circassians
and Kurds to murder and plunder them. Since the Berlin
Treaty, the Sultan, calling the European Kings, Emperors and
Princes heathen hogs and Christian dogs, directly and indirectly, he has killed nearly 200,000 Armenian Christians. But
still 500,000 Armenians remain today who need only daily
bread. That was his reform.

I often hear it said in this country, "Let us help the poor
Armenians," and I feel very indignant. Poor Armenians!

There are poor among the Armenians as among all nations, but the Armenians as a body are not poor; they are the richest people in Turkey. That is one reason why they are plundered and killed. I do not want the American people to help the Armenians as a poor, ignorant, miserable people, but because they deserve help as a rich, noble, Christian nation, being rusted out by plunder and murder, for the benefit of, and by means of a horde of savages.

After the last war, and loss of the provinces, the Sultan encouraged the Mohammedan population of European Turkey to emigrate to Asiatic Turkey, that they might not live under Christians, and that they might increase the number of Mohammedans in the Asiatic part. The slaughter of the Armenians and the confiscation of their property forms part of the scheme to make room for them. Before his time the Armenians in Armenia outnumbered the Turks; but the massacres, the occupation of the farms and houses by the savages let loose on them, and the emigration of many more Armenians to Persia and Russia, have greatly diminished their numbers. Of course they are not permitted to emigrate; they simply fly. About 200,000 have actually perished. As to the forced conversions the Sultan does not care a particle for Islamism, but wants to please the Muslim and finds this an agreeable way to do it. As to the converts from Islamism to Christianity, they are ordered to go to Constantinople and are killed there. Hundreds and thousands of the Mohammedan Turks are Christians in secret, but do not dare to confess it. These are the ones who helped and protected the Armenians during the recent atrocities. Some six or seven years ago a number of such professed the Christian religion publicly; they were at once ordered to go to Constantinople and every one of them was murdered by order of the Sultan. When the representatives of the Christian powers asked about them the Sultan denied that they had come there at all. This was the method of their assassination: The Sultan has several pleasure boats, and in one of those boats he fitted up an air-tight room with an air-pump; each night one of the converts was taken from prison and put into this room, the air was pumped out, and he was suffocated; then an iron chain was hooked around him and he was thrown into the Bosphorus. One by one all of them were so murdered. How did the author of this book discover the secret? Well, when in Constantinople I had an intimate friend among the engineers. The engineer of this death boat told my friend about it and he told me.

And the Sultan is not simply a murderer by proxy and official order; he is a murderer himself personally. When in Constantinople I learned from several authoritative sources that he killed with his own revolver several of his servants for no cause whatever, but merely from suspicion or rage. He always keeps a revolver in his pocket, and whomever in the palace he suspects he shoots.

VIII. The eighth cause of the horrors to the Armenians, these are come through the great powers of the European.

During the last several years Constantinople has been the great battle ground of European diplomacy. England was the first in the field. The occasion of her action was the destruction of the Armenian villages and the massacres of many of the people in the Kurdish mountains near Sassoun, in August and September, 1894. The facts were denied by the Turkish government, and she demanded an investigation and such reforms as should insure the safety and well-being of the Armenians. She invited Russia and France to unite with her in securing both these ends. They consented. Italy expressed a wish to join them, but this offer was declined. Austria and Germany were not invited, and did not wish to be, as they had no interest in Asiatic Turkey.

England, France and Russia worked together in apparent harmony, secured a Turkish commission of investigation and appointed their own delegates to oversee its action. This commission, appointed in November, 1894, continued its sittings until July, 1895, and a report of its doings has just been published in an English Blue Book. Meanwhile the English,

Russian and French ambassadors devoted their attention to the elaboration of a scheme of reforms for the six provinces in which the Armenians were most numerous. This was completed and presented to the Sultan as the minimum of reforms, which the three powers could accept in harmony and his immediate acceptance of them demanded. This was in May, 1895. After a delay of more than two weeks, the Sultan returned an evasive and unsatisfactory answer. Up to this point the three powers seem to have worked together in harmony. The other powers, when appealed to by the Sultan, declined to interfere.

The question then arose what was to be done. Should these demands be presented as an ultimatum, and the Sultan be forced to accept them and carry them out? or should they be left where they were as so much good advice, which he might take or reject? England was in favor of coercion, but Russia and France opposed it. Just at this time the Liberal government in England resigned: the Conservatives came in with a practical interregnum until after the election in July. Lord Salisbury took up the question as he found it. Russia and France persisted in their refusal to admit of the use of force, and gave this assurance to the Sultan. Still the three powers pressed their demands diplomatically, and the English fleet came into the vicinity of the Dardanelles. Germany expressed her sympathy with the Sultan, but still advised him to come to terms with the three powers. At the end of September came the outbreak at Constantinople and the massacre of some two hundred Armenians in the streets. Three weeks later the Sultan accepted, with some unimportant modifications, the scheme of reforms presented to him in May, 1895, and here ended the alliance of England, France and Russia. There had been no real harmony between them for some time. Russia and France remained in it not to help the Armenians, but to control the action of England, and, if possible, prevent her sending her fleet to Constantinople, still there was no positive acknowledged break.

Meanwhile there had been massacres at Trebezand, Ak-Hissar, Baiburt, Giumushkhane, Erzingan, Diarbekr, and other places, which showed that the situation was far more grave than any one in Europe had supposed.

The excitement in England was intense. It was believed that there was a deliberate purpose to exterminate the Armenians, and the English government believed that armed intervention was necessary to dethrone the Sultan, or at least to limit his power. Exactly what happened between the first of October and the middle of November between the great powers we do not know. There is reason to believe that Germany proposed to England to join the Triple Alliance, in which case the four powers would go to Constantinople together. England refused and Germany resented it, and threw all her influence into the scale with Russia. At this point was formed the concert of the six powers, which was simply a mutual agreement that no power should act independently, and all the fleets gathered in the Ægean to watch each other. By the end of December it was evident that nothing would be done, and one by one they stole silently away, leaving the Sultan apparently master of the situation. There is no doubt that all through the year the Sultan showed consummate skill in this diplomatic conflict, and a better knowledge of the situation than most of the statesmen concerned in it. Technically he won the battle. England has been beaten and humiliated and the Sultan is in close alliance with Russia, France and Germany, stronger, if he can trust his allies, than ever before. The Continental governments have had a perfectly free hand in this conflict, because there has been no popular feeling of sympathy for the Armenians. The Continental press has either ignored the massacres or represented them as due to the revolutionary spirit of the Armenians. "Any way," they have said, "who are the Armenians? What interest have we in these Asiatics?"

But can the Sultan trust his allies? In fact he has but one; France and Germany are simply bidding against one

another for the friendships of Russia and follow her lead at
Constantinople. The real victor in this conflict is not Turkey
but Russia—who has played the part of a disinterested friend
of the Sultan so well that she has for the first time in history
driven England off the field and became the sole protector of
the Ottoman Empire, thus realizing the dream of centuries.
The first result of this triumph is a close alliance of Russia
with Bulgaria, Servia and Montenegro, and the overthrow of
Austrian influence in the Balkan peninsular to be consum-
mated this week at Sofia.

Russia is now supreme in this part of the world and can
do what she pleases. What she will do with her newly acquired influence remains to be seen. She will do nothing
for the Armenians, that is certain. She has not professed any
interest in them. She has before her three possible courses
of action from which she must choose one. She may seize
upon the present opportunity, the best she has ever had to
come to Constantinople.

First, perhaps, as the friend and support of the Sultan;
but any way, come to stay. The alliance with the Balkan
states makes this easy, even if the Sultan should be inclined to
resist. But he will not. It is only necessary to stir up serious
trouble in Constantinople to make the coming appear as a
friendly act of a trusted ally. If no effort is made to put a
stop to the troubles in the interior or here, this will be an indication that this plan is in favor at the Russian embassy here,
if not at St. Petersburg, and may be realized soon.

Second, possibility for Russia is to make her alliance with
Turkey and the Balkan states as agreeable to them as possible,
to do her best to restore and preserve order, and with them
as allies to guard her rear and flank, to attack Austria and bring
all the Southern Slavs under her own rule, or at least under her
protection. This is the dream of the Pan-Slavists, who are
the strongest and most active party in Russia. This would
mean a general European war, for Germany and Italy are
bound by treaty to defend Austria from any such attack.

France would improve her opportunity to recover Alsace and
Lorraine. England pretends to believe that the old Austrian
Alliance is no longer of any value to her, but the chances are
that she would become involved in such a war.

The third possibility for Russia is to maintain the present
state of things here—to continue to play with France and Germany, giving encouragement to both and securing the aid of
both to destroy English influence in China and to gain a commanding position there herself, with some compensation to
France and Germany, this might lead to a war with England.

"It is plain that Russia cannot do more than one of these
things, and to decide which is the most desirable and practic-
able will demand the highest statesmanship. My own opinion is
that no deliberate choice will be made, but that, as in most
Russian affairs, the decision will be left to chance and be determined by some accident, by a massacre in Constantinople,
by some resentful action on the part of Austria in connection
with the Balkan states, or by some event in the far East.
Russia is never in a hurry. The Czar has determined to have
grand coronation ceremonies in May, and will hardly be inclined to stir up trouble anywhere before that time.

The great powers have each of them some general ideas
of what they consider to be their interests. Each has a policy
of some kind. But now that the telegraph has put an end to
all independent action on the part of ambassadors, and everything is managed by the foreign ministers, diplomacy has become a hand to mouth affair. There is very little planning
for the future or for the people of the East.

Listen to what the haughty young ruler of Germany says:
"It is better that the Armenians be killed than the peace of
Europe disturbed."

The Sultan, to begin with, has proved himself to be one
of the boldest and most skilful diplomatists in Europe, and
his point of view is so totally different from that of Christian
rulers that no one can calculate in what direction it will lead
him.

With such elements of uncertainty in the methods of diplomacy and in the men who direct it, it would be folly to venture upon any predictions for the future. Things may drift on for months or years very much as they are today, or some unforeseen incident may change the whole face of . Europe.

It is perfectly true that the government, whose deeds we have to impeach, is a Mohammedan government, and it is perfectly true that the sufferers under those outrages, under those actions, are Christian sufferers. The Mohammedan subjects of Turkey suffer a great deal, but what they suffer is only in the way of the ordinary excesses and defects of an intolerably bad government—perhaps the worst on the face of the earth. Well, I say, the great powers gave chance or privilege to Turkish Sultan to ruin himself, and also the population of Turkey.

CHAPTER IX.

THE MASSACRE AND MARTYRDOM OF ARMENIA.

Turkish atrocities in Armenia are not new things. The previous brief history of this people, especially since the introduction of Christianity into Armenia, has furnished the reader with sufficient facts to convince him that the real troubles and atrocities of this nation began from the time of their conversion to Christianity, and has come down to the present time.

What the Armenians are now is not less than what they have suffered in the fifth century from the hands of the fire-worshipping Persians. Had they then received Zoroastrianism, forced upon them, they might have changed the entire aspect of the history of Western Asia, or had they embraced Mohammedanism in the seventh century, when fanatic missionary soldiers of Mohammed fell upon them, sword in hand, and massacred thousands upon thousands in cold blood, because they refused to accept the sensual religion of a sensual and bloody man, again the history of Western Asia might have been differently written from the present. They have gone on for centuries and left but a fraction of the population it once had. But let us disregard old history and come to the subject of the present, those that were begun about the last of August, 1894, and to the end of August, 1896, which are horrible atrocities, and oppressions which had been done among the Armenians. Practically that begins with Hamid II., the present Sultan. He began his persecutions nearly twenty years ago, but on a small scale. He had continually devised new methods of getting rid of the Armenians without responsibility. Finally he hit on the plan of arming the Kurds and letting them loose with full power to do their worst. He summoned the Kurdish chiefs, hundreds of them, to Constantinople, and entertained them in the palace, armed them with modern rifles, and sent them to Armenia on their mission. The pretence under which he did it was worthy of him; he called them the "Hamidish Cavalry," and pretended that they were a sort of mounted police who were to keep order and protect the Armenians, but the Armenians knew well what they were for. The European travellers and newspaper correspondents took it all seriously and talked of his "civilizing the Kurds," etc. Now these were only the chiefs; each chief had a large following of tribesmen, so that about 30,000 Kurds in all were given arms and ordered to go to work exterminating the Armenians.

This work began in 1891, but on a small scale, and in a very crafty way so that it should not have the appearance of a premeditated massacre; then it was stopped till about 1894, when they were encouraged to begin again, publicly, and with full swing. It was decided to begin in Sassoun, a district far from the sea, with no roads and a sparse population; if successful in escaping the report there, he could carry out the massacre through all Armenia, for which "reforms" were asked and promised. He ordered Zekü Pasha to have his soldiers ready, and meantime to have the "Hamidish Cavalry," the Kurdish chiefs and tribesmen ready to attack and kill all the Armenians in Sassoun. This city lies between Moosh and Bitlis, in a mountainous country, and the Armenians in Sassoun are almost a brave people. The district has about sixty villages and towns, and more than 12,000 people in 1894 had been killed. The chief commander, Zekü Pasha, and the regular soldiers and the armed Kurds, surrounded the district from all sides, and in about a month had slaughtered the entire population. It was reported that Zekü carried on his breast an order from the Sultan as follows: "Whoever spares man, woman or child is disloyal." After he had finished his task he received great rewards from the Sultan, and is now one of his most esteemed commanders. Before the massacre of the people at Sassoun, the Sultan's order to Zekü Pasha was to

spare neither man, woman nor child, but as the men met the
enemy first, they were killed first. When the women's turn
came, the Turks and Kurds abused all they could get hold of
and then told them that if they would deny Christ and accept
Mohammedianism, and become their wives, they should live, but
if they refused, every one of them, according to the Sultan's
order, should be killed. "Now," said they, "choose between
Islam and death." The noble Armenian Christian women
said: "We are Christians; we can never deny Christ. Jesus
Christ is our Saviour, He came down from heaven and died
on the cross for us; for that dying and loving Christ, we are
Christians, we are ready to die for Him who died for us," and
they added further "We are no better than our husbands were;
you killed them, please kill us too." Then the horrible
butchery began on these defenseless women. A good many of
them were slaughtered and a good many of them ran to
different churches, hoping that perhaps they might find protection in some way in those holy walls, or hoping that God in
his great mercy might shelter them, but the ferocious Kurds
and Turkish soldiers pursued them, sword in hand, violated
them even in the churches, and cut their throats there until
the floors were streaming with blood, then they poured kerosene on the building and burned them.

They went to one village and killed every man, the
women, of course, knowing that their fate was soon to be worse
than their husband's. One of the leading women named
Shaheg, perceiving that the Turks and Kurds were getting
ready to seize and ravish them, called the other women and
said: "Sisters, our husband's are killed, and you know what is
in store for us and our children. Don't let us fall into the
hands of those savage beasts, we have to die anyway, and can
die easier, and without being defiled first, and perhaps tortured. Let us go to the precipice and jump off." So saying,
she took her baby on her arm, ran to the rock, and threw herself over. The others followed her, and thus all were killed.
In the meantime the Turks captured many boys and girls, six

or eight of ten years of age, held them by an arm or foot, and hacked them to pieces with their swords. Sometimes they stood the boys in a row and shot them, to see how many could be killed by a single bullet. They wrenched babies from their mothers' arms, cut their throats while the mothers shrieked and pleaded, and boiling them in kettles, forced the mothers to eat the flesh. They cut open women about to become mothers, tore out the unborn babes, and marched triumphantly with the ghastly trophies on their spears, crucifying head downward, and pouring boiling water on them, leaving them so till death came; flaying alive, cutting off arms, feet, nose, ears and other members, and leaving them to die; thrusting red-hot wires into and through their bodies. They pulled out the eyes of several Christian pastors, saying: "Now dance for us." They poured kerosene on them and burned them to death. They put a Bible and a cross before others and ordered them to first spit and then trample on both and deny Christ, on their refusal they were butchered. The handsomest girls and young matrons were not murdered, but worse; each one was kept as a spoil of some Turk or Kurd, who carried her to his house and made a slave and concubine of her.

This is another specimen of Mohammed religion, and it all happens because the Armenians are Christians. They boasted of it, they plumed themselves on it, they praised the Sultan for ordering them to do it, and he praised them for doing it and decorated all the officers.

THE MASSACRE OF 1894.

"The Armenians of Sassoun were fully aware of the hostile intention of the government, but they could not imagine it to be one of utter extermination.

"The Porte had prepared its plans, Sassoun was doomed. The Kurds were to come in much greater number, the government was to furnish the provision and ammunition, and the regular army was to second them in case of need.

"The various tribes received invitations to take part in the great expedition, and the chiefs, with their men, arrived one after the other. The total number of the Kurds who took part in the campaign may be estimated at 30,000. The Armenians believed in the beginning that they had to do only with the Kurds. They found out later that an Ottoman regular army, with provisions, rifles, cannons, and kerosene oil, was standing at the back of the Kurds.

"The plan was to destroy first Shenig, Semal, Guelliegoozan, Aliantz, etc., and then to proceed toward Dalvorig. The Kurds, notwithstanding their immense numbers, proved to be unequal to the task. The Armenians held their own, and the Kurds got worsted. After a two weeks' fight between Kurd and Armenian, the regular army entered into an active compaign. Mountain pieces began to thunder. The Armenians, having nearly exhausted their ammunition, took to flight. Kurd and Turk pursued them, and massacred men, women and children. The houses were searched and then set on fire. Certain groups of men, with tax receipts in their hands, went to the camp and asked to be protected, but were slaughtered.

"A great number of villages outside of the Dalvorig district, which had in no wise been concerned in the conflicts of the previous years, were also attacked, to the unspeakable horror of the population. The troops climbed up even the Mount Antok, where a multitude of fugitives had taken refuge, and massacred them. A number of women and girls were taken to the church of Guelliegoozan, and after being frightfully abused, were tortured to death.

"When the work of destruction was nearly accomplished in the other districts, some of the Kurdish armies were set on Dalvorig. The people defended themselves against the overwhelming number of the barbarians, but after four or five days they saw other tribes and regular Turkish troops marching on them from every side, and they took to flight, but were overtaken and massacred. The scene was most horrible. The enemy took a special delight in butchering the Dalvorig people. An immense crowd of Turkish and Kurdish soldiery fell upon the villages, busily searching the houses and rooting out hidden treasures, and then setting fire to the village. While the troops were so occupied, a number of the fugitives fled wildly to get out of the district, and tried to hide themselves in caves, between rocks, or among bushes. Three days after the complete destruction of the Dalvorig villages, the Kurds and the regular soldiers divided among themselves the result of the plunder, and the Kurds returned to their own mountains."

As my use of English is defective, I take the liberty here of quoting from a long letter by E. J. Dillon to the Contemporary Review, January, 1896.

Dr. Dillon is an Englishman who was the special correspondent of the London "Daily Telegraph," a most accurate and conscientious reporter, who writes as an eye-witness:

"If a detailed description were possible of the horrors which our exclusive attention to our own mistaken interests let loose upon Turkish Armenians, there is not a man within the kingdom of Great Britain whose heart-strings would not be touched and thrilled by the gruesome stories of which it would be composed.

"During all those seventeen years, written law, traditional custom, the fundamental maxims of human and divine justice were suspended in favor of a Mohammedan saturnalia. The Christians, by whose toil and thrift the empire was held together, were despoiled, beggared, chained, beaten, and banished or butchered. First their movable wealth was seized, then their landed property was confiscated, next the absolute necessaries of life were wrested from them, and finally honor, liberty and life were taken with as little ado as if these Christian men and women were wasps or mosquitoes. Thousands of Armenians were thrown into prison by governors like Tahsin Pasha and Bahri Pasha, and tortured and terrorized till they delivered up the savings of a lifetime, and the support of the helpless families, to ruffianly parasites. Whole villages were attacked in broad daylight by the Imperial Kurdish cavalry without pretext or warning, the male inhabitants turned adrift or killed, and their wives and daughters transformed into instruments to glut the foul lusts of these beastial murderers. In a few years the provinces were decimated, Aloghkerd, for instance, being almost entirely 'purged' of Armenians. Over 20,000 woe-stricken wretches, once healthy and well-to-do, fled to Russia or Persia in rags and misery, deformed, diseased, or dying; on the way they were seized over and over again by the soldiers of the Sultan, who deprived them of the little money they possessed, nay, of the clothes they were wearing, outraged the married women in the presence of their sons and daughters, deflowered the tender girls before the eyes of their mothers and brothers, and then drove them over the frontier to starve and die. Those who remained for a time behind were no better off. Kurdish brigands lifted the last cows and goats of the peasants, carried away their carpets and their valuables, raped their daughters and dishonored their wives. Turkish tax-gatherers followed these, gleaning what the brigands had left, and, lest anything should escape their avarice, bound the men, flogged them till their bodies were a bloody, mangled mass, cicatrized the wounds with red-hot ramrods, plucked out their beards, hair by hair, tore the flesh from their limbs with pincers, and, often, even then, dissatisfied with the financial results of their exertions, hung the men whom they had thus beggared and maltreated from the rafters of the room, and kept them there to witness with burning shame, impotent rage, and incipient madness, the dishonoring of their wives and the deflowering of their daughters, some of whom died miserably during the hellish outrage.

"In accordance with the plan of extermination, which has been carried out with such signal success during these long years of Turkish vigor and English sluggishness, all those Armenians who possessed money, or money's worth, were for a time allowed to purchase immunity from prison, and from all that prison life in Asia Minor implies. But as soon as terror

GROUP OF ARMENIANS AT VAN.

and summary confiscation took the place of slow and elaborate extortion, the gloomy dungeons of Erzeroum, Erzinghan, Marsovan, Hassankaleh and Van were filled till there was no place to sit down, and scarcely sufficient standing room. And this means more than English people can realize, or any person believe who has not actually witnessed it. It would have been a torture for Turkish troopers and Kurdish brigands, but it was more than death to the educated school-masters, missionaries, priests and physicians, who were immured in these noisome hot-beds of infection, and forced to sleep night after night standing on their feet, leaning against the foul, reeking corner of the wall which all the prisoners were compelled to use as ...
The very worst class of Tartar and Kurdish criminals were turned in here to make these hell-chambers more unbearable to the Christians. And the experiment was everywhere successful. Human hatred and diabolical spite, combined with the most disgusting sights, and sounds, and stenches, with their gnawing hunger and their putrid food, their parching thirst and the slimy water, fit only for sewers, rendering their agony maddening. Yet these were not criminals nor alleged criminals, but upright Christian men, who were never even accused of an infraction of the law. No man who has not seen these prisons with his own eyes, and heard these prisoners with his own ears, can be expected to conceive, much less realize, the sufferings inflicted and endured. The loathsome diseases, whose terrible ravages were freely displayed; the still more loathsome vices, which were continually and openly practiced; the horrible blasphemies, revolting obscenities, and ribald jests which alternated with cries of pain, songs of vice, and prayers to the unseen God, made these prisons, in some respects, nearly as bad as the Black Hole of Calcutta, and in others infinitely worse. In one corner of this foul fever-nest a man might be heard moaning and groaning with the pain of a shattered arm or leg; in another, a youth is convulsed with the death spasms of cholera or poison; in the centre, a knot of Turks, whose dull eyes are fired with bestial lust, surround a Christian boy, who

pleads for mercy with heart-harrowing voice while the human fiends actually outrage him to death.

"Into these prisons venerable old ministers of religion were dragged from their churches, teachers from their schools, missionaries from their meeting-houses, physicians and peasants from their firesides. Those among them who refused to denounce their friends, or consent to some atrocious crime, were subjected to horrible agonies. Many a one, for instance, was put into a sentry-box bristling with sharp spikes, and forced to stand there motionless, without food or drink, for twenty-four and even thirty-six hours, was revived with stripes whenever he fell fainting to the prickly floor, and was carried out unconscious at the end. It was thus that hundreds of Armenian Christians, whose names and histories are on record, suffered for refusing to sign addresses to the Sultan accusing their neighbor and relatives of high treason. It was thus that Azo was treated by his judges, the Turkish officials, Talib Eenffdi, Captain Reshid, and Captain Hadji Fehim Agha, for declining to swear away the lives of the best men of his village. A whole night was spent in torturing him. He was first bastinadoed in a room close to which his female relatives and friends were shut up so that they could hear his cries. Then he was stripped naked, two poles extending from his armpits to his feet were placed on each side of his body and tied tightly. His arms were next stretched out horizontally and poles arranged to support his hands. This living cross was then bound to a pillar, and the flogging began. The whips left livid traces behind. The wretched man was unable to make the slightest movement to ease his pain. His features alone, hideously distorted, revealed the anguish he endured. The louder he cried, the more heavily fell the whip. Over and over again he entreated his tormentors to put him out of pain, saying, 'If you want my death kill me with a bullet, but for God's sake don't torture me like this!' His head alone being free, he at last, maddened by excruciating pain, endeavored to dash out his brains against the pillar, hoping in this way

to end his agony. But this consummation was hindered by
the police. They questioned him again; but in spite of his
condition, Azo replied as before: 'I cannot defile my soul with
the blood of innocent people. I am a Christian.' Enraged at
his obstinacy, Talib Effendi, the Turkish official, ordered the
application of other and more effective tortures. Pincers were
fetched to pull out his teeth, but Azo remaining firm, this
method was not long persisted in. Then Talib commanded
his servants to pluck out the prisoner's moustachios by the
roots, one hair at a time. This order the gendarmes executed,
with roars of infernal laughter. But this treatment proving
equally ineffectual, Talib instructed the men to cauterize the
unfortunate victim's body. A spit was heated in the fire.
Azo's arms were freed from their supports, and two brawny
policemen approached, one on each side, and seized him.
Meanwhile another gendarme held to the middle of the
wretched man's hand the glowing spit. While his flesh was
thus burning, the victim shouted out in agony, 'For the love
of God kill me at once!'

"Then the executioners, removing the red-hot spit from
his hands, applied it to his breast, then to his back, his face,
his feet, and other parts. After this, they forced open his
mouth, and burned his tongue with red-hot pincers. During
these inhuman operations, Azo fainted several times, but on
recovering consciousness maintained the same inflexibility of
purpose.

Meanwhile, in the adjoining apartment, a heartrending
scene was being enacted. The women and the children,
terrified by the groans and cries of the tortured man, fainted.
When they revived, they endeavored to rush out and call for
help, but the gendarmes, stationed at the door, barred their
passage, and brutally pushed them back.

"Nights were passed in such hellish orgies and days in in-
venting new tortures or refining upon the old, with an ingenuity which reveals unimagined strata of malignity in the

human heart. The results throw the most sickening horrors of the Middle Ages into the shade. Some of them cannot be described, nor even hinted at. The shock to people's sensibilities would be too terrible. And yet they were not merely described to, but endured by men of education and refinement, whose sensibilities were as delicate as ours.

"And when the prisons in which these and analogous doings were carried on had no more room for new-comers, some of the least obnoxious of its actual inmates were released for a bribe, or, in case of poverty, were expeditiously poisoned off.

"In the homes of these wretched people the fiendish fanatics were equally active and equally successful. Family life was poisoned at its very source. Rape and dishonor, with nameless accompaniments, menaced almost every girl and woman in the land. They could not stir out of their houses in broad daylight to visit the bazaars, or to work in the fields, nor even lie down at night in their own homes, without fearing the fall of that Damocles' sword ever suspended over their heads. Tender youth, childhood itself, was no guarantee. Children were often married at the age of eleven, even ten, in the vain hope of lessening this danger. But the protection of a husband proved unavailing; it merely meant one murder more, and one 'Christian dog' less. A bride would be married in church yesterday, and her body would be devoured by the beasts and birds of prey to-morrow,—a band of ruffians, often officials, having within the intervening forty-eight hours seized her and outraged her to death. Others would be abducted, and, having for weeks been subjected to the loathsome lusts of lawless Kurds, would end by abjuring their God and embracing Islam; not from any vulgar motive of gain, but to escape the burning shame of returning home as pariahs and lepers, to be shunned by those near and dear to them forever. Little girls of five and six were frequently forced to be present during these horrible scenes of lust, and they, too, were often sacrificed before the eyes of their mothers, who would have gladly, madly accepted death, ay, and damnation, to save their tender offspring from the corroding poison.

"One of the abducted young women who, having been outraged by the son of the Deputy-Governor of Khnouss, Hussein Bey, returned, a pariah, and is now alone in the world, lately appealed to her English sisters for such aid as a heathen would give to a brute, and she besought it in the name of our common God. Lucine Mussegh—this is the name of that outraged young woman whose Protestant education gave her, as she thought, a special claim to act as a spokes-woman of Armenian mothers and daughters—Lucine Mussegh besought, last March, the women of England to obtain for the women of Armenia the 'privilege' of living a pure and chaste life! This was the boon which she craved—but did not, could not obtain. The interests of 'higher politics,' the civilizing missions of the Christian powers, are, it seems, incompatible with it! 'For the love of the God whom we worship in common,' wrote this outraged, but still hopeful, Armenian lady, 'help us, Christian sisters! Help us before it is too late, and take the thanks of the mothers, the wives, the sisters, and the daughters of my people, and with them the gratitude of one for whom, in spite of her youth, death would come as a happy release.'

"Neither the Christian sisters nor the Christian brethren in England have seen their way to comply with this strange request. But it may perhaps interest Lucine Messegh to learn that the six great powers of Europe are quite unanimous, and are manfully resolved, come what will, to shield His Majesty the Sultan from harm, to support his rule, and to guarantee his kingdom from disintegration. These are objects worthy of the attention of the great powers; as for the privilege of leading pure and chaste lives—they cannot be importuned about such private matters.

"In due time they began. Over 60,000 Armenians have been butchered, and the massacres are not quite ended yet. In Trebizond, Erzeroum, Erzinghan, Hassankalek, and numberless other places the Christians were crushed like grapes during the vintage. The frantic mob, seething and surging in the streets of the cities, swept down upon the defenseless Armenians, plundered their shops, gutted their houses, then joked and jested with the terrified victims, as cats play with mice. As rapid, whirling motion produces apparent rest, so the wild frenzy of those fierce fanatical crowds resulting in a condition of seeming calmness, composure, and gentleness, which, taken in connection with the unutterable brutality of their acts, was of a nature to freeze men's blood with horror. In many cases they almost caressed their victims, and actually encouraged them to hope while preparing the instruments of slaughter."

After the horrible scenes at Sassoun, and other places, the Armenian protests shamed the European powers, who signed the treaty of Berlin, to send a commission and investigate the atrocities. It found the stories quite true, laid the facts before the Sultan—and that was the end of it. The Armenians asked, "Since you admit the truth of these things, why do you not punish the criminals, stop the outrages, and compel the payment of indemnity to those who were outraged and who lost their dear ones and their property?" The powers were deaf to all this. Then the Armenians prepared an appeal (several months ago) and carried it to the Sublime Porte, asking it to do them justice. As soon as the Sultan heard of this, he ordered his soldiers to fire on them if they presented it. The appeal was presented, and before the eyes of the European Ambassadors in Constantinople, the brave soldiers of the kind-hearted Sultan butchered about 3,000 Armenian Christians, several thousand were imprisoned, and several hundred were murdered in the Central Prison. Then the cold, wise, and considerate European powers began to move very slowly, not for the sake of the Armenians, but for their own, their citizens in Constantinople and elsewhere.

They ordered the Sultan to reform Armenia, brought their fleets to the Dardanelles near Constantinople to overawe him, prepared a scheme of reform for Armenia, and made huge threats to the Sultan if he did not accept it. But he knew that this pretended concert of the powers for Armenian reform was a mere trick and a sham, as I have persistently asserted all

along in the face of my hopeful European and American
friends; in fact, the Russian government at this very time was
secretly urging him to stand firm and refuse to accept the reforms. He did so, broached a scheme of his own as a substitute, and the powers accepted it as such; and then the whole
thing was dropped, the Sultan did nothing whatever about it,
as he had never intended to. The European countries were
hoodwinked, and the Armenian massacres and conflagrations,
plundering and deflowering, went on at a greater pace than
ever. Then the powers dropped the Armenian question, and
took up that of gunboats in the Bosphorus, to protect their
citizens against a rising in Constantinople; that they forced the
Sultan to permit, because their own interests were concerned
in it,—which shows that they could have forced him to stop
exterminating the Armenians if they had cared. All joined in
this except Germany; the German Emperor is the Sultan's
friend, and backs him up. So now, Germany, Russia, and the
Sultan are hand in hand, leagued to prevent any of the miserable victims of his tyranny from escaping his clutches, and the
Sultan has the best possible encouragement to go on killing
the Armenians. The German Emperor says, "Better the Armenians be killed than have a war in Europe and lose the
lives of some of my soldiers." The Czar says, "Time must be
given to the Sultan to reform his country." Lord Salisbury
says, "The Sultan has promised, and we must wait and see
what he will do." And the Sultan, cursing every Emperor
and lord of them all as a set of Christian hogs, orders the soldiers and the Kurds to go on with the good work in Armenia.
And when we come to America, the Monroe doctrine obliges it
to quarrel over Venezuela, and not only refuse help itself, but
give Lord Salisbury a good excuse to give none either.

Such is the situation; the massacres are going on in Armenia and the Armenians in despair are crying, "O Lord, how
long, how long!"

Mass meetings are good as far as they go; raising money
and sending it to relieve the Armenians is good as far as it

goes; the Red Cross Society is good as far as it goes; there are no objections to any of them; they are all noble and Christian. But, reader, don't you think all these good movements with good motives will hurt the Armenian cause, as there is nothing to aid that cause directly? All these mass-meetings merely irritate the Sultan into carrying on the murders more strenuously, since there is no force back of them. Don't you think the Armenian question being discussed in the United States Congress, and resolutions made without any action, will hurt the Armenians more than anything else? If you can't tread down the Sultan, don't stir him up. Miss Clara Barton, that noble woman, is in Armenia to help the Armenians. The Red Cross Society is there and is feeding the Armenians. I thank her, every Armenian thanks her. But do you think that that will relieve the situation? Spring has come, and what now? Will the Armenians have any crops? Did they, or could they sow any seed? Is there any farmer left alive? Has any farmer, if he is alive, any oxen or horses? If he has, will he dare go to his field, sow, reap, and thresh? Reader, consider all these things, and reconsider them, and I am sure you will come to the same conclusion I did many years ago, that Turkey does not need a Red Cross Society, not like the mediæval crusades, but a Protestant American crusade in the nineteenth century. Let me illustrate this Armenian question by the following parable:—

Suppose a lamb is torn by a wolf, and the wolf lies in wait to finish it. You go to the lamb with a bundle of grass in your hand, pat it and say, "Here, poor lamb, I pity you, I give you grass; take it and eat." Then you leave the lamb and go away. Do you think you have helped the lamb? As soon as you have gone the wolf will come and tear the lamb to pieces. If you are going to help the lamb, you must kill the wolf, else no matter how much grass you give the wounded lamb, it will do it no good. You will do no good by sending Red Cross societies to Armenia to feed the Armenians if you have not the power of the will to keep the wild beasts off. You will feed them, and then the wolves will kill them

Now I will pass in review some of the leading cities in Armenia where there have been great persecutions. Before beginning, however, I must state that it is impossible to give an accurate census of the population in the Armenian cities, or the number who have been massacred; for the Turkish government never takes a correct census, and never gives or will give the true number of those it has murdered. But I think I can make a fair approximation of both. I will begin with the city of Harpoot.

HARPOOT AND ITS VICINITY.

This is one of the most important Armenian districts, because the Armenians outnumber the Mohammedans there; in the cities the Turks are the more numerous, but there are many Armenian town and villages which make up. The district has about 150,000 people, most of them Armenians, and about 40,000 were killed in the recent massacre. Harpoot is built on three hills, and has a commanding view. Here is located a great American missionary institution, the Euphrates College; it has three departments, the college, the Theological Seminary, and the Girls' Seminary. There were twelve buildings, eight of which were burned in the outrages, a loss of $100,000.

Almost all the outlying villages were burned, and the movables carried off. Women were made preys, boys and girls were kidnapped; the horrors can never be described. I give here a few words from a private letter, written to a Mohammedan Turk to his brother in this country. I have the letter in my possession, written in the Turkish language. He says:

"My dear brother: All the Christian villages which belong to Harpoot district, we plundered and destroyed, and killed the inhabitants. We killed them both with our swords and with our rifles. The bullets of our rifles poured upon them like rain; none of them are left, neither any dwelling was left, we burnt all their houses. We thank God that not a single Mohammedan was killed. Everywhere throughout Armenia the Christians were punished in the same manner."

Another testimony from another Mohammedan, an officer; he says nearly 40,000 were killed in Harpoot province, February 26, 1896:—

"A petition in behalf of the Armenians was given to the powers in the hope of improving their condition. An imperial firman was issued for carrying out the reforms suggested by the powers. On this account the Turkish population was much excited, and thought that an Armenian principality was to be established, and they began to show great hostility to the poor Armenians, who had been obedient to them and with whom they had lived in peace for more than 600 years. To the anger of the people were added the permission and help of the government; and so, before the reforms were undertaken, the whole Turkish population was aroused, with the evil intent of obliterating the Armenian name; and so the Turks of the province, joining with the neighboring Kurdish tribes by the thousand, armed with weapons which are allowed only to the army, and with the help and under the guidance of Turkish officials, in an open manner, in the daytime, attacked the Armenian houses, shops, stores, monasteries, churches, schools, and committed the fearful atrocities set forth in the accompanying table. They killed bishops, priests, teachers, and common people with every kind of torture, and they showed special spite toward ecclesiastics by treating their bodies with extra indignity, and in many cases they did not allow their bodies to be buried. Some they burned, and some they gave as food to dogs and wild beasts.

"They plundered churches and monasteries, and they took all the property of the common people, their flocks and herds, their ornaments and their money, their house furnishings and their food, and even the clothing of the men and women in

their flight. Then after plundering them, they burned many
houses, churches, monasteries, schools and markets, sometimes using petroleum, which they had brought with them to
hasten the burning; large stone churches which would not
burn they ruined in other ways.

"Priests, laymen, women, and even small children were
made Moslems by force. They put white turbans on the men
and circumcised them in a cruel manner. They cut the hair
of the women in bangs, like that of Moslem women, and made
them go through the Mohammedan prayers. Married women
and girls were defiled, against the sacred law, and some were
married by force, and are still detained in Turkish houses.
Especially in Palu, Severek, Malatia, Arabkir, and Choon-
koosh, many women and girls were taken to the soldiers' bar-
racks and dishonored. Many, to escape, threw themselves
into the Euphrates, or committed suicide in other ways.

"It is clear that the majority of those killed in Harpoot,
Severek, Husenik, Malatia, and Arabkir were killed by the
soldiers, and also that the schools and churches of the missionaries and Gregorians in the upper quarter of Harpoot City, together with the houses, were set on fire by cannon balls.

"It is impossible to state the amount of pecuniary loss.
The single city of Egin has given 1,200 (some say 1,500) Turkish pounds as a ransom.

"These events have occurred for the reasons I have mentioned. I wish to show by this statement, which I have written from love to humanity, that the Armenians gave no occasion for these attacks."

The Turk, whose document is thus translated, figures that
the total deaths in the province of Harpoot during the scenes,
have been 39,334; the wounded 8,000; houses burned, 28,562;
and the number of the destitutes is 94,870.

In a letter just received (Jan. 18, 1896) from the Rev.
H. N. Barnum, D.D., of Harpoot, Eastern Turkey, where the
property of the American Board was burned, he says that
reports have been secured from 176 villages in the vicinity of

Harpoot. These villages contained 15,400 houses belonging
to Christians. Of this number 7,054 have been burned, and
15,845 persons are reported killed. Dr. Barnum adds: "The
reality, I fear, will prove to be much greater."

The statistics of the last outrages will never be accurately
known, but the most careful figures thus far received, the partial, are as told. In the table below I will try to show the population of the ten provinces and the houses and shops plundered
and destroyed or burned in the ten provinces, namely: Erze-
rim, Bitlis, Diarbekr, Van, Harpoot, Sivas, Trebizond, Angora, Adana, and Aleppo:

Total population of the ten provinces............... 5,898,300
Armenians in the ten provinces................... 1,192,000
Total houses and shops plundered and destroyed or
 burned in the provinces.................... 62,661
Number killed in the ten provinces............. 83,895
Number forced to accept Islam in the ten provinces 40,950
Number left entirely destitute in the ten provinces.. 315,060
Number of the widow women.................. 65,650
Number of Armenian Orphans................. 55,000

It thus appears that about nine-tenths of the outrages occurred within the first six provinces to which the reform scheme
applied. The Sultan professed to accept the reforms on October 16th, 1896, and the above figures show with what energy,
zeal and good faith he carried them out; for most of the work
was done within two months of that date. There can be no
doubt that the Sultan deserves credit for these "reforms," for
he claims it himself, assuring Lord Salisbury, in a letter made
public at his request, that they were being executed under his
personal direction. Kurds and soldiers have constantly declared that they were simply obeying the Sultan's orders and
that this was the case is clear from the fact that no one has
been punished for disobedience, not even the officials in whose
presence the American colony at Harpoot was bombarded,

plundered and burnt out of home 1805 in Nov. It has repeatedly been preached that these outbreaks were carefully pre-arranged by disarming Christians and by prescribing limits as to place, time, duration and method of execution.

It is from this spirit, the book of Koran, that the blood of many innocent persons has been shed in Turkey; it is from this spirit that children and delicate women have been ill treated and butchered.

Let it be fully understood throughout the Christian world that the massacre is a religious demand which the Turks have to complete.

As a Christian tries to be faithful to Christ and his teachings, so the Turks are trying to be faithful to their prophet and his teachings also.

They go to the mosques and pray "Allah (God) help me or help us, strengthen our hands and sharpen our swords to kill the infidel Armenians." Then they come out from the mosques and begin to kill, plunder, outrage and commit every sort of indescribable atrocities on the peaceable and defenceless Armenians; but it will grow worse than ever since so called Christian nations have given the Sultan public notice that they will not interfere with him. Do not be deceived by his lying reports. There were no Armenian rebellions; they could not rebel; they did not kill the Turks; they never dreamed of such madness. This awful fate has fallen on them purely and simply for being Christians.

This is the Fetva or secret sentence which comes out from the Shaikhull Islam: If the Giavoure or Kaffirs, which means blasphemers, do not accept the true religion they should be killed and their property be appropriated by the true believers.

Of course they cannot help it; it is their faith, a religion for barbarians.

Their teachers or Hojas go to the mosques and preach to them this way: "You Mohammedans love your fellow believers, but hate and kill all others; they are Giavoures, heathen dogs and hogs." To kill a Christian is just the same as to kill a hog for them.

The Hojas say that first you ask them to accept our faith; if they do you must not harm them, but if they will not, kill them, because they have no right to live in a Mohammedan country. It is a great virtue the more Christians you kill, and the greater reward you will have from Allah (or God) and his prophet Mohammed.

The Turks slaughter Armenians to earn this reward; there is no nationality like Turks which ever respects or gratify the females.

If a woman falls into their hands she need not hope to keep her virtue and religion; they violate her first, then force her to become a Mohammedan after all.

In the years of 1894 and 1895 in a good many places in Armenia or Turkey, a number of able-bodied young Armenians were captured, bound, covered with brushwood and burned alive, but thousands surrendered themselves and plead for mercy. Many of them were shot down on the spot and the remainder were dispatched with sword and bayonet.

Lots of women, variously estimated from 60 to 160, were locked up in a church and the soldiers were commanded to let loose, kill them. Most of them were outraged to death in a different way.

Once, when a number of young women were in one place, locked up, the Turks advised them that if they were carried off to the harems or their houses they could get along with them very nicely, but if you refused you would be killed, so they did.

Children were placed in a row, one behind another, and a bullet fired through the line, apparently to see how many could be shot down with one bullet; houses were surrounded by soldiers, set on fire and the inmates forced back into the flames at the point of the bayonet as they tried to escape. A number of men of one village, during their escape, took the women and children, about five hundred in number, and placed them in a sort of grotto in a ravine; after several days the soldiers found them and butchered those who had not died of hunger.

Fifty young women and girls were selected from one village and placed in a church, when the soldiers were ordered to do with them as they liked, after which they were butchered.

In another village fifty choice women were set aside and urged to change their faith and become Hanums (or lady) in Turkish harems, but they indignantly refused to deny Christ, preferring the fate of their fathers and husbands. People were crowded into the houses, which were then set on fire; in one instance a little boy ran out of the flames, but was caught on a bayonet and thrown back. Children were frequently held up by the hair and cut in two, or had their jaws torn apart. Women with children were ripped open, and older children were pulled apart by their legs.

A handsome recently wedded couple fled to a hill top; soldiers followed and told them that they were pretty and would be spared if they would accept Islamism, but the thought of the horrible death they knew would follow did not prevent them from confessing Christ.

"THE INEXPIABLE WRONG, THE UNUTTERABLE SHAME."

If the Turks and the Kurds only killed and killed clean, there would be less indignation in the heart of mankind. But they, of all savages, least hearken to the well-known prayer—

"Spare us the inexpiable wrong, the unutterable shame
That turns the coward's heart to steel, the sluggard's blood to
    flames."

In all the atrocities of the Armenian charnel-house nothing can for a moment vie in hideous and unspeakable horror the continuous and never-ending string of narratives of the foulest of outrages on women and children.

It is assumed too often that the continual liability to violation with impunity of generation after generation would have somewhat deadened the sense of female honour in the unfortunate Armenians. Dr. Dillon, however, confirming many other witnesses, says that this is by no means the case.

I have seen and conversed with hundreds and hundreds of Armenian women lately, and I have found no signs of the tempering process. Whatever vices or virtues may be predicated of Armenian women, chastity must be numbered among their essential characteristics. They carry it to an incredible extreme. In many places an Armenian woman never speaks to any man but her husband, unless the latter is present. Even to her nearest and dearest male relatives and connections she has nothing to say; and her purity, in the slums of Erzeroum as in the valleys of Sassoum, is above suspicion. Yet these are the people who are being continually outraged by Kurds and Turks, oftentimes until death releases them.

"English people have not even a remote notion of the extent to which young married women and girls are outraged all over Armenia by Turkish soldiers, imperial Zaptiehs, Kurdish officers and brigands;—and outraged with such accompaniments of nameless brutality that their agonies often culminate in a horrible death. Girls of eleven and twelve—nay, of nine—are torn from their families and outraged in this way by a band of 'men' whose names are known, and whose deeds are approved by the representatives of law and order. Indeed, these representatives are themselves the monsters, the bestial poison of whose loathsome passion is destroying 'the subtle, pure, and innocent spirit of life.'

"Rape, violation, outrages that have no name, and whose authors should have no mercy, are become the commonplaces of daily life in Armenia. And the Turkish 'gentleman' smiles approval. I have myself, says Dr. Dillon, collected over 300 of these cases, and I have heard of countless others.

"The following case is one in which I took a very lively interest because I am well acquainted with the victim and her family. Her name is Lucine Mussegh, her native village Khnoossaberd, Born in 1878, Lucine was sent at an early age Armenian Missionary school at Erzeroum, where she was taught the doctrines of evangelical Christianity, her father, Aghadjan Kemalian, having always manifested a strong sympathy for Protestantism. Armenian parents are continually scheming for the purpose of shielding their daughters from violation by the Turks and Kurds. Lucine, to escape this danger, was taken from school at the age of fourteen, and wedded to a boy of her own age, Milikean by name, and having lived some time with him under his father's roof, was sent to the Protestant school once more. One night, during her husband's absence from home, she was seized by some men, dragged by the hair, gagged, and taken to the house of Hussni Bey. This man is the son of the Deputy-Governor of the place. He dishonored the young woman and sent her home next day, but her husband refused to receive her any more, and she is now friendless and alone in the world.

"Lucine's father presented a complaint to the colonel of the Hamidehs, and a petition to the parish priest. The Metropolitan Archbishop of Erzeroum likewise took the matter in hand, and appealed to the Governor-General of the Vilayet, and to the Court Khnouss. But all to no purpose. Lucine is now a pariah. In her Appeal to the Women of England, which is too long and too naive to find a place here, Lucine says:

We suffered in patience when our corn, butter, and honey were seized, and we were left poor and hungry; we bowed our heads in sorrowful resignation when our kith and kin were cut down by the Kurds and Turks. Are we also to be silent and submissive now that our race is being poisoned at its source? Now that child-mothers and baby-daughters are being defiled and brutalised by savages? Say, Christian sisters, is there in truth no remedy? . . . . We ask for no revenge, for no privileges; we ask only that . . . . but need I be more explicit to English matrons, wives and sisters? . . . . Although we are Armenians we are Christians; I was brought up in a Protestant school, as you were; I drew my moral sustenance from the Bible, as you did; I was taught to feel and think, as you were . . . For the love of God, then, whom we worship in common, help us, Christian sisters, before it is too

late, and take the thanks of the motherss, wives, sisters, and
daughters of my people, and with them the gratitude of one
for whom, in spite of her youth, death would come as a happy
release.

(Signed)   LUCINE MUSSEGH.

"I have also received a piteous appeal to women of England from some hundreds of Armenian women of the District
of Khnouss, begging as an inestimable favor to be shielded
from the brutal treatment to which they are all subjected. It
is needless to publish it here. Written appeals are seldom very
forcible. If the reader had seen the wretched women themselves, as I saw them, and heard them tell their gruesome tales
in the simplest of words, punctuated by sobs and groans, em-
phasised by misery and squalor, they would be in a condition to
form some idea of the state of things in Armenia, which in the
good old times of theocracy would have brought down consuming fire from heaven. In the village of Begli Akhmed,
for example, I met a woman of about twenty-eight clothed
in ragged pieces of dirty carpets, with a pale emaciated boy
of twelve, suffering from a terrible cough, who looked like a
typhus patient aged only six or seven. I asked her to tell her
story, and this is what she said:

My name is Atlass Manookian; I come from the village
of Khrt (Khnouss District). We were very well off, but the
Kurds took away everything we had. Everything, Effendi;
still my poor husband worked for me and the child here, though
they told us to go. One day I was bringing bread to my husband in the field, they struck me on the head and dishonored
me. That was in the daytime. .   .

"'It was at noon, mother, when father used to eat his
bread, that they did that to you,' broke in the ghost of a child.
I never in my life witnessed anything more horrible than the
sight of those two friendless, hopeless wretches, as they stood
there trembling in the cold, the dying child thus simply bearing

witness that his mother was dishonored in the fields by a number of neighboring Kurds. She then went on: 'I complained to the head officer, Sheikh Moorad, but the Binbashi beat me cruelly about the head and back, and knocked me down. Then, last spring, when my husband was sowing corn, Ali Mahmed came up and killed him.' 'With an axe, mother,' said the boy. 'We are now alone in the world, wandering and begging, and nobody knows us,' said the woman. Having given her some coins, I hurried away, vainly striving to shake off the horrible impression which clung to me, like a hideous ghost, for weeks afterwards.

"Let me close this awful chapter with one despairing cry. It was written November 14, 1894, to an Armenian missionary by one of his old pupils:—

"'I implore and earnestly entreat that you will remember one of your former pupils, and hear my cry for sympathy and protection. I have been outraged. Oh, woe is me, eternal pain and sorrow to my young heart! Evil disposed and lawless men have robbed me of the bloom and beauty of my wifely purity. It was H—— Bey, the son of the Kaimakam (the local Turkish Governor residing in the village). It was in the evening between six and seven o'clock. I was engaged in my household work. I stepped outside the door, when I suddenly found myself in the grasp of four men. They smothered my cries and threatened my life, and by force carried me off to a strange house. Oh what black hours were those till the sweet light of the sun once more arose! Though this is written with ink, believe me, it is written in blood and tears.'"

By the few examples here given, the true nature of the Mohammedanism may be closely ascertained, that religion as you may observe gives many opportunities for the corruption of the morality of mankind, and with it endangers the property of the people.

A private letter from a young lady to her dear brother of Cæsarea, Asia Minor, in Turkey, Dec. 31, 1895:

My Dear Brother: Before the horrible massacre, everybody was in fear; several families would gather in one house to protect themselves, and all Armenian stores were closed for twenty days; but as the government guaranteed that there would be no danger, and told everybody to attend to their business, and open their shops, they did so. It was the 16th of November, on Saturday, that all peoples opened their shops again, and the transaction of business commenced in full force. At 2 p. m., at the doors of market, bugles sounded, and several hundred bashr-bozook (irregular soldiers), were at the doors of the bazaar, every one of them having in his hands stilettos, swords, yataghans, guns, revolvers, hammers, axes, hatchets, sickles, poinards, daggers, and heavy sticks with twenty or thirty nails fastened to them.

Then they blew horns, the signal to start the massacre, cries were heard, first kill, cut and butcher the Gianours; the property already belongs to us; cut, cut, kill, don't care plundering. Then they rushed into the market and slaughtered all they met. Oh; you can imagine what became of those who fell into the hands of those brutes. Alas! alas! how unspeakable! They butchered them like cattle; cut their heads off like onions. Some tried to run, but could not; others tried to escape but were brought back and killed. The bazaar was full of dead bodies. People hid themselves among the goods, and in the cellars and were saved; ten or fifteen days after, people were found there in a starving condition, not having dared to come out. They killed at once in a factory thirty-eight men; in Kayanjilar everybody was slain. After the massacre was over the Governor, Yerrick Pasha, sent soldiers around, and they discovered many people hiding and took them back to the Government house, (Saray), examined their pockets for revolvers and knives, and not finding any the governor sent them to their homes.

They plundered the bazaar of all its goods, and then, oh, my Lord; they rushed upon the house, and upon women in Turkish baths. I believe you don't know the meaning of Turkish bath. In Turkey, as a rule, twice, or once a week, and generally on Saturday, good many Armenian women go to Turkish baths to wash themselves. On that Saturday in Turkish baths more than four hundred Armenian women, young ladies and girls. At meantime a good many bashi-bazook came in Turkish baths. . . . I cannot describe this; when I think of it, my whole body trembles. The people in the baths were killed and wounded, and they carried away the young ladies and girls; every one was killed that they came in contact with. The houses were plundered of all their contents and buildings were torn down, and houses full of people were burned. Oh, how terrible. What I say you cannot imagine to be so; you may think it is a dream, because your eyes have not seen nor your ears heard the screams, wailings, weeping, shrieks and groaning, that even your forefathers never heard, but of which our ears are full day and night.

Some of the kidnapped girls were brought back by the Government, but most of them were wounded and half dead from fright. Thank God, we are safe, but we are not better than those girls. We are lost, lost, ruined, no work, no business, every one of us looking for safety. Happy, happy be you that are in America and have nothing to fear. They say to me, you ought to be with your brother in America now. If the way was opened everybody would like to go.

If you are not in good circumstances there, you must feel satisfied and give thanks to God always. We also have to thank God that we are still living. It is one month now that we have not been able to go out in the street. O, Lord, help us. Oh; what shall we come to? Oh my dear brother, if you can help us in any way please do so; make lectures, get some help; everybody is dying of hunger. I cannot write any longer; we leave all to your conscience. I do not write this letter only to you, but to all. Do whatever you can for us; we are in a terrible condition. I thank you, my brother, for the money that you sent to me; thank you very much.

Your Sister.

A letter has been written by the missionary lady from Oarfa, Jan. 28, 1896:

Dear Friend: Your only remaining brother sends you a letter, but no letters can begin to explain the sad state of this city. The massacre of Dec. 28 and 29 has left all homes except Catholics and Syrians entirely empty of any comforts. Many families have not one bed even; all cooking utensils, clothing, bedding, carpets, etc., were taken. Most have a little Zakhere left, though some have not that. We are feeding about 175 of the most needy, and more will come to us every week. The loss by death is between 4,000 and 5,000. Our pastor, the Rev. Hogop Abauhayatian, Dr. Kivore, and brother Haratoun, Sarkis varjebed chubukian and b rother and son, Garabed, Raumian, Habbangan Avedis, and brother Sarkis, old sexton Garabed and other sexton, ogas, Magar Kivore and brother Bogos and Berber Manofa and two sons, Eskiyiyan Morderas, Zarman Boamian's three sons, are some of the dead. In all, our Protestant dead are 115. Some of our people perished in the Gregarian Church, where 1,500 or 2,000 went for refuge Saturday night, and on Sunday were murdered or burned, very few escaping.

It was the most awful of all the terrible events of those two days. Thank God, two hundred and forty were saved by coming to me. Sixty of them were men. I could not keep the men in my house or yard, because it was forbidden by the guards, but hid them elsewhere, and fed them for three or four days. The government carefully protected me, and killed as many of my friends as possible. We have our house and all the schoolrooms full of the wounded and the most forlorn.

Our Oarfa redeaf leave tomorrow; we have now soldiers now for guard of the city; and Christians epecially. Oarfa redeafs have been poor guards, and but for them the awful work would not have been accomplished. The pastor of Severek, the Rev. Marderas, the Rev. Vartan remains alive in Adayaman. Both in Severek and Adayaman the number of the killed was very great. In Birijik, about 200 were killed, and

all remaining have become Moslems; they have been circumcised.

In Aintab about 300 were killed, 847 shops plundered,
and 417 houses, and about 400 wounded.

During our first disturbance, six to seven hundred shops
were plundered, and about 175 houses. Then the Christians used arms to defend themselves. Since then all arms
have been taken by the government from the Christians, and
the leaders were forced to sign a paper stating the city as "in
peace and harmony, thanks to the rulers," etc.; twenty-five
signed it, and now almost all of those have been killed.

Our pastor signed for Protestants.

Only two of the Gregarian priests rema'n, and they are
wounded. The bishop is alive, but feeble a١ ١ does not work
publicly now. Their state is very bad. \Ve desire your
prayers, and the aid of all who can give us ٪. lp by money at
this time. Sincerely your Friend.

Before the coming end of this book, I would like to say
a few words about the same especial martyrs.

During the wholesale massacre of the Christian Armenians, a good many thousands, the brave and faithful Christian
men and women, they are never deny their Saviour of Jesus
Christ before the swords of their enemies, most of them they
are bravely confessed their Christian faith and their martyrs,
as the follows.

Ourfa, Dec. 29, 1895. During the massacre on that day,
while every Armenian was running with their life, six of them
entered the house of Rev. Absuhayatian of that city to find
shelter there. In the meantime, fifteen Mohammedans, well
armed, came to the house of Rev. Absuhayatian and asked him
to come out. When he did so they told him how well they
thought of him and for such a good man as he is it would be
advisable to accept the religion of Mussalman, in answer to this
Rev. Absuhaytian said: "No, I cannot do that. I cannot deny
my Redeemer." The Mohammedans repeated their request
three times and each time the answer they received was the
same, and the last time Rev. Absuhayatian said: "I cannot

give up my faith, and would rather die a Christian." As he
finished these last words a bullet went through his left breast,
fired by one of the Mohammedans, who was standing some
distance from the victim. Following the shooting, others
struck him and stabbed him with their daggers and swords until the victim was utterly helpless. Then they went inside of
the house, found the six men hidden there, these they killed and
wounded to death, also Rev. Absuhayatian, about twelve hours
afterward, died a martyr for Christianity.

Severek, Nov. 23, 1895. While Rev. Mardiros was in his
house a band of Kurds and Mohammedans walked into the
house and requested that he should accept the religion of Islam
(or Islamism), Rev. Mardiros said, "No, cannot comply with
your request, nor can I deny my Lord and my Saviour." At
this time they took one of his sons and killed him there; then
they asked him (Rev. Mardiros) if he was ready to accept Islamism, for if he did his life will be spared. To this they received
again a negative answer, and they brought the second son and
murdered him there in the presence of his father; and Rev.
Mardiros was asked the third time if he was now willing to
accept the right religion. They received the same negative
answer. Then a Kurd struck him with his sword, and the
poor sufferer raised his voice and said, "I am a Christian. My
name is Mardiros, and I have received this name while I was
being baptized to be a martyr for Christ. At that moment
some one of the crowd struck his head with an axe, and the
victim fell to the ground dead.

Ourfa, 3,500 attendants in an Armenian church were
burnt to ashes by kerosene oil.

Beridjik, a Christian young man, was repeatedly requested to turn to Islamism, but he persistently refused to
do so, saying, "I am a Christian, and I cannot accept your
false prophet." His head was put into a large stone mortar
and was smashed to death.

Marash, an elderly gentleman of my acquaintance, advised his two sons while they were being murdered before his

eyes that through fear of death they should not deny Christ; it is better for them to die and be martyrs for Christ; and they were made martyrs, and the father also was killed, to follow his sons. And again, my brother-in-law in Marash, with his two sons, were invited to accept Mohammedanism. On refusal of such request all three were killed. They soon found his son-in-law and killed him also. The bloodthirsty mob found twenty-six persons hidden in one house. After killing them all, they tied ropes around their feet and dragged the dead bodies through the streets as they do the body of an animal.

These are only a few of the true happenings of everyday massacres in Armenia, and tens of thousands of such bloody works can be gathered. While at this time the blood of these martyrs is crying out to us of the cruel injustice to them, their spirits beneath the altar of the Heavenly Throne are crying still louder and saying, "O, Lord! when wilt Thou revenge our enemies?" Truly, the number of martyrs of Christianity in Armenia and in the entire Ottoman Empire during 1894 and 1895 has been greater than has been known to other nations.

Sivas, Nov. 12, 1895.—Rev. Gorabed Kilyjian died a martyr, his life being offered him three times if he would deny Christ. He bore noble testimony before many witnesses, then fell in their presence, sealing his faith and testimony with his blood.

The nature of the pacification which may be expected if Turkey is left free to carry out its schemes for these provinces may be judged from the following list of educated and influential ministers, who have been put to death for refusing to embrace Mohammedanism. In every case the offer of life on these terms was made; in several cases time was allowed for consideration of the proposal; and in each case faith in Jesus Christ was the sole crime charged against the victim.

1. Rev. Krikor, pastor at Ichme, killed Nov. 6, 1895.
2. Rev. Krikor Tamzarien.

3. Rev. Boghos Atlasian, killed November 13.

4. Rev. Mardiros Siraganian, of Abakir, killed Nov. 13.

5. Rev. Garabed Kilijjian of Sivas, killed Nov. 12.

6. ·Rev. Mr. Stepan, of the Anglican Church at Marash, killed Nov. 18.

7. The preacher of the village of Hajin, killed at Marash, Nov. 18.

8. Rev. Krikor Baghdasarian, retired preacher at Harpoot, Nov. 18.

9. Retired preacher at Divrik, killed Nov. 8.

10. Rev. Garabed Resseian, pastor at Cherwouk, Nov.

12. Pastor at Cutteroul, Nov. 6.

13. Preacher at Cutteroul, Nov. 6.

14. Rev. Sarkis Narkashjian, pastor at Chounkoush, Nov. 14.

15. The pastor of the church at Severek, November.

16. The pastor of the church at Adiyaman.

17. Rev. Hohannes Hachadorian, pastor at Kilisse, Nov. 7.

18. The preacher at Karabesh, near Diarbekr, Nov. 7.

19. Rev. Mardiros Tarzian, pastor at Keserik, near Harpoot, November.

THE BLOT ON THIS NINETEENTH CENTURY.

Dear reader, do you know how many thousand Christians have been killed during this nineteenth century? It stands about as follows:

1822, Greeks, especially in the Island of Sco........ 55,000
1850, Nestorians and Armenians, in Kurdistan...... 12,000
1860, Maronites and Syrians, Lebanon and Damascus 11,000
1876, Bulgarians in Bulgaria..................... 13,500
1894, Armenians, in Armenia and Sassoun......... 12,000
1895-6, Armenians, in Constantinople and all over in
    Asia Minor, more than...................... 71,895

1896 and 1897, Greeks, in Island of Crete and Greece,
at the last war, over........................... 55,000

The total number........................... 240,395

In a word the nineteenth century has been a bloody and blotted era for the eastern Christians, because up to this date over 240,000 men and women and innocent children have been killed and butchered in cold blood by the brutal and immoral Islamism. Therefore many thousands of such bloody words can be gathered. While at this date the blood of those martyrs is crying out for the cruel injustice to them and to the orphans and widows left behind them, their spirits also, beneath the altar of the Heavenly Throne, are crying still louder and saying, "O Lord, when wilt thou revenge our enemies." Truly the number of martyrs of Christianity in Armenia and of the entire Ottoman Empire during the 19th century has been greater than has been known to other nations.

TABULAR VIEW OF THE ARMENIAN MASSACRES.

From 1894 to 1896, 26 of August.

NAME OF TOWN AND THE VILLAGES.	DATE OF MASSACRE.	NUMBER KILLED.	BY WHOM DONE.
Sassoun and Villages	1894	More than 12,000	Soldiers, Kurds and Turks.
Constantinople	1895, Sept. 30	" " 3,000	Police, Softas and Turks.
Ak-Hissar	" Oct. 9	" " 150	Moslem villagers.
Trebizond	" " 8	" " 800	Soldiers, Lazes and Turks.
Baiburt and Villages	" " 13	" " 1,200	Lazes and Turks.
Gumushane and Vill's	" " 11	" " 150	Turks and Kurds.
Erzingian and Villages	" " 21	" " 1,000	Soldiers and Turks.
Bitlis and Villages	" " 25	" " 1,200	Soldiers, Kurds and Turks.
Harpoot and Vicinities	" Nov. 11	" " 15,845	" " " "
Sivas and Vicinities	" " 12	" " 1,500	Soldiers and Turks.
Palu and Villages	" Oct. 25	" " 4,000	Soldiers, Kurds and Turks.
Diarbekr and Vicinities	" " 25	" " 3,500	" " " "
Albostan	" "	" " 150	Turks and Kurds.
Eerzerum and Vicinities	" " 30	" " 3,000	Soldiers and Turks.
Onrfa and Villages	{ " Nov. 3 } { " Dec. 28 }	" " 3,500	Kurds, Turks and Soldiers.
Kara, Hessar	" Oct. 25	" " 500	Circassians and Turks.
Maltia	" Nov. 6	" " 250	Turks and Kurds.
Marash and Villages	" " 18	" " 1,200	
Aintab and Kilis	" " 15	" " 1,150	Soldiers and Turks.
Guoroon	" " 10	" " 3,500	Kurds and Turks.
Daranda	" " 9	" " 750	" " "
Ashody	" " 9	" " 125	" " "
Arabkir	" " 6	" " 2,000	" " "
Argana	" "	" " 150	" " "
Soverek	" Dec. 19	" " 250	" " "
Birejeck, Jibin and Orul	" Nov. 19	" " 500	" " "
Adnyaman and Basny	" " 17	" " 1,300	" " "
Azizia and Gamerac	" " 13	" " 500	" " "
Divrigy and Villages	" " 13	" " 250	Kurds, Circassians, Turks.
Baknur Madany	" " 12	" " 200	" " "
Mush	" " 12	" " 150	" " "
Tokat	" "	" " 350	" " "
Amasia	" "	" " 250	" " "
Yozgat and Villages	" " 19	" " 1,575	" " "
Egun	" " 13	" " 250	Kedifs and Turks.
Zaytoon, Gaban	1896 again.	" " 2,250	Kurds and Turks.
Furnuz, Doongala	} 1895	" " 3,000	Soldiers and Turks.
Shivilgy, Nuorpat	}		
Gaoksoom. Shardarasy and Hajine	{ " Nov. 25	" " 800	Soldiers, Ofshar Turks.
Adana and Vicinity	" " 26	" " 150	Circassians and Turks.
Cæsarea and Neegda	" " 16	" " 1,200	" " "
And some other places	"	" " 150	Turks

During the three years from 1894 to 1896, 26 of August, the total number of the massacres of the Christian Armenians in Asia Minor and Turkey, 83,895.

The statistics of the last outrages will never be accurately known, but by the most careful figures thus far received, the partial are as told. In the table below I wish to show the population of the ten provinces, and the houses and shops are plundered, and destroyed or burned in the ten provinces, namely: *Erzerum, Bitlis, Diarbekr, Van, Harpoot, Sivas, Trebizond, Angora, Adana,* and *Aleppo.*

www.ingramcontent.com/pod-product-compliance
Lightning Source LLC
Chambersburg PA
CBHW060549030726
47498CB00005B/1325